JAMES JOYCE

Stephen Hero

Part of the first draft of
A Portrait of the Artist as a Young Man

Edited with an Introduction by
Theodore Spencer

Revised edition with additional material
and a Foreword by
John J. Slocum and Herbert Cahoon

D1026205

A TRIAD GRAFTON BOOK
A Division of the Collins Publishing Group

LONDON GLASGOW
TORONTO SYDNEY AUCKLAND

Grafton Books
A Division of the Collins Publishing Group
8 Grafton Street, London W1X 3LA

Published by Grafton Books 1977
Reprinted 1981, 1982, 1984, 1986 (twice)

First published in Great Britain by
Jonathan Cape Ltd 1944

ISBN 0-586-04477-9

Printed and bound in Great Britain by
Collins, Glasgow

Set in Monotype Bembo

Contents

FOREWORD TO THE REVISED EDITION

The personal library of James Joyce, with the literary manuscripts which he had chosen to preserve, was left in Trieste in the care of his brother Stanislaus when Joyce moved to Paris in June 1920. Subsequently, at Joyce's request, his brother sent him the greater portion of the library including the bulk of the surviving pages of the early draft of *A Portrait of the Artist as a Young Man*, known as *Stephen Hero*. Joyce turned over many of these manuscripts to Miss Sylvia Beach, publisher of *Ulysses*. Stanislaus Joyce retained a certain number of manuscript items including twenty-five additional pages of *Stephen Hero* which were purchased by John J. Slocum in 1950 and are here printed for the first time. These pages, as numbered by Joyce, precede numerically the 383 pages edited by the late Theodore Spencer and are numbered 477-8, 481-9, 491-7, 499-505; the first manuscript page of the text Spencer published in 1944 is numbered 519. In this edition, however, the additional material follows the originally published text.

This newly discovered portion of the manuscript is actually an episode by itself, although still incomplete; this unity may be the reason that it was preserved by James Joyce. The first eight lines of manuscript on page 477 were destined to become, with a few changes, the last part of the diary entry of April 16th at the conclusion of *A Portrait*. The remainder of the manuscript tells of a visit that Stephen Daedalus made to his godfather, Mr Fulham, in Mullingar, Westmeath, sometime after he had begun his studies at University College in 1898. The words, 'Departure for Paris', words that mark the end of *A Portrait*, have been written by Joyce in blue crayon across the page at the conclusion of the first eight lines. It is probable, though by no means certain, that the pages preceding page 477 were discarded as they were used in the creation of *A Portrait*. It is also probable that the missing pages from this episode included descriptions or dialogues that eventually found their way into *A Portrait*. Joyce's known economy of episode and phrase was such that even the rejected portions of his manuscripts usually contributed heavily to a published work.

Mullingar, in the centre of Ireland, has none of the urban polish of the other two Irish cities Joyce describes in his work, Dublin and Cork, and he perhaps intended at first to use these scenes of provincial life to fill out his picture of Ireland. He knew Mullingar well, having accompanied his father there during the summers of 1900 and 1901, when John Joyce was charged with the duty of straightening out the confused Mullingar election lists. James Joyce's copy of D'Annunzio's *The Child of Pleasure*, now in the Yale University Library, bears Joyce's signature and the words, 'Mullingar July.5.1900.'; the manuscript of his translation of Hauptmann's *Vor Sonnenaufgang* is inscribed, 'Summer, 1901. MS/Mullingar. Westmeath.' Joyce alters the actual events considerably by representing Mullingar as the home of Stephen's godfather, Mr Fulham. (Joyce's godfather was Philip McCann, who had no connection with Mullingar and had died in 1898.) This fiction is continued in the later pages of *Stephen Hero*, where Mr Fulham is mentioned repeatedly as the source of money for Stephen's university expenses. It is conceivable that an undiscovered patron is represented by the figure of the godfather.

Many of the incidents in these pages must have had their origins in Joyce's 'epiphanies', those unostentatious moments of revelation which Joyce was in the habit of recording for future use. The descriptions of the lame beggar and of Mr Garvey of the *Examiner* are based directly upon two surviving 'epiphanies' now in the Joyce Collection of the Lockwood Memorial Library of the University of Buffalo. In turn these pages sometimes affect later work. So Nash, who appears in this Mullingar episode, and Mr Tate, who is mentioned in it, return in *A Portrait*. There is an echo of Captain Starkie's story of the old peasant in the April 14th entry of Stephen's diary in the last chapter of *A Portrait*. Stephen's remark to Mr Heffernan, 'My own mind is more interesting to me than the entire country', is close to his remark to Bloom in *Ulysses*, 'You suspect that I may be important because I belong to the *Faubourg Saint-Patrice* called Ireland for short . . . But I suspect that Ireland must be important because it belongs to me'. It is close, too, to Joyce's remark to Yeats in 1902 that his own mind 'was much nearer to God than folklore'. Finally, Mullingar is mentioned several times in *Ulysses* because Milly Bloom is said to be working there in a photographer's shop.

But Joyce never used the bulk of the Mullingar episode, perhaps because he came to feel that the role of Stephen showing off against the provincials had something disagreeable in it. There are also hints that he originally intended to give Mr Fulham a more important role in his book; when his plans changed, the episode became a little irrelevant.

These new pages do not add any new dimensions to the character of Stephen, but the arguments and situations, in which Stephen, as usual, emerges triumphant, contain some excellent expositions of his attitudes towards religion, Irish nationalism and his countrymen. The sensitive, self-righteous, honest and cruel young man is beautifully displayed.

In preparing these pages for publication we have followed the editorial procedures of Professor Spencer as set forth in his editorial note. We are grateful to Professor Richard Ellmann of Northwestern University for his advice and criticism, to the late Stanislaus Joyce, and to the Estate of James Joyce and the Yale University Library, owner of the manuscript, for permission to publish these additional pages.

JOHN J. SLOCUM
HERBERT CAHOON

INTRODUCTION TO THE FIRST EDITION

I

In 1935, Miss Sylvia Beach, the first publisher of *Ulysses*, issued a catalogue from her bookshop, *Shakespeare and Company*, 12 Rue de l'Odéon, Paris, in which she offered for sale, among other things, certain manuscripts of James Joyce. One of these consisted of pp. 519–902 of an early version of *A Portrait of the Artist as a Young Man*, in Joyce's handwriting. These pages were bought by the Harvard College Library in the autumn of 1938, and are here printed with the permission of Joyce's executors, and of the Harvard College Library.

There is some confusion about the date of this manuscript. In her catalogue Miss Beach, to whom Joyce originally gave it, says that it dates from 1903, and adds the following sentence: 'When the manuscript came back to its author, after the twentieth publisher had rejected it, he threw it in the fire, from which Mrs Joyce, at the risk of burning her hands, rescued these pages.' This story is to some extent supported by Mr Herbert Gorman, who says in his life of Joyce, writing of the year 1908[1]: 'Joyce burned a portion of *Stephen Hero* [as the book was then called] in a fit of momentary despair and then started the novel anew in a more compressed form.'[2] No surviving page of the manuscript shows any signs of burning.

Joyce himself was not very communicative on the subject. When the present writer wrote to him about the manuscript at the end of 1938, he received a reply from Joyce's secretary which said: 'Apparently the very large MS. of about 1000 pages of the first draft of *A Portrait of the Artist as a Young Man*, which he calls a schoolboy's

[1] Herbert Gorman: *James Joyce*, Farrar & Rinehart, New York, 1940, p. 196.

[2] See Publisher's Note, p. 24.

production written when he was nineteen or twenty, has been sold in lots to different institutions in America. He feels that he can do nothing in the matter except to state this fact which he certainly can scarcely be blamed for not having foreseen at the moment of the presentation he made of it [*sic*].'

Since Joyce was born in 1882, the ages here mentioned suggest that the manuscript was written in 1901–02, instead of 1903, as Miss Beach's catalogue says. Both dates, however, are apparently too early. Mr Gorman, whose book was checked by Joyce, tells us that when Joyce left Ireland in 1904, he took with him a first chapter and notes for *Stephen Hero*, and he prints a letter from Joyce to Grant Richards written on March 13th, 1906, which speaks of the book as half finished:

> You suggest I should write a novel in some sense autobiographical. I have already written a thousand pages of such a novel, as I think I told you, 914 pages to be accurate. I calculate that these twenty-five chapters, about half the book, run into 150,000 words. But it is quite impossible for me in present circumstances to think the rest of the book much less to write it.

From this account it seems clear that *Stephen Hero* was written between 1904 and 1906.

The discrepancy between the different dates may be reconciled, I believe, by remembering that when Joyce left Ireland he took with him 'notes' for his book. Mr Gorman reprints some of them (pp. 135ff). It seems highly probable that there were also fuller notes than these, consisting of transcripts of conversations, etc., which were incorporated without much change into the manuscript: the reader of the following pages will undoubtedly agree that much of the talk sounds as if it had been taken down immediately after it had been spoken. If this is so, then we can think of the manuscript as representing the work of the years 1901 to 1906. It is a very clean copy, with only a few corrections, and Joyce's handwriting is remarkably legible.

The first 518 pages have apparently disappeared for good; I doubt very much if they have been 'sold in lots to different institutions in

America'.[1] Probably the story of their having been burnt is correct – although there is no evidence in Mr Gorman's book to indicate that the manuscript was ever sent to twenty publishers. Yet though the loss of the early pages is greatly to be regretted, the 383 pages that remain have a kind of unity in themselves. As Joyce planned it, *Stephen Hero* was to be 'an autobiographical book, a personal history, as it were, of the growth of a mind, his own mind, and his own intensive absorption in himself and what he had been and how he had grown out of the Jesuitical garden of his youth. He endeavoured to see himself objectively, to assume a godlike poise of watchfulness over the small boy and youth he called Stephen and who was really himself'. (Gorman, p. 133.) The Harvard manuscript describes about two years of Stephen's life; it begins shortly after he enters the National University, and it breaks off just as Stephen's emancipation from all that the University implies reaches a kind of climax. It does not give us a picture of the 'small boy', but it gives us a very vivid and coherent picture of the 'youth' who is called Stephen Daedalus, but who, in his appearance, his actions and his thought is so evidently James Joyce.

It can be seen at a glance that this early version is very different from the version eventually published as *A Portrait of the Artist as a Young Man*. The period covered by the 383 pages of the manuscript occupies only the last 80 pages of the published version (Jonathan Cape, illustrated edition, 1956) – the manuscript account of Stephen's two years at the University is at least as long as the whole history of his development in its final form. It portrays many characters and incidents which the published version leaves out, and it describes the growth of Stephen's mind in a far more direct and less elliptical form than that with which we are familiar. Consequently, though Joyce rejected it, and in his later years scorned it – from the reader's point of view, unjustifiably – as a 'schoolboy's production', the

[1] Mr Gorman agrees with me on this point. I quote a letter from him of January 21st, 1941: 'I . . . believe that what you have is all that Miss Beach possessed. Neither do I believe that any other portion of the draft exists. When Mr Joyce's secretary (I presume you mean M. Paul Léon) wrote you that "lots" had been sold to "different institutions in America", I think his informant (presumably Mr Joyce) had mixed up in his mind other material that Miss Beach was selling.'

interest of the manuscript to admirers of Joyce is great. It not only gives us a wonderfully convincing transcript of life, it throws light on Joyce's whole development as an artist by showing us more clearly than we have been able to see before what the beginning of that development was like.

2

Every reader of the present text will want to make his own comparisons between its picture of Stephen Daedalus and the picture given by the final version; I do not want to forestall any such critical pleasure by making exhaustive comparisons myself. Nevertheless there are certain characteristics of the manuscript which are of such special interest that they may, I hope not too obtrusively, be briefly pointed out in advance.[1]

The most obvious of these characteristics is the wealth of detail with which incidents and people are described. For example the Daedalus family is much more clearly seen than in the final form of the book; the family gives a richly sordid background to the arrogant growth of Stephen's mental independence through his University years: in the final version, the members of his family have virtually disappeared from the scene by the time Stephen has gone to the University. In the *Portrait* we have nothing like the description of Mr Wilkinson's house (pp. 165ff.); we hear nothing of Stephen's intimacy with his brother Maurice; the pathetic and shocking account of the illness and death of Stephen's sister Isabel (pp. 167ff.) is entirely omitted; nothing is said of Stephen's attempt to convert his family to an admiration of Ibsen (pp. 89ff.). Even when the same incidents are mentioned, the present text usually treats them in a different manner – a more direct and dramatic manner – than that used in the *Portrait*. A typical illustration of this is the handling of Stephen's refusal to perform his Easter duty. In the present text (pp. 136ff.) the argument between Stephen and his mother is given as a dialogue – no doubt as it actually occurred – and it is a very effective piece of writing. But in the *Portrait* (Cape ed., p. 243) the scene, which is a crucial one in Stephen's history, is merely referred to in a conversation with Cranly.

[1] Mr Harry Levin has already used the manuscript to excellent critical effect in his *James Joyce, a Critical Introduction*, Faber & Faber, 1944.

We can easily understand, of course, what Joyce was aiming at when he discarded his first draft and rewrote the material in this fashion. He was aiming at economy, and he was trying to place his centre of action as much as possible inside the consciousness of his hero. To do this he evidently decided to sacrifice the method – which is, after all, the method of *Dubliners* rather than that of the *Portrait* – of objectively presenting one episode or character after another. As a result the *Portrait* has more intensity and concentration, a more controlled focus, than the earlier version. In the *Portrait*, as Mr Levin observes, 'drama has retired before soliloquy'. The diffuseness of real life is controlled and ordered by being presented from a single point of view. Furthermore the method used in the *Portrait* of merely hinting at an episode or conversation instead of describing it in full (compare the way Giordano Bruno is introduced in the *Portrait*, p. 253, with the way he is introduced in the present version, p. 175) – this method makes Stephen's thoughts and actions more suggestive than they are as Joyce describes them here. In the *Portrait* we are looking at a room through a keyhole instead of through an open door: the vague shapes which we can with difficulty see in the dark corners add portentousness to what our framed and limited vision can perceive. In the present version the door is open, and everything is made as visible as possible. To change the image: we here see things in daylight, instead of under a spotlight; here there is less emphasis, less selection, less art.

But the increased pressure of concentration to be found in the *Portrait*, however desirable or admirable it may be, is gained at a loss. For example: in the *Portrait* we are introduced to Stephen's friends – Cranly, Lynch and the rest – as items, so to speak, in Stephen's mind. They are not pictured for us; Joyce expects us to take them for granted, as features in Stephen's landscape which need no further identification beyond their names and their way of speaking. But in the present text these friends are much more clearly identified; Joyce introduces us to them by describing their appearance and their points of view; they have an independent reality of their own, like the people in *Dubliners*; they are not merely sounding boxes or slot-machines, as they are in the *Portrait*, for the ideas of the all-important Stephen.

This is particularly true of the girl to whom Stephen is physically (though not otherwise) attracted. In the *Portrait* she has only initials –

15

E. C. – and Stephen's reveries centre round a virtually anonymous young girl. But in the present text the girl is named Emma Clery, and she has a living personality which is lacking in her merely initial-led successor. There are several scenes in the present text – particularly that on pp. 70ff. – where we see Emma very clearly indeed, and as a result Stephen's relations with her become, like his relations with other people, more dramatic than they are in the final version.[1]

The most striking differences which the reader will notice between the two versions is in the way Stephen himself is described. In the present text he is emotionally and intellectually a cruder and more youthful figure than in his creator's eyes he was later to become; he is more like the average undergraduate and, in spite or because of the fact that he is portrayed more diffusely, he is on the whole a more sympathetic person, proud and arrogant as he may be. He has more weaknesses and does more foolish things (such as his pursuit of Emma) than are entirely consistent with the self-possession of his later por-trait. He has a hero-worship for Ibsen, which is scarcely mentioned later, and his reaction from his Jesuit training makes him rage in a more sophomoric fury against what he calls the 'plague of Catholi-cism'. He is more dependent on his family for approval and support.

In the development of Stephen Daedalus, as presented in both the earlier and later versions, there are five main themes, all closely re-lated to the central theme of Stephen himself. The themes are these: Stephen's family; his friends, male and female; the life of Dublin; Catholicism; Art. Stephen's development as an individual may be described as a process which sloughs off the first four in order that the fifth may stand clear. When this happens, and art is defined, the artist may then return to the first four for his subject matter. In fact he *has* to return to them if his function as an artist is to be fulfilled.

But before he can do this he has to determine what sort of man the artist is and also what art is: the two, for autobiographical purposes, are in many respects the same. It is not only Stephen Hero who mat-

[1] In the present text, Stephen meets Emma at the house of a Mr Daniel, where he sometimes goes on Sunday evenings. Nothing is said about Mr Daniel and his household in the *Portrait*, but Joyce transfers, in a shortened form, his description of Mr Daniel's living-room to describe 'her' house (*Portrait*, p. 223). The change is a typical example of Joyce's economy and concentration in the published work.

ters – Joyce mentions 'that old English ballad *Turpin Hero*, which begins in the first person and ends in the third person' (*Portrait*, p. 219); – it is the portrait of the *artist* as well. Stephen as hero is an adolescent; Stephen as artist is an adult. That is, perhaps, the major difference between the two versions of his career.

Yet the aesthetic theory with which we are familiar in the *Portrait* is already fully outlined in *Stephen Hero*, and no doubt one of the chief interests of the present text for most readers will consist in discovering how differently it is presented here from the way it is presented in the *Portrait*. In the *Portrait* Stephen outlines his aesthetic programme in a conversation with Lynch, and the intellectual integrity and hardness of Stephen's ideas are contrasted with the coarse ejaculations and comments of his companion. This is an effective way of sustaining interest in an abstract exposition, and by setting Stephen's seriousness against Lynch's humour, what might be heavy or monotonous becomes lively and entertaining. The theory is presented objectively and with a comic background. But in the *Portrait* Stephen merely expounds his views; we are made to feel that he is so convinced of their truth that it doesn't in the least matter to him whether anybody else agrees with him or not. Cold fish that he is, he is above approval or disapproval; he is already prepared for 'silence, exile and cunning'.

Not so the younger Stephen of the present text. To him the setting forth of his ideas is a matter of great personal importance, and he delivers them, not in the casual form of a conversation with a friend, but in the form of a public paper to a literary society; it is a public event, an event for which Stephen prepares with great care. Furthermore his ideas are not contrasted merely with one other man's semi-humorous comments: they are contrasted with the conventionality of Catholicism and the passage (pp. 96ff.) which describes Stephen's conversation on the subject with the President of the University is one of the best in the book. Stephen's ideas are also contrasted, in the present text, with the intellectual paralysis of Dublin. For when he delivers his paper, which, word for word, he had so carefully planned, it gets only an indifferent and misunderstanding response; the philistines cannot be conquered on their own ground, and Stephen falls back more than ever on his own resources.[1]

[1] In the manuscript Stephen does, to be sure, discuss his aesthetic theory with a friend; see pp. 218ff. But it is interesting to note that the

The advantages of presenting the theory in such a fashion are obvious. We follow Stephen as he develops it through his conversations with his brother Maurice, the situation comes to a crisis in the delivery of the paper, and we are interested, as we are interested in a drama, as we wait to hear how the audience will react. We share Stephen's disappointment and disillusionment. Yet the method has its disadvantages as well: the development of Stephen's theory is spread out over a long period, it is intercepted by other episodes (the five main themes are interwoven throughout), and its exposition does not occupy, as in the *Portrait*, a crucial place in Stephen's career. In the *Portrait* the statement of Stephen's theory is an immediate prologue to his abandonment of Ireland, and hence is a climax to the whole book; in the present version, however dramatically it may be described, it is only one episode among many.

In fact the way the theory is finally presented in the *Portrait* is an illustration of the theory itself. One of Stephen's central ideas is that only improper art is 'kinetic'; it moves us to something, which true art should not do; on the contrary, the true 'esthetic emotion' is static, and the true artist is essentially impersonal: 'The artist, like the God of the creation, remains within or behind or beyond or above his handiwork, invisible, refined out of existence, indifferent, paring his fingernails' (*Portrait*, p. 219). It is in this impersonal static, non-kinetic fashion that Stephen expounds his theory to Lynch. But in the present text it is expounded kinetically. Stephen is personally interested in the success of his paper, his intellectual fortunes seem to depend on it, and we are moved – not necessarily to do something – but to sympathy and concern for the outcome. The later text is, as usual, more mature, and shows Joyce, as the earlier version does not, illustrating his theory by his practice.[1]

---

friend is Cranly, not Lynch, that the conversation comes long after the main theory is expounded in the public essay, and that Stephen is personally disappointed in Cranly's failure to be interested in the argument.

[1] There are traces of Stephen's paper on aesthetics left in the *Portrait*. On p. 191 the dean of studies asks Stephen: 'When may we expect to have something from you on the esthetic question?' And on p. 215 Donovan says to Stephen: 'I hear you are writing some essay about

3

There is one aspect of Stephen's aesthetic theory which appears in the manuscript alone, and is left out of the *Portrait* entirely. In my opinion the passage describing it is the most interesting and revealing in the entire text. It is the passage on pp. 216ff. beginning with the words, 'He was passing through Eccles' Street', which explains Joyce's theory of epiphanies.[1]

I ask the reader to turn to this passage, and read it.

This theory seems to me central to an understanding of Joyce as artist, and we might describe his successive works as illustrations, intensifications and enlargements of it. *Dubliners*, we may say, is a series of epiphanies describing apparently trivial but actually crucial and revealing moments in the lives of different characters. The *Portrait* may be seen as a kind of epiphany – a showing forth – of Joyce himself as a young man; *Ulysses*, by taking one day in the life of the

---

esthetics.' These remarks, like several others in the *Portrait* (for example the references to 'that certain young lady' [Emma] and Father Moran, p. 206) take on richer connotations – and sometimes can only be fully understood – if we read them with a knowledge of the present text in mind.

[1] This theory is mentioned once in *Ulysses*, John Lane, 1937, pp. 36–7. Stephen is meditating: 'Remember your epiphanies on green oval leaves, deeply deep; copies to be sent if you died to all the great libraries of the world, including Alexandria?' Dr Gogarty also refers to it in his autobiography, *As I was Walking down Sackville Street* (p. 285). Gogarty is spending the evening with Joyce and others; Joyce says 'Excuse me', and leaves the room. 'I don't mind being reported,' Gogarty writes, 'but to be an unwilling contributor to one of his Epiphanies is irritating.

'Probably Fr Darlington had taught him, as an aside in his Latin class – for Joyce knew no Greek – that "Epiphany" meant "a showing forth". So he recorded under "Epiphany" any showing forth of the mind by which he considered one gave oneself away.

'Which of us had endowed him with an "Epiphany" and sent him to the lavatory to take it down?'

average man, describes that man, according to Joyce's intention, more fully than any human being had ever been described before; it is the epiphany of Leopold Bloom, just as, years earlier, the trivial conversation overheard on a misty evening in Eccles' Street (where, incidentally, Mr Bloom lived) was the epiphany of those two people's lives, shown forth in a moment. And *Finnegans Wake* may be seen as a vast enlargement, of course unconceived by Joyce as a young man, of the same view. Here it is not any one individual that is 'epiphanized'; it is all of human history, symbolized in certain types the representatives of which combine with one another as the words describing them combine various meanings, so that H. C. Earwicker and his family, his acquaintances, the city of Dublin where he lives, his morality and religion, become symbols of an epiphanic view of human life as a whole, and the final end of the artist is achieved.

And if we keep this theory in mind, as a further aspect of the static theory of art developed throughout the present text, it helps us to understand what kind of writer Joyce is. A theory like this is not of much use to a dramatist, as Joyce seems to have realized when he first conceived it. It is a theory which implies a lyrical rather than a dramatic view of life. It emphasizes the radiance, the effulgence, of the thing itself revealed in a special moment, an unmoving moment, of time. The moment, as in the macrocosmic lyric of *Finnegans Wake*, may involve all other moments, but it still remains essentially static, and though it may have all time for its subject matter it is essentially timeless.

4

But this fragment of *Stephen Hero* does not have to be considered in relation to Joyce's later writing to be thought worth preserving. It can stand on its own merits as a remarkable piece of work. Though it is not as carefully planned and concentrated as the *Portrait*, it has a freshness and directness, an accuracy of observation and an economy and sharpness of style that make it, in spite of its occasional immaturities, something to be enjoyed and admired for its own sake. It is one of the best descriptions of a growing mind that has ever been written.

THEODORE SPENCER

PUBLISHER'S NOTE

More recent research has given us another version of this story. Richard Ellmann, in his biography *James Joyce* (O.U.P., 1959), maintains that the manuscript was thrown into the fire 'after a particularly unpleasant exchange about writing and eating . . .', and that it was rescued not by Mrs Joyce, but by the author's sister Eileen. This account of the incident is supported by Harriet Weaver and confirmed by James Joyce's executors.

EDITORIAL NOTE

There are two kinds of correction in the manuscript as Joyce left it. One kind consists of revisions made in copying it from the rough draft: certain words are deleted, others have been changed. These corrections have been indicated in the text by placing the original version in brackets with the amended version following. There are also some obvious errors – repetitions of words, omitted words and faults of punctuation. These are of no interest and I have silently set them right.

The second kind of correction has been more difficult to handle. Joyce evidently went through the manuscript with a red or blue crayon in his hand and slashed strokes beside, under or across certain phrases, sentences and paragraphs. Presumably he did not like them and intended to change them or get rid of them. Some indication of where these slashes occur is obviously necessary if an accurate presentation is to be given of the manuscript and of Joyce's feelings about it. Consequently wherever there is a slash I have put a small superior 'c' (for 'crayon') – in the manner of a quotation mark – at the beginning and end of the slashed passage. The slashes are made very broadly, as if in haste or impatience, so that it is not always easy to decide where, in Joyce's mind, the unsatisfactoriness began and stopped. But the general indications are clear enough, and the slashes were evidently made by Joyce himself since he used the same crayon to make an occasional verbal correction, and the handwriting in such cases is his.

I am greatly indebted to Mr John Kelleher, of the Society of Fellows, Harvard University, for putting his knowledge of all things Irish at my disposal. The reader who cares to identify the characters mentioned in the present text with their prototypes in real life should consult Mr Gorman's *James Joyce* (pp. 53ff.).

T. S.

STEPHEN HERO

STEPHEN HERO

[The Manuscript begins here]

... anyone spoke to him mingled a too polite disbelief with its expectancy. ᶜ His [stiff] coarse brownish hair was combed high off his forehead but there was little order in its arrangement. [The face] A girl might or might not have called him handsome: the face was regular in feature and its pose was almost softened into [positive distinct] beauty by a small feminine mouth. In [the] a general survey of the face the eyes were not prominent: they were small light blue eyes which checked advances. They were quite fresh and fearless but in spite of this the face was to a certain extent the face of a debauchee. ᶜ

The president of the college was a sequestrated person who took the chairs at reunions and inaugural meetings of societies. His visible lieutenants were a dean and a bursar. The bursar, Stephen thought, fitted his title: a heavy, florid man with a ᶜ black-grey cap of hair. ᶜ He performed his duties with great unction and was often to be seen looming in the hall watching the coming and going of the students. He insisted on punctuality: a minute or so late once or twice – he would not mind that so much; he would clap his hands and make some cheery reproof. But what made him severe was a few minutes lost every day: it disturbed the proper working of the classes. Stephen was nearly always more than a quarter of an hour late and [so] when he arrived the bursar had usually gone back to his office. One morning, however, he arrived at the school earlier than usual. Walking up the steps before him was a fat [young] student, a very hard-working, timorous young man with a bread-and-jam complexion. The bursar was standing in the hall with his arms folded across [the] his chest and when he caught sight of the fat young man he looked significantly at the clock. It was eight minutes past eleven.

— Now then, Moloney, you know this won't do. Eight minutes

late! Disturbing your class like that – we can't have that, you know. Must be in sharp for lecture every morning in future.

The jam overspread the bread in Moloney's face as he stumbled over some excuses about a clock being wrong and then scurried upstairs to his class. Stephen delayed a little [while] time hanging up his overcoat while the large priest eyed him solemnly. Then he turned his head quietly towards the bursar and said

— Fine morning, sir.

The bursar at once clapped his hands and rubbed them together and clapped them together again. The beauty of the morning and the appositeness of the remark both struck him at the same time and he answered cheerily:

— Beautiful! Fine bracing morning now! and he fell to rubbing his hands again.

One morning [he] Stephen arrived three quarters of an hour late and he thought it his decenter plan to wait till the French lecture should begin. As he was leaning over the banisters, waiting for the twelve o'clock bell to ring a young man began to ascend the winding-stairs slowly. At a few steps from the landing he halted and turned a square rustic face towards Stephen.

— Is this the way to the Matriculation class, if you please, he asked in a brogue accenting the first syllable of Matriculation.

Stephen directed him and the two young men began to talk. The new student was named Madden and came from the county of Limerick. His manner without being exactly diffident was a little scared and he seemed grateful for Stephen's attentions. After the French lecture the two walked across the green together and Stephen brought the newcomer into the National Library. Madden took off his hat at the turnstile and as he leaned on the counter to fill up the docket for his book Stephen remarked the peasant strength of his jaws.

The dean of the college was professor of English, Father Butt. He was reputed the most able man in the college: he was a philosopher and a scholar. He read a series of papers at a total abstinence club to prove that Shakespeare was a Roman Catholic: he had also written against another Jesuit father who had very late in life been converted to the Baconian theory of the authorship of the plays. Father Butt had always his hands full of papers and his soutane very

soiled with chalk. He was an elderly greyhound of a man and his
vocal ligaments, like his garb, seemed to be coated with chalk. He
had a plausible manner with everyone and was particularly –

[*Two pages missing*]

of verse are the first conditions which the words must submit to, the
rhythm is the esthetic result of the senses, values and relations of the
words thus conditioned. The beauty of verse consisted as much in the
concealment as in the revelation of construction but it certainly could
not proceed from only one of these. For this reason he found Father
Butt's reading of verse and a schoolgirl's accurate reading of verse
intolerable. Verse to be read according to its rhythm should be read
according to the stresses; that is, neither strictly according to the feet
nor yet with complete disregard of them. All this theory he set himself to explain to Maurice and Maurice, when he had understood the
meanings of the terms and had put these meanings carefully together, agreed that Stephen's theory was the right one. There was only
one possible way of rendering the first quatrain of Byron's poem:

> My dáys are in the yéllow léaf
> The flowers and frúits of lóve are góne
> The wórm, the cańker and the gríef
> Are míne alone.

The two brothers tried this theory on all the verse they could remember and it yielded wonderful results. Soon Stephen began to
explore the language for himself and to choose, and thereby rescue
once for all, the words and phrases most amenable to his theory.
ᶜ He became a poet with malice aforethought. ᶜ

He was at once captivated by the seeming eccentricites of the prose
of Freeman and William Morris. He read them as one would read a
thesaurus and made a ᶜ garner ᶜ of words. He read Skeat's Etymologi-
cal Dictionary by the hour and his mind, which had from the first
been only too submissive to the infant sense of wonder, was often
hypnotized by the most commonplace conversation. People seemed
to him strangely ignorant of the value of the words they used so
glibly. And pace by pace as this indignity of life forced itself upon him
he became enamoured of an idealizing, a more veritably human tradition. The phenomenon seemed to him a grave one and he began to

see that people had leagued themselves together in a conspiracy of ignobility and that Destiny had scornfully reduced her prices for them. He desired no such reduction for himself and preferred to serve her on the ancient terms.

There was a special class for English composition and it was in this class that Stephen first made his name. The English essay was for him the one serious work of the week. His essay was usually very long and the professor, who was a leader-writer on the *Freeman's Journal*, always kept it for the last. Stephen's style of writing, [that] though it was over affectionate towards the antique and even the obsolete and too easily rhetorical, was remarkable for a certain crude originality of expression. He gave himself no great trouble to sustain the boldnesses which were expressed or implied in his essays. He threw them out as sudden defence-works while he was busy constructing the enigma of a manner. For the youth had been apprised of another crisis and he wished to make ready for the shock of it. On account of such manœuvres he came to be regarded as a very unequilibrated [youth] young man who took more interest than young men usually take in theories which might be permitted as pastimes. Father Butt, to whom the emergence of these unusual qualities had been duly reported, spoke one day to Stephen with the purpose of 'sounding' him. Father Butt expressed a great admiration for Stephen's essays all of which, he said, the professor of English composition had shown him. He encouraged the youth and suggested that in a short time perhaps he might contribute something to one of the Dublin papers or magazines. Stephen found this encouragement kindly meant but mistaken and he launched forth into a copious explanation of his theories. Father Butt listened and, even more readily than [Stephen] Maurice had done, agreed with them all. Stephen laid down his doctrine very positively and insisted on the importance of what he called the literary tradition. ° Words, he said, have a certain value in the literary tradition and a certain value in the market-place – a debased value. ° Words are simply receptacles for human thought: in the literary tradition they receive more valuable thoughts than they receive in the market-place. Father Butt listened to all this, rubbing his chalky hand often over his chin and ° nodding his head and said that Stephen evidently understood the importance of tradition.^c Stephen quoted a phrase from Newman to illustrate his theory.

— In that sentence of Newman's, he said, the word is used according to the literary tradition: it has there its full value. In ordinary use, that is, in the market-place, it has a different value altogether, a debased value. 'I hope I'm not detaining you.'

— Not at all, not at all!

— No, no . . .

— Yes, yes, Mr Daedalus, I see . . . I quite see your point . . . detain . . .

The very morning after this Father Butt returned Stephen's monologue in kind. It was a raw nipping morning and when Stephen, who had arrived too late for the Latin lecture, strolled into the Physics Theatre he discovered Father Butt kneeling on the hearthstone engaged in lighting a small fire in the huge grate. He was making neat wisps of paper and carefully disposing them among the coals and sticks. All the while he kept up a little patter explaining his operations and at a crisis he produced from the most remote pockets of his chalkey soutane three dirty candle-butts. These he thrust in different openings and then looked up at Stephen with an air of triumph. He set a match to a few projecting pieces of paper and in a few minutes the coals had caught.

— There is an art, Mr Daedalus, in lighting a fire.

— So I see, sir. A very useful art.

— That's it: a useful art. We have the useful arts and we have the liberal arts.

Father Butt after this statement got up from the hearthstone and went away about some other business leaving Stephen to watch the kindling fire and Stephen brooded upon the fast melting candle-butts and on the reproach of the priest's manner till it was time for the Physics lecture to begin.

The problem could not be solved out of hand but the artistic part of it at least presented no difficulties. In reading through *Twelfth Night* for the class Father Butt skipped the two songs of the clown without a word and when Stephen, determined on forcing them on his attention, asked very gravely whether they were to be learned by heart or not Father Butt said it was improbable such a question would be on the paper:

— The clown sings these songs for the duke. It was a custom at that time for noblemen to have clowns to sing to them . . . for amusement.

He took *Othello* more seriously and made the class take a note of the moral of the play: an object lesson in the passion of jealousy. Shakespeare, he said, had sounded the depths of human nature: his plays show us men and women under the influence of various passions and they show us the moral result of these passions. We see the conflict of these human passions and our own passions are purified by the spectacle. The dramas of Shakespeare have a distinct moral force and *Othello* is one of the greatest of tragedies. Stephen trained himself to hear all this out without moving hand or foot but at the same time he was amused to learn that the president had refused to allow two of the boarders to go ᶜ to a performance of *Othello* at the Gaiety Theatre on the ground that there were many coarse expressions in the play.ᶜ

The monster in Stephen had lately taken to misbehaving himself and on the least provocation was ready for bloodshed. Almost every incident of the day was a goad for him and the intellect had great trouble keeping him within bounds. But the episode of religious fervour which was fast becoming a memory had resulted in a certain outward self-control which was now found to be very useful. Besides this Stephen was quick enough to see that he must disentangle his affairs in secrecy and reserve had ever been a light penance for him. His reluctance to debate scandal, to seem impolitely curious of others, aided him in his real indictment and was not without a satisfactory flavour of the heroic. Already while that fever-fit of holiness lay upon him he had encountered but out of charity had declined to penetrate disillusioning forces. These shocks had driven him from breathless flights of zeal shamefully inwards and the most that devotional exercises could do for him was to soothe him. This soothing he badly needed for he suffered greatly from contact with his new environment. He hardly spoke to his colleagues and performed the business of the class without remark or interest. Every morning he rose and came down to breakfast. After breakfast he took the tram for town, settling himself on the front seat outside with his face to the wind. He got down off the tram at Amiens St Station instead of going on to the Pillar because he wished to partake in the morning life of the city. This morning walk was pleasant for him and there was no

32

face that passed him on its way to its commercial prison but he strove to pierce to the motive centre of its ugliness. It was always with a feeling of displeasure that he entered the Green and saw on the far side the gloomy building of the college.

As he walked thus through the ways of the city he had his ears and eyes ever prompt to receive impressions. It was not only in Skeat that he found words for his treasure-house, he found them also at haphazard in the shops, on advertisements, in the mouths of the plodding public. He kept repeating them to himself till they lost all instantaneous meaning for him and became wonderful vocables. He was determined to fight with every energy of soul and body against any possible consignment to what he now regarded as the hell of hells – the region, otherwise expressed, wherein everything is found to be obvious – and the saint who formerly was ᶜ chary of speech ᶜ in obedience to a commandment of silence could just be recognized in the artist who schooled himself to silence lest words should return him his discourtesy. Phrases came to him asking to have themselves explained. He said to himself: I must wait for the Eucharist to come to me: and then he set about translating the phrase into common sense. He spent days and nights hammering noisily as he built a house of silence for himself wherein he might await his Eucharist, days and nights gathering the first fruits and every peace-offering and heaping them upon his altar whereon he prayed clamorously the burning token of satisfaction might descend. In class, in the hushed library, in the company of other students he would suddenly hear a command to begone, to be alone, a voice agitating the very tympanum of his ear, a flame leaping into divine cerebral life. He would obey the command and wander up and down the streets alone, the fervour of his hope sustained by ejaculations until he felt sure that it was useless to wander any more: and then he would return home with a deliberate, unflagging step piecing together meaningless words and phrases with deliberate unflagging seriousness.[1]

[1] In the MS 'End of First Episode of V' is written in red crayon at this point.

Their Eminences of the Holy College are hardly more scrupulous solitaries during the ballot for Christ's vicar than was Stephen at this time. He wrote a great deal of verse and, in default of any better contrivance, his verse allowed him to combine the offices of penitent and confessor. He sought in his verses to fix the most elusive of his moods and he put his lines together not word by word but letter by letter. He read Blake and Rimbaud on the values of letters and even permuted and combined the five vowels to construct cries for primitive emotions. To none of his former fervours had he given himself with such a whole heart as to this fervour; ^c the monk now seemed to him no more than half the artist. He persuaded himself that it is necessary for an artist to labour incessantly at his art if he wishes to express completely even the simplest conception and he believed that every moment of inspiration must be paid for in advance. He was not convinced of the truth of the saying [*Poeta nascitur, non fit*] 'The poet is born, not made' but he was quite sure of ^c the truth of this at least: [*Poema fit, non nascitur*] 'The poem is made, not born.' The burgher notion of the poet Byron in undress pouring out verses [like] just as a city fountain pours out water seemed to him characteristic of most popular judgments on esthetic matters and he combated the notion at its root ^c by saying solemnly to Maurice – Isolation is the first principle of artistic economy. ^c

Stephen did not attach himself to art in any spirit of youthful dilettantism but strove to pierce to the significant heart of everything. ^c He doubled backwards into the past of humanity and caught glimpses of emergent art as one might have a vision of the plesiosaurus emerging from his ocean of slime. He seemed almost to hear the simple cries of fear and joy and wonder which are antecedent to all song, the savage rhythms of men pulling at the oar, ^c to see the rude scrawls and the portable gods of men whose legacy Leonardo and Michelangelo inherit. And over all this chaos of history and legend, of fact and supposition, he strove to draw out a line of order, to reduce the abysses of the past to order by a diagram. The treatises which were recommended to him he found valueless and trifling; the Laocoon of Lessing irritated him. He wondered how the world could accept as valuable contributions such [fantas] fanciful generalizations. What finer certitude could be attained by the artist if he believed that ancient art was plastic and that modern art was pictorial – ancient art in this context meaning art between the Balkans and the Morea and modern art meaning art anywhere between the Caucusus and the Atlantic except in the sacrosanct region. A great contempt devoured him for the critics who considered 'Greek' and 'classical' interchangeable terms and so full was he of intemperate anger that [all week Saturday] when Father Butt gave *Othello* as the subject for the essay of the week Stephen lodged on the following Monday a profuse, downright protest against the 'masterpiece'! The young men in the class laughed and Stephen, as he looked contemptuously at the laughing faces, thought of a self-submersive reptile.

No-one would listen to his theories: no-one was interested in art. The ᶜ young men in the college ᶜ regarded art as a continental vice and they said in effect, 'If we must have art are there not enough subjects in Holy Writ?' – for an artist with them was a man who painted pictures. It was a bad sign for a young man to show interest in anything but his examinations or his prospective 'job'. It was all very well to be able to talk about it but really art was all 'rot': besides it was probably immoral; they knew (or, at least, they had heard) about studios. They didn't want that kind of thing in their country. Talk about beauty, talk about rhythms, talk about esthetic – they knew what all the fine talk covered. One day a big countrified student came over to Stephen and asked:

— ᶜ Tell us, aren't you an artist?

Stephen gazed at the idea-proof young man, without answering. ℒ

— Because if you are why don't you wear your hair long? ᶜ

A few bystanders laughed at this and Stephen wondered for which of the learned professions the young man's father designed him.

In spite of his surroundings Stephen continued his labours of research and all the more ardently since he imagined they had been ᶜ put under ban.ᶜ It was part of that ineradicable egoism which he was afterwards to call redeemer that he conceived converging to him the deeds and thoughts of his microcosm. Is the mind of youth medieval that it is so divining of intrigue? Field-sports (or their equivalent in the world of mentality) are perhaps the most effective cure and Anglo-Saxon educators favour rather a system of hardy brutality. But for this fantastic idealist, eluding the grunting booted apparition with a bound, the mimic warfare was no less ludicrous than unequal in a ground chosen to his disadvantage. Behind the rapidly indurating shield the sensitive answered: Let the pack of enmities come tumbling and sniffing to my highlands after their game. There was his ground and he flung them disdain from flashing antlers.[1]

Indeed he felt the morning in his blood: he was aware of some movement already proceeding ᶜ out in Europe.ᶜ Of this last phrase he was fond for it seemed to him to unroll the measurable world before the feet of the islanders. Nothing could persuade him that the world was such as Father Butt's students conceived it. He had no need for the cautions which were named indispensable, no reverence for the proprieties which were called the bases of life. He was an enigmatic figure in the midst of his shivering society where he enjoyed a reputation. His comrades hardly knew how far to venture with him and professors pretended to think his seriousness a sufficient warrant against any practical disobedience. On his side chastity, having been found a great inconvenience, had been quietly abandoned and the youth amused himself in the company of certain of his fellow-students among whom (as the fame went) wild living was not unknown. The Rector of Belvedere had a brother who was at this time a student in the college and one night in the gallery of the Gaiety (for Stephen had become a constant 'god') another Belvedere boy, ᶜ who was also a student in the college, bore scandalous witness into Stephen's ear.ᶜ

[1] This phrase occurs in Joyce's satirical poem, 'The Holy Office', which was written at about the same time as the present text. See Gorman, p. 140:

> 'So distantly I turn to view
> The shamblings of that motley crew,
> Those souls that hate the strength that mine has
> Steeled in the school of old Aquinas.
> Where they have crouched and crawled and prayed
> I stand, the self-doomed, unafraid,
> Unfellowed, friendless and alone,
> Indifferent as the herring-bone,
> Firm as the mountain-ridges where
> I flash my antlers on the air.'

— I say, Daedalus . . .

— Well?

— I wonder what MacNally would say if he met his brother – you know the fellow in the college?

— Yes . . .

— I saw him in Stephen's Green the other day with a tart. I was just thinking if MacNally saw him . . .

The informant paused: and then, afraid of over-implication and with an air of a connoisseur, he added seriously:

— Of course she was . . . all right.

Every evening after tea Stephen left his house and set out for the city, Maurice at his side. The elder smoked cigarettes and the younger ate lemon drops and, aided by these animal comforts, they beguiled the long journey with philosophic discourse. Maurice was a very attentive person and one evening he told Stephen that he was keeping a diary of their conversations. Stephen asked to see the diary but Maurice said it would be time enough for that at the end of the first year. Neither of the youths had the least suspicion of themselves; they both looked upon life with frank curious eyes (Maurice naturally serving himself with Stephen's vision when his own was deficient) and they both felt that it was possible to arrive at a sane understanding of so-called mysteries if one only had patience enough. On their way in every evening the heights of argument were traversed and the younger boy aided the elder bravely in the building of an entire science of esthetic. They spoke to each other very decisively and Stephen found Maurice very useful for raising objections. When they came to the gate of the Library they used to stand to finish some branch of their subject and often the discussion was so protracted that Stephen would decide that it was too late to go in to read and so they would set their faces for Clontarf and return in the same manner. Stephen, after certain hesitations, showed Maurice the first-fruits of his verse and Maurice asked who the woman was. Stephen looked a little vaguely before him before answering and in the end had to answer that he didn't know who she was.

To this unknown verses were now regularly inscribed and it seemed that the evil dream of love which Stephen chose to commemorate in these verses lay veritably upon the world now in a season of ᶜ damp violet mist. He had abandoned his Madonna,ᶜ he had forsaken his word and he had withdrawn sternly from his little world and surely it was not wonderful that his solitude should propel him to frenetic outbursts of a young man's passion and to outbursts of loneliness? This quality of the mind which so reveals itself is called (when incorrigible) a decadence but if we are to take a general view of [life] the world we cannot but see a process to life through corruption. There were moments for him, however, when such a process would have seemed intolerable, life on any common terms an intolerable offence, and at such moments he prayed for nothing and lamented for nothing but he felt with a sweet sinking of consciousness that if the end came to him it was in the arms of the unknown that it would come to him:

<blockquote>
ᶜ The dawn awakes with tremulous alarms,
How grey, how cold, how bare!
O, hold me still white arms, encircling arms!
And hide me, heavy hair!

Life is a dream, a dream. The hour is done
And antiphon is said.
We go from the light and falsehood of the sun
To bleak wastes of the dead.ᶜ
</blockquote>

Little by little Stephen became more irregular in his attendances at the college. He would leave his house every morning at the usual hour and come into the city on the tram. But always at Amiens St Station he would get down and walk and as often as not he would decide to follow some trivial indication of city life instead of entering the oppressive life of the college. He often walked thus for seven or eight hours at a stretch without feeling in the least fatigued. The damp Dublin winter seemed to harmonize with his inward sense of unreadiness and he did not follow the least of feminine provocations through tortuous, unexpected ways any more zealously than he followed through ways even less satisfying the nimble movements of the elusive one. What was that One: arms of love that had not love's malignity, laughter running upon the mountains of the morning, an hour wherein might be encountered the incommunicable? And if the heart but trembled an instant at some approach to that he would cry, youthfully, passionately 'It is so! It is so! Life is such as I conceive it.' He spurned from before him the stale maxims of the Jesuits and he swore an oath that [never] they should never establish over him an ascendancy. He spurned from before him a world of the higher culture in which there was neither scholarship nor art nor dignity of manners – a world of trivial intrigues and trivial triumphs. Above all he spurned from before him the company of [the] decrepit youth – and he swore an oath that never would they establish with him a compact of fraud. Fine words! fine oaths! crying bravely and passionately even in the teeth of circumstances. For not infrequently in the pauses of rapture Dublin would lay a sudden hand upon his shoulder, ° and the chill of the summons would strike to his heart. One day he passed on his homeward journey through Fairview. At the fork of the roads before the swampy beach a big dog was recumbent. From time to time he lifted his muzzle in the vaporous air, uttering a prolonged sorrowful howl. ° People had gathered on the footpaths to hear him. [and] Stephen made one of them till he felt the first drops of rain, and then he continued his way in silence under the dull surveillance of heaven, hearing from time to time behind him the strange lamentation.

It was natural that the more the youth sought solitude for himself the more his society sought to prevent his purpose. Though he was still in his first year he was considered a personality and there were even many who thought that though his theories were a trifle ardent they were not without meaning. Stephen came seldom to lectures, prepared nothing and absented himself from term examinations and not merely was no remark passed on these extravagances but it was supposed probable that he represented really the artistic type and that he was, after the fashion of that little known tribe, educating himself. It must not be supposed that the popular University of Ireland lacked an intelligent centre. Outside the compact body of national ° revivalists there were here and there students who had certain ideas of their own and were more or less tolerated by their fellows.° For instance there was a serious young feminist named McCann – a blunt brisk figure, wearing a Cavalier beard and shooting-suit, and a steadfast reader of the *Review of Reviews*. The students of the college did not understand what manner of ideas he favoured and they considered that they rewarded his originality sufficiently by calling him 'Knicker-bockers'. There was also the College orator – a most amenable young man who spoke at all meetings. Cranly too was a personality and Madden had soon been recognized as the ᶜ spokesman ᶜ of the patri-otic party. Stephen may be said to have occupied the position of notable-extraordinary: very few had ever heard of the writers he was reported to read and those who had knew them to be mad fel-lows. At the same time as Stephen's manner was so unbending to all it was supposed that he had preserved his sanity entire and safely braved temptations. People began to defer to him, to invite him to their houses and to present serious faces to him. His were simply theories and, as he had as yet committed no breach of the law, he was respectfully invited to read a paper before the Literary and Historical Society of the college. The date was fixed for the end of March and the title of the paper was announced as 'Drama and Life'. Many risked the peril of rebuff to engage the young eccentric in talk but Stephen preserved a disdainful silence. One night as he was returning from a party a reporter of one of the Dublin papers, who had been intro-duced that evening to the prodigy, approached him and after a few exchanges said to him tentatively:

— I was reading of that writer . . . what's this you call him . . . Maeterlinck the other day . . . you know?

— Yes . . .

— I was reading, *The Intruder* I think was the name of it . . . Very . . . curious play . . .

Stephen had no wish to talk to the man about Maeterlinck and on the other hand he did not like to offend by the silence which the remark and the tone and the intention all seemed to deserve so he cast about quickly in his mind for some noncommittal banality with which to pay the debt. At last he said:

— It would be hard to put it on the stage.

The journalist was quite satisfied at this exchange as if it was just this impression and no other which Maeterlinck's play had produced upon him. He assented with conviction:

— O yes! . . . next to impossible . . .

Allusions of such a kind to what he held so dear at heart wounded

Stephen deeply. It must be said simply and at once that at this time Stephen suffered the most enduring influence of his life. The spectacle of the world which his intelligence presented to him with every sordid and deceptive detail set side by side with the spectacle of the world which the monster in him, now grown to a reasonably heroic stage, presented also had often filled him with such sudden despair as could be assuaged only by melancholy versing. He had all but decided to consider the two worlds as aliens one to another – however disguised or expressed the most utter of pessimisms – when he encountered through the medium of hardly procured translations the spirit of Henrik Ibsen. He understood that spirit ᶜ instantaneously.ᶜ Some years before this same instantaneous understanding had occurred when he had read the very puzzled, apologetic account which Rousseau's English biographer had ᶜ given of the young philosopher's ᶜ stealing his mistress's spoons and allowing a servant-girl to be accused of the theft at the very moment when he was beginning his struggle for Truth and Liberty. Just as then with the [perverted] perverse philosopher so now: Ibsen had no need of apologist or critic: the minds of the old Norse poet and of the perturbed young Celt met in a moment of radiant simultaneity. Stephen was captivated first by the evident excellence of the art: he was not long before he began to affirm, out of a sufficiently scanty knowledge of the tract, of course, that Ibsen was the first among the dramatists of the world. In translations of the Hindu or Greek or Chinese theatres he found only anticipations of or attempts and in the French classical, and the English romantic, theatres anticipations less distinct and attempts less successful. But it was not only this excellence which captivated him: it was not that which he greeted gladly with an entire joyful spiritual salutation. It was the very spirit of Ibsen himself that was discerned moving behind the impersonal manner of the artist: [Ibsen with his profound self-approval, Ibsen with his haughty, disillusioned courage, Ibsen with his minute and wilful energy.] a mind of sincere and boylike bravery, of disillusioned pride, of minute and wilful energy.[1] Let the world solve itself in whatsoever fashion it pleased, let its putative Maker justify Himself

[1] The changed wording is written in pencil in the margin, perhaps at a later date than that of the MS.

by whatsoever processes seemed good to Him, one could scarcely advance the dignity of the human attitude a step beyond this answer. Here and not in Shakespeare or Goethe was the successor to the first poet of the Europeans, here, as only to such purpose in Dante, a human personality had been found united with an artistic manner which was itself almost a natural phenomenon: and the spirit of the time united one more readily with the Norwegian than with the Florentine.

The young men of the college had not the least idea who Ibsen was but from what they could gather here and there they surmised that he must be one of the ᶜ atheistic writers whom the papal secretary puts on the *Index*. It was a novelty to hear anyone mention such a name ᶜ in their college but as the professors gave no lead in condemnation they concluded that they had better wait. Meanwhile they were somewhat impressed: many now began to say that though Ibsen was immoral he was a great writer and one of the professors was heard to say that when he was in Berlin last summer on his holidays there had been a great deal of talk about some play of Ibsen's which was being performed at one of the theatres. Stephen had begun to study Danish instead of preparing his course for the examination and this fact was magnified into a report that he was a competent Danish scholar. That youth was astute enough to profit by rumours which he took no trouble to contradict. He smiled to think that these people in their hearts feared him as an infidel and he marvelled at the quality of their supposed beliefs. Father Butt talked to him a great deal and Stephen was nothing loth to make ᶜ himself the herald ᶜ of a new order. He never spoke with heat and he argued always as if he did not greatly care which way the argument went, at the same time never losing a point. The Jesuits and their flocks may have said to themselves: the ᶜ youthful-seeming-independent ᶜ we know, and the appeasable patriot we know, but what are you? They played up to him very well, ᶜ considering their disadvantages, and Stephen could not understand why they took the trouble to humour him.ᶜ

— Yes, yes, said Father Butt one day after one of these scenes, I see . . . I quite see your point . . . It would apply of course to the dramas of Turgénieff?

Stephen had read and admired certain translations of Turgénieff's novels and stories and he asked therefore with a genuine note in his voice:

— Do you mean his novels?

— Novels, yes, said Father Butt swiftly, . . . his novels, to be sure . . . but of course they are dramas . . . are they not, Mr Daedalus?

Very often Stephen used to visit at a house in Donnybrook the atmosphere of which was compact of liberal patriotism and orthodox study. There were several marriageable daughters in the family and whenever any promise [was] on the part of a young student was signalled he was sure to receive an invitation to this house. The young feminist McCann was a constant visitor there and Madden used to visit occasionally. The father of the family was an elderly man who played chess on week evenings with his grown-up sons and assisted on Sunday evenings at a round of games and music. The music was supplied by Stephen. There was an old piano in the room and when the room was tired of games one of the daughters used to come over smilingly to Stephen and ᶜ ask him to sing them some of his beautiful songs. The keys of the piano were worn away and sometimes the notes would not sound but the tone was soft and mellow and Stephen used to sit down and sing his beautiful songs to the polite, tired, unmusical audience.ᶜ¹ The songs, for him at least, were really beautiful – the old country songs of England and the elegant songs of the Elizabethans. The 'moral' of these songs was sometimes a little dubious and Stephen's ear used to catch at once the note of qualification in the applause that followed them. The studious daughters found these songs very quaint but Mr Daniel said that Stephen should sing operatic music if he wanted to have his voice heard properly. In spite of the entire absence of sympathy between this circle and himself Stephen was very much at ease in it and he was as they bade him be, very much 'at home' as he sat on the sofa counting the lumps of horsehair with the ends of his ᶜ fingers, and listening to the conversation.ᶜ The young men and the daughters amused themselves tolerably under Mr Daniel's eye but whenever there was an approach to artistic matters during the process of their games Stephen with egoistic

¹ The words 'loth to depart' are written in red crayon in the margin opposite these sentences.

humour imagined his presence acting as a propriety. He could see seriousness developing on the shrewd features of a young man who had to put a certain question to one of the daughters:

— I suppose it's my turn now . . . Well . . . let me see . . . (and here he became as serious as a young man, who has been laughing very much for a full five minutes, can become) . . . Who is your favourite poet, Annie?

Annie thought for a few moments: there was a pause. Annie and the young man were 'doing' the same course.

— . . . German?

— . . . Yes.

Annie thought for another few moments while the table waited to be edified.

— I think . . . Goethe.

McCann used very often to organize ᶜ charades ᶜ in which he used to take the most violent parts. The charades were very farcical and everyone took his part with goodwill, Stephen as well as the others. Stephen would [play often] play his quiet deliberative manner off against McCann's uproarious acting and for this reason the two were often 'picked' together. These charades wearied Stephen a little but McCann was very much given to organizing them as he was of the opinion that amusement is necessary for the bodily welfare of mankind. The young feminist's Northern accent always excited laughter and his face, adorned with its Cavalier beard, was certainly capable of brazen grimaces. In the college McCann [was] had never been assimilated on account of his 'ideas' but here he partook of the inner life of the family.[1] In this house it was the custom to call a young visitor ᶜby his Christian nameᶜ a little too soon and though Stephen was spared the compliment, McCann was never spoken of as anything but 'Phil'. Stephen used to call him 'Bonny Dundee' nonsensically associating [the] his brisk name and his ᶜbrisk manners with the soundᶜ of the line:

Come fill up my cup, come fill up my can.

[1] Opposite this paragraph the words, 'fancy dress ball: Emma', are written in red crayon.

44

Whenever the evening assumed the character of a serious affair Mr Daniel would be asked to recite something for the company. Mr Daniel had formerly been the manager of a theatre in Wexford and he had °often spoken at public meetings° through the country. He recited national pieces in a stern declamatory fashion amid attentive silence. The daughters also recited. During these recitations Stephen's eye never moved from the picture of the Sacred Heart which hung right above the head of the reciter's head. The Miss Daniels were not so imposing as their father and their dress was [*word crossed out so as to be illegible*] somewhat colleen. ° Jesus, moreoever, exposed ° his heart somewhat too obviously in the cheap print: and Stephen's thoughts were usually fascinated to a pleasant stupor by these twin futilities. A parliamentary charade was frequent. Mr Daniel had sat for his country some years before and for this reason he was chosen to impersonate the Speaker of the House. McCann always represented a member of the Opposition and he spoke point-blank. Then a member would protest and there would be a make-believe of parliamentary manners.

— Mr Speaker, I must ask . . .
— Order! Order!
— You know it's a lie!
— You must withdraw, Sir.
— As I was saying before the honourable gentleman interrupted we must . . .
— I won't withdraw.
— I must ask honourable members to preserve order in the House.
— I won't withdraw.
— Order! Order!

Another favourite was 'Who's Who'. A person goes out of the room and the rest of the company choose the name of someone who is supposed to have special attractions for the absent player. This latter, when he returns to the company, has to ask questions all round and try to guess the name. This game was generally used to the discomfiture of the young male guests for the manner in which it was played suggested that each young student had an affair of the heart with some young lady within tolerable distance of him: but the young men, who were at first surprised by these implications, ended by looking as if they thought that the sagacity of the other players had just forestalled them in an unexpected, not unpleasant, discovery. No such suggestion could be seriously made by the company to fit Stephen's case and so the first time he played the game they chose differently for him. The [company was] players were unable to answer his questions when he returned to the room: such questions as: 'Where does the person live?' 'Is the person married or single?' 'What age is the person?' could not be answered by the circle until McCann had been consulted in a swift undertone. The answer 'Norway' gave Stephen the clue at once and so the game ended and the company proceeded to divert themselves as before this serious interruption. Stephen sat down beside one of the daughters and, while admiring the rural comeliness of her features, waited quietly for her first word which, he knew, would destroy his satisfaction. Her large handsome eyes looked at him for a while as if they were ᶜ about to trust him ᶜ and then she said:

— How did you guess it so quickly?

—I knew you meant him. But you're wrong about his age.

Others had heard this: but she was impressed by a possible vastness of the unknown, complimented to confer with one who conferred directly with the exceptional. She leaned forward to speak with soft seriousness.

— Why, how old is he?

— Over seventy.

— Is he?

Stephen now imagined that he had explored this region sufficiently and he would have discontinued his visits had not two causes induced him to continue. The first cause was the unpleasant character of his home and the second was the curiosity occasioned by the advent of a new figure. One evening while he was musing on the horsehair sofa he heard his name called and stood up to be introduced. A dark ᶜ full-figured ᶜ girl was standing before him and, without waiting for Miss Daniel's introduction, she said:

— I think we know each other already.

She sat beside him on the sofa and he found out that she was studying in the same college with the Miss Daniels and that she always signed her name in Irish. She said Stephen ᶜ should learn Irish too ᶜ and join the League. A young man of the company, [with] whose face wore always the same look of studied purpose, spoke with her across

Stephen addressing her familiarly by her Irish name. Stephen therefore spoke very formally and always addressed her as 'Miss Clery'.
She seemed on her part to include him in the ° general scheme of her
nationalizing charm: and when he helped her into her jacket she
allowed his hands to rest for a moment against the warm flesh of her
shoulders.°

XVII

Stephen's home-life had by this time grown sufficiently unpleasant: the direction of his development was against the stream of tendency of his family. The evening walks with Maurice had been prohibited for it had become evident that Stephen was corrupting his brother to idle habits. Stephen was harassed very much by enquiries as to his progress at the College and Mr Daedalus, meditating upon the evasive answers, had begun to express a fear that his son was falling into bad company. The youth was given to understand that if he did not succeed brilliantly at the coming examination his career at the University would come to a close. He was not greatly troubled by this warning for he knew that his fate was, in this respect, with his godfather and not with his father. He felt that the moments of his youth were too precious to be wasted in a dull mechanical endeavour and he determined, whatever came of it, to prosecute his intentions to the end. His family expected that he would at once follow the path of remunerative respectability and save the situation but he could not satisfy his family. He thanked their intention: it had first fulfilled him with egoism; and he rejoiced that his life had been so self-centred. He felt [also] however that there were activities which it ° would be a peril ° to postpone.

Maurice accepted this prohibition with a bad grace and had to be restrained by his brother from overt disobedience. Stephen himself bore it lightly because he could ease himself greatly in solitude and for human channels, at the worst, he could resort to a few of his college-companions. He was now busily preparing his paper for the Literary and Historical Society and he took every precaution to ensure in it a maximum of explosive force. It seemed to him that the students might need only the word to enkindle them towards liberty or that, at least, his trumpet-call might bring to his side a certain minority of the elect. McCann was the Auditor of the Society and as he was anxious to know the trend of Stephen's paper the two used often to leave the Library at ten o'clock and walk towards the Auditor's lodgings, discussing. McCann enjoyed the reputation of a fearless, free-spoken young man but Stephen found it difficult to bring him to any fixed terms on matters which were held to be dangerous ground. McCann would talk freely on feminism and on rational life: he believed that the sexes should be educated together in order to accustom them early to each other's influences and he believed that women should be afforded the same opportunities as were afforded to the so-called superior sex and he believed that women had the right to compete with men in every branch of social and intellectual activity. He also held the opinion that a man should live without using any kind of stimulant, that he had a moral obligation to transmit to posterity sound minds in sound bodies, and that he should not allow himself to be dictated to on the subject of dress by any conventions. Stephen delighted to riddle these theories with agile bullets.

— You would have no sphere of life closed to them?

— Certainly not.

— Would you have the soldiery, the police and the fire-brigade recruited also from them?

— There are certain social duties for which women are physically unfitted.

— I believe you.

— At the same time they should be allowed to follow any civil profession for which they have an aptitude.

— Doctors and lawyers?

— Certainly.

— And what about the third learned profession?

— How do you mean?

— Do you think they would make good confessors?

— You are flippant. The Church does not allow women to enter the priesthood.

— O, the Church!

Whenever the conversation reached this point McCann refused to follow it further. The discussion usually ended in [an impasse] a deadlock:

— But you go mountain-climbing in search of fresh air?

— Yes.

— And bathing in the summertime?

— Yes.

— And surely the mountain air and the salt water act as stimulants!

— Natural stimulants, yes.

— What do you call an unnatural stimulant?

— Intoxicating drinks.

— But they are produced from natural vegetable substances, aren't they?

— Perhaps, but by an unnatural process.

— Then you regard a brewer as a high thaumaturgist?

— Intoxicating drinks are manufactured to satisfy artificially induced appetites. Man, in the normal condition, has no need for such props to life.

— Give me an example of man in what you call 'the normal condition'.

— A man who lives a healthy, natural life.

— Yourself?

— Yes.

— Do you then represent normal humanity?

— I do.

— Then is normal humanity short-sighted and tone-deaf?

— Tone-deaf?

— Yes: I think you are tone-deaf.

— I like to hear music.

— What music?

— All music.

— But you cannot distinguish one air from another.

— No: I can recognize some airs.

— For instance?

— I can recognize 'God save the Queen'.

— Perhaps because all the people stand up and take off their hats.

— Well, admit that my ear is a little defective.

— And your eyes?

— They too.

— Then how do you represent normal humanity?

— In my manner of life.

— Your wants and the manner in which you satisfy them, is it?

— Exactly.

— And what are your wants?

— Air and food.

— Have you any subsidiary ones?

— The acquisition of knowledge.

— And you need also religious comforts?

— Maybe so . . . at times.

— And women . . . at times?

— Never!

This last word was uttered with a moral snap of the jaws and in such a business-like tone of voice that Stephen burst out into a fit of loud laughter. As for the fact, though he was very suspicious in this matter, Stephen was inclined to believe in McCann's chastity and much as he disliked it he chose to contemplate it rather than the contrary phenomenon. He almost trembled to think of that unhorizoned doggedness working its way backwards.

McCann's insistence on a righteous life and his condemnation of licence as a sin against the future both annoyed and stung Stephen. It annoyed him because it savoured so strongly of *paterfamilias* and it stung him because it seemed to judge him incapable of that part. In McCann's mouth he considered it unjust and unnatural and he fell back on a sentence of Bacon's. The care of posterity, he quoted, is greatest in them that have no posterity; and for the rest he said that he ᶜ could not understand what right the future had to hinder him from any passionate exertions in the present.ᶜ

— That is not the teaching of Ibsen, said McCann.

— Teaching! cried Stephen.

— The moral of *Ghosts* is just the opposite of what you say.

— Bah! You regard a play as a scientific document.

— *Ghosts* teaches self-repression.

— O Jesus! said Stephen in agony.

— This is my lodging, said McCann, halting at the gate. I must go in.

— You have connected Ibsen and Eno's fruit salt forever in my mind, said Stephen.

— Daedalus, said the Auditor crisply, you are a good fellow but you have yet to learn the ᶜ dignity of altruism and the responsibility of the human individual. ᶜ

Stephen had decided to address himself to Madden to [find out] ascertain where Miss Clery was to be found. He set about this task carefully. Madden and he were often together but their conversations were rarely serious and though the rustic mind of one was very forcibly impressed by the metropolitanism of the other both young men were on relations of affectionate familiarity. Madden who had previously tried in vain to infect Stephen with nationalistic fever was surprised to hear these overtures of his friend. He was delighted at the prospect of making such a convert and he began to appeal eloquently to the sense of justice. Stephen allowed his critical faculty a rest. The so-desired community for the realizing of which Madden sought to engage his personal force seemed to him anything but ideal and the liberation which would have satisfied Madden would by no means have satisfied him. The Roman, not the Sassenach, was for him the tyrant of the islanders: and so deeply had the tyranny eaten into all souls that the intelligence, first overborne so arrogantly, was now eager to prove that arrogance its friend. The watchcry was Faith and Fatherland, a sacred word in that world of cleverly inflammable enthusiasms. With literal obedience and with annual doles the Irish bid eagerly for the honour which was studiously withheld from them to be given to nations which in the [present] past, as in the [past] present, had never bent the knee but in defiance. While the multitude of preachers assured them that high honours were on the way and encouraged them ever to hope. The last should be first, according to the Christian sentiment, and whosoever humbled himself, exalted and in reward for several centuries of obscure fidelity the ᶜ Pope's Holiness ᶜ had presented a tardy cardinal to an island which was for him, perhaps, only the ᶜ afterthought of Europe.ᶜ[1]

Madden was prepared to admit the truth of much of this but he gave Stephen to understand that the new movement was politic. If the least infidelity were hoisted on the standard the people would not flock to it and for this reason the promoters desired as far as possible to work hand in hand with the priests. Stephen objected that this working hand in hand with the priests had over and over again ruined the chances of revolutions. Madden agreed but now at least the priests were on the side of the people.

— Do you not see, said Stephen, that they encourage the study of Irish that their flocks may be more safely protected from the ᶜ wolves of disbeliefᶜ; they consider it is an opportunity to withdraw the people into a past of literal, implicit faith?

[1] In Joyce's notes for *Stephen Hero* printed by Gorman (p. 135), appear the words: 'Ireland – an afterthought of Europe'.

— But really our peasant has nothing to gain from English Literature.

— Rubbish!

— Modern at least. You yourself are always railing . . .

— English is the medium for the Continent.

— We want an Irish Ireland.

— It seems to me you do not care what banality a man expresses so long as he expresses it in Irish.

— I do not entirely agree with your modern notions. We want to have nothing of this English civilization.

— But the civilization of which you speak is not English – it is Aryan. The modern notions are not English; they point the way of Aryan civilization.

— You want our peasants to ape the gross materialism of the Yorkshire peasant?

— One would imagine the country was inhabited by cherubim. Damme if I see much difference in peasants: they all seem to me as like one another as a peascod is like another peascod. The Yorkshire-man is perhaps better fed.

— Of course you despise the peasant because you live in the city.

— I don't despise his office in the least.

— But you despise him – he's not clever enough for you.

— Now, you know, Madden, that's nonsense. To begin with he's as cute as a fox – try to pass a false coin on him and you'll see. But his cleverness is all of a low order. I really don't think that the Irish peasant ᶜ represents ᶜ a very admirable type of culture.

— That's you all out! Of course you sneer at him because he's not up-to-date and lives a simple life.

— Yes, a life of dull routine – the calculation of coppers, the weekly debauch and the weekly piety – a life lived in cunning and fear between the shadows of the parish chapel and the asylum!

— The life of a great city like London seems to you better?

— The [English] intelligence of an English city is not perhaps at a very high level but at least it is higher than the mental swamp of the Irish peasant.

— And what about the two as moral beings?

— Well?

— The Irish are noted for at least one virtue all the world over.

— Oho! I know what's coming now!

— But it's a fact – they are chaste.

— To be sure.

— You like to run down your own people at every hand's turn but you can't accuse them . . .

— Very good: you are partly right. I fully recognize that my countrymen have not yet advanced [to] as far as the machinery of Parisian harlotry because . . .

— Because . . .?

— Well, because they can do it by hand, that's why!

— Good God, you don't mean to say you think . . .

— My good youth, I know what I am saying is true and so do you know it. Ask Father Pat and ask Dr Thisbody and ask Dr Thatbody. I was at school and you were at school – and that's enough about it.

— O, Daedalus!

This accusation laid a silence on the conversation. Then Madden spoke:

— Well, if these are your ideas I don't see what you want coming to me and talking about learning Irish.

— I would like to learn it – as a language, said Stephen lyingly. At least I would like to see first.

— So you admit you are an Irishman after all and not one of the red garrison.

— Of course I do.

— And don't you think that every Irishman worthy of the name should be able to speak his native tongue?

— I really don't know.

— And don't you think that we as a race have a right to be free?

— O, don't ask me such questions, Madden. You can use these phrases of the platform but I can't.

— But surely you have some political opinions, man!

— I am going to think them out. I am an artist, don't you see? Do you believe that I am?

— O, yes, I know you are.

— Very well then, how the devil can you expect me to settle everything all at once? Give me time.

So it was decided that Stephen was to begin a course of lessons in

Irish. He bought the O'Growney's primers published by the Gaelic League but refused either to pay a subscription to the League or to wear the badge in his buttonhole. He had found out what he had desired, namely, the class in which Miss Clery was. People at home did not seem opposed to this new freak of his. Mr Casey taught him a few Southern songs in Irish and always raised his glass to Stephen saying 'Sinn Fein' instead of 'Good Health'. Mrs Daedalus was probably pleased for she thought that the superintendence of priests and the society of harmless enthusiasts might succeed in influencing her son in the right direction: she had begun to fear for him. Maurice said nothing and asked no questions. He did not understand what made his brother associate with the patriots and he did not believe that the study of Irish seemed in any way useful to Stephen: but he was silent and waited. Mr Daedalus said that he did not mind his son's learning the language so long as it did not keep him from his legitimate work.

One evening when Maurice came back from school he brought with him the news that the retreat would begin in three days' time. This news suddenly delivered showed Stephen his position. He could hardly believe that in a year his point of view had changed so completely. Only twelve months ago he had been clamouring for forgiveness and promising endless penances. He could hardly believe that it was no other than he who had clung so fiercely to the sole means of salvation which the Church vouchsafes to her guilty children. He marvelled at the terror which had then possessed him. One evening during the retreat he asked his brother what kind of sermons the priest was giving. The two were standing together looking into the window of a stationer's shop and it was a picture of S. Anthony in the window which had led to the question. Maurice smiled broadly as he answered:

— Hell to-day.

— And what kind of a sermon was it?

— Usual kind of thing. Stink in the morning and pain of loss in the evening.

Stephen laughed and looked at the square-shouldered boy beside him. Maurice announced facts in a dry satirical voice and his cloudy complexion did not change colour when he laughed. He made Stephen think of the pictures in 'Silas Verney'. His sombre gravity, his careful cleansing of his much-worn clothes, and the premature disillusionment of his manner all suggested the human vesture of some spiritual or philosophical problem transplanted from Holland. Stephen did not know in what stage the problem was and he thought it wiser to allow it its own path of solution.

— Do you know what the priest told us also? asked Maurice after a pause.

— What?

— He said we weren't to have companions.

— Companions?

— ᶜ That we weren't to go for walks in the evenings with any special companions. If we wanted to take a walk, he said, a lot of us were to go together.ᶜ

Stephen halted in the street and struck the palms of his hands together.

—What's up with you? said Maurice.

— I know what's up with them, said Stephen. They're afraid.

— Of course they're afraid, said Maurice gravely.

— By the by of course you have made the retreat?

— O, yes. I'm going to the altar in the morning.

— Are you really?

— Tell the truth, Stephen. When mother gives you the money on Sunday to go in to short twelve in Marlboro' St do you really go to Mass?

Stephen coloured slightly.

— Why do you ask that?

— Tell the truth.

— No . . . I don't.

— And where do you go?

— O anywhere . . . about the town.

— So I thought.

— You're a 'cute fellow, said Stephen in a sidewise fashion. Might I ask do you go to mass yourself?

— O, yes, said Maurice.

They walked on [then] for a short time in silence. Then Maurice said:

— I have bad hearing.

Stephen made no remark.

— And I think I must be a little stupid.

— How's that?

In his heart Stephen felt that he was condemning his brother. In this instance he could not admit that freedom from strict religious influences was desirable. It seemed to him that anyone who could contemplate the condition of his soul in such a prosaic manner was not worthy of freedom and was fit only for the severest ᵉ shackles of the Church.ᵉ

— Well to-day the priest was telling us a true story. It was about the death of a drunkard. The priest came in to see him and talked to him and asked him to say he was sorry and to promise to give up drink. The man felt that he was going to die in a few moments but he sat upright in the bed, the priest said, and pulled out a black bottle from under the bedclothes . . .

— Well?

— and said 'Father, if this was to be the last I was ever to drink in this world I must drink it.'

— Well?

— So he drained the bottle dry. That very moment he dropped dead, said the priest lowering his voice. 'That man fell dead in the bed, stone dead. He died and went . . .' He spoke so low that I couldn't hear but I wanted to know where the man went so I leaned forward to hear and hit my nose a waliop against the bench in front. While I was rubbing it the fellows knelt down to say the prayer so I didn't hear where he went. Amn't I stupid?

Stephen exploded in laughter. He laughed so loudly that the people who were passing turned to look at him and had to smile themselves by attraction. He put his hands to his sides and the tears almost fell out of his eyes. Every glimpse he caught of Maurice's solemn olive-coloured face set him off on a new burst. He could say nothing between times but – 'I'd have given anything to have seen it – "Father, if this was the last" . . . and you with your mouth open. I'd have given anything to have seen it.'

The Irish class was held every Wednesday night in a back room on the second floor of a house in O'Connell St. The class consisted of six young men and three young women. The teacher was a young man in spectacles with a very sick-looking face and a very crooked mouth.

He spoke in a high-pitched voice and with a cutting Northern accent. He never lost an opportunity of sneering at seoninism[1] and at those who would not learn their native tongue. He said that Beurla[2] was the language of commerce and Irish the speech of the soul and he had two witticisms which always made his class laugh. One was the 'Almighty Dollar' and the other was the 'Spiritual Saxon'. Everyone regarded Mr Hughes as a great enthusiast and some thought he had a great career before him as an orator. On Friday nights when there was a public meeting of the League he often spoke but as he did not know enough Irish he always excused himself at the beginning of his speech for having to speak to the audience in the language of the [gallant] 'Spiritual Saxon'. At the end of every speech he quoted a piece of verse. He scoffed very much at Trinity College and at the Irish Parliamentary Party. He could not regard as patriots men who had taken oaths of allegiance to the Queen of England and he could not regard as a national university an institution which did not express the religious convictions of the majority of the Irish people. His speeches were always loudly applauded and Stephen heard some of the audience say that they were sure he would be a great success at the bar. On enquiry, Stephen found that Hughes, who was the son of a Nationalist solicitor in Armagh, was a law-student at the King's Inns.

The Irish class which Stephen attended was held in a very sparely furnished room lit [with] by a gasjet which had a broken globe. Over the mantelpiece hung the picture of a priest with a beard who, Stephen found, was Father O'Growney. It was a beginners' class and its progress was retarded by the stupidity of two of the young men. The others in the class learned quickly and worked very hard. Stephen found it very [hard] troublesome to pronounce the gutturals but he did the best he could. The class was very serious and patriotic. The only time Stephen found it inclined to levity was at the lesson which introduced the word 'gradh'. The three young women laughed and the two stupid young men laughed, finding something very funny in the Irish word for 'love' or perhaps in the notion itself. But Mr Hughes and the other three young men and Stephen were all very grave. When the excitement of the word had passed Stephen's

---

[1] 'West Britonism.' From *Seon*, John; especially John Bull.
[2] The English language.

attention was attracted to the younger of the stupid young men who was still blushing violently. His blush continued for such a long time that Stephen began to feel nervous. ° The young man grew more and more confused and what was worst was that he was making all this confusion for himself for no-one in the class but Stephen seemed to have noticed him. He continued so till the end of the hour never once daring to raise his eyes from his book and when he had occasion to use his handkerchief he did so stealthily with his left hand.°

The meetings on Friday nights were public and were largely patron-ized by priests. The organizers brought in reports from different districts and the priests made speeches of exhortation. Two young men would then be called on for songs in Irish and when it was time for the whole company to break up all would rise and sing the Rallying-Song. The young women would then begin to chatter while their cavaliers helped them into their jackets. A very stout black-bearded citizen who always wore a wideawake hat and a long bright green muffler was a constant figure at these meetings.[1] When the company was going home he was usually to be seen surrounded by a circle of young men who looked very meagre about his bulk. He had the voice of an ox and he could be heard at a great distance, criticizing, denouncing and scoffing. His circle was the separatist centre and in it reigned the irreconcilable temper. It had its headquarters in Cooney's tobacco-shop where the members sat every evening in the 'Divan' talking Irish loudly and smoking churchwardens. To this circle Madden who was the captain of a club of hurley-players reported the muscular condition of the young irreconcilables under his charge and the editor of the weekly journal of the irreconcilable party[2] reported any signs of Philocelticism which he had observed in the Paris newspapers.

By all this society liberty was held to be the chief desirable; the members of it were fierce democrats. The liberty they desired for themselves was mainly a liberty of costume and vocabulary: and Stephen could hardly understand how such a poor scarecrow of liberty could bring [to their] serious human beings to their knees in worship. As in the Daniels' household he had seen people playing at

[1] This is Michael Cusack, the 'Citizen' of *Ulysses*, and founder of the Gaelic Athletic Association.

[2] Arthur Griffith and *The United Irishman*.

being important so here he saw people playing at being free. He saw that many political absurdities arose from the lack of a just sense of comparison in public men. The orators of this patriotic party were not ashamed to cite the precedents of Switzerland and France. The intelligent centres of the movement were so scantily supplied that the analogies they gave out as exact and potent were really analogies built haphazard upon very inexact knowledge. The cry of a solitary Frenchman (A bas l'Angleterre!) at a Celtic re-union in Paris would be made by these enthusiasts the subject of a leading article in which would be shown the imminence of aid for Ireland from the French Government. A glowing example was to be found for Ireland in the case of Hungary, an example, as these patriots imagined, of a long-suffering minority, entitled by every right of race and justice to a separate freedom, finally emancipating itself. In emulation of that achievement bodies of young Gaels conflicted murderously in the Phoenix Park with whacking hurley-sticks, thrice armed in their just quarrel since their revolution had been blessed for them by the Anointed, and the same bodies were set aflame with indignation [at] by the unwelcome presence of any young sceptic who was aware of the capable aggressions of the Magyars upon the Latin and Slav and Teutonic populations, greater than themselves in number, which are politically allied to them, and of the potency of a single regiment of infantry to hold in check a town of twenty thousand inhabitants.

Stephen said one day to Madden:

— I suppose these hurley-matches and walking tours are preparations for the great event.

— There is more going on in Ireland at present than you are aware of.

— But what use are camàns?[1]

— Well, you see, we want to raise the physique of the country.

Stephen meditated for a moment and then he said:

— It seems to me that the English Government is very good to you in this matter.

— How is that may I ask?

— The English Government will take you every summer in batches to different militia camps, train you to the use of modern

---

[1] Hurley sticks.

60

weapons, drill you, feed you and pay you and then send you home again when the manœuvres are over.

— Well?

— Wouldn't that be better for your young men than hurley-practice in the Park?

— Do you mean to say you want young Gaelic Leaguers to wear the redcoat and take an oath of allegiance to the Queen and take her shilling too?

— Look at your friend, Hughes.

— What about him?

— One of these days he will be a barrister, a Q.C., perhaps a judge – and yet he sneers at the Parliamentary Party because they take an oath of allegiance.

— Law is law all the world over – there must be someone to administer it, particularly here, where the people have no friends in Court.

— Bullets are bullets, too. I do not quite follow the distinction you make between administering English law and administering English bullets: there is the same oath of allegiance for both professions.

— Anyhow it is better for a man to follow a line of life which civilization regards as humane. Better be a barrister than a redcoat.

— You consider the profession of arms a disreputable one. Why then have you Sarsfield Clubs, Hugh O'Neill Clubs, Red Hugh Clubs?[1]

— O, fighting for freedom is different. But it is quite another matter to take service meanly under your tyrant, to make yourself his slave.

— And, tell me, how many of your Gaelic Leaguers are studying for the Second Division and looking for advancement in the Civil Service?

— That's different. They are only civil servants: they're not . . .

[1] Named after Irish military heroes. Patrick Sarsfield (d. 1693) was a general in the war against King William III, and was idolized by all classes of Irishmen in his time. Hugh O'Neill, Earl of Tyrone (1540?–1616) was the ablest and most famous of Irish leaders in the wars against England. Red Hugh – Hugh Roe O'Donnell (1571?–1602) – was an associate of O'Neill. He was the last of the old Gaelic kings.

61

— Civil be damned! They are pledged to the Government, and paid by the Government.

— O, well, of course if you like to look at it that way . . .

— And how many relatives of Gaelic Leaguers are in the police and the constabulary? Even I know nearly ten of your friends [that] who are sons of Police inspectors.

— It is unfair to accuse a man because his father was so-and-so. A son and a father often have different ideas.

— But Irishmen are fond of boasting that they are true to the traditions they receive in youth. ° How faithful all you fellows are to Mother Church! Why would you not be as faithful to the tradition of the helmet as to that of the tonsure? °

— We remain true to the Church because it is our national Church, the Church our people have suffered for and would suffer for again. The police are different. We look upon them as aliens, traitors, oppressors of the people.

— The old peasant down the country doesn't seem to be of your opinion when he counts over his greasy notes and says 'I'll put the priest on Tom an' I'll put the polisman on Mickey'.[1]

— I suppose you heard that sentence in some 'stage-Irishman' play. It's a libel on our countrymen.

— No, no, it is Irish peasant wisdom: he balances the priest against the polisman and a very nice balance it is for they are both of good girth. A compensative system!

— No West-Briton could speak worse of his countrymen. You are simply giving vent to old stale libels – the drunken Irishman, the baboon-faced Irishman that we see in *Punch*.

— What I say I see about me. The publicans and the pawnbrokers who live on the miseries of the people spend part of the money they make in sending their sons and daughters into religion to pray for them. One of your professors in the Medical School who teaches you Sanitary Science or Forensic Medicine or something – God knows what – is at the same time the landlord of a whole streetful of brothels not a mile away from where we are standing.

— Who told you that?

[1] In Joyce's notes, as printed by Gorman (p. 135), occurs the phrase: 'Priests and police in Ireland.'

— A little robin-redbreast.

— It's a lie!

— Yes, it's a contradiction in terms, what I call a systematic compensation.

Stephen's conversations with the patriots were not all of this severe type. Every Friday evening he met Miss Clery, or, as he had now returned to the Christian name, Emma. She lived near Portobello and any evening that the meeting was over early she walked home. She often delayed a long time chatting with a low-sized young priest, a Father Moran, who had a neat head of curly black hair and expressive black eyes. This young priest was a pianist and sang sentimental songs and was for many reasons a great favourite with the ladies. Stephen often watched Emma and Father Moran. Father Moran, who sang tenor, had once complimented Stephen saying he had heard many people speak highly of his voice and hoping he would have the pleasure of hearing him some time. Stephen had said the same thing to the priest adding that Miss Clery had told him great things of *his* voice. At this the priest had smiled and looked archly at Stephen. 'One must not believe all the complimentary things the ladies say of us' he had said. 'The ladies are a little given to – what shall I say – fibbing, I am afraid.' And here the priest had bit his lower rosy lip with two little white even teeth and smiled with his expressive eyes and altogether looked such a pleasant tender-hearted vulgarian that Stephen felt inclined to slap him on the back admiringly. Stephen had continued talking for a few minutes and once when the conversation had touched on Irish matters the priest had become very serious and had said very piously 'Ah, yes. ᶜ God bless the work!' ᶜ Father Moran was no lover of the old droning chants, he told Stephen. Of course, he said, it is very grand music severe style of music [*sic*]. But he held the opinion that the Church must not be made too gloomy and he said with a charming smile that the spirit of the Church was not gloomy. He said that one could not expect the people to take kindly to severe music and that the people needed more human religious music than the Gregorian and ended by advising Stephen to learn 'The Holy City' by Adams.

— There is a song now, beautiful, full of lovely melody and yet – religious. It has the religious sentiment, a touching ᶜ melody, power – soul, in fact.ᶜ

Stephen watching this young priest and Emma together usually worked himself into a state of unsettled rage. It was not so much that he suffered personally as that the spectacle seemed to him typical of Irish ineffectualness. Often he felt his fingers itch. Father Moran's eyes were so clear and tender-looking, Emma stood to his gaze in such a poise of bold careless ° pride of the flesh ° that Stephen longed to precipitate the two into each other's arms and shock the room even though he knew the pain this impersonal generosity would cause himself. Emma allowed him to see her home several times but she did not seem to have reserved herself for him. The youth was piqued at this for above all things he hated to be compared with others and, had it not been that her body seemed so compact of pleasure, he would have preferred to have been ignominiously left behind. Her loud forced manners shocked him at first until his mind had thoroughly mastered the stupidity of hers. She criticized the Miss Daniels very sharply, assuming, much to Stephen's discomfort, an identical temper in him. She coquetted with knowledge, asking Stephen could he not persuade the President of his College to admit women to the college. Stephen told her to apply to McCann who was the champion of women. She laughed at this and said with ° genuine dismay ° 'Well, honestly, isn't he a dreadful-looking artist?' She treated femininely everything that young men are supposed to regard as serious but she made polite exception for Stephen himself and for the Gaelic Revival. She asked him wasn't he reading a paper and what was it on. She would give anything to go and hear him: she was awfully fond of the theatre herself and a gypsy woman had once read her hand and told her she would be an actress. She had been three times to the pantomime and asked Stephen what he liked best in pantomime. Stephen said he liked a good clown but she said that she preferred ballets. Then she wanted to know did he go out much to dances and pressed him to join an Irish dancing-class of which she was a member. Her eyes had begun to ° imitate the expression ° of Father Moran's – an expression of tender ° significance ° when the conversation was at the lowest level of banality. Often as he walked beside her Stephen wondered how she had employed her time since he had last seen her and he congratulated himself that he had caught an impression of her when she was at her finest moment. In his heart he deplored the change in her for he would have liked nothing so well

64

as an adventure with her now but he felt that even that warm ample body could hardly compensate him for her distressing pertness and middle-class affectations. ᶜ In the centre of her attitude towards him he thought he discerned a point of defiant illwill and he thought he understood the cause of it. ᶜ He had swept the moment into his memory, the figure and the landscape into his treasure-room, and conjuring with all three had brought forth some pages of ᶜ sorry verse.ᶜ One rainy night when the streets were too bad for walking she took the Rathmines tram at the Pillar and as she held down her hand to him from the step, thanking him for his kindness and wishing him goodnight, that ᶜ episode of their childhood seemed to magnetize ᶜ the minds of both at the same instant. The change of circumstances had reversed their positions, giving her the upper hand. He took her hand caressingly, caressing one after another the three lines on the ᶜ back of her kid glove and numbering her knuckles,ᶜ caressing also his own past towards which this inconsistent hater of [antiquity] inheritances was always lenient. They smiled at each other; and again in the centre of her amiableness he discerned a [centre] point of illwill and he suspected that by her code of honour she was obliged to insist on the forbearance of the male and to despise him for forbearing.

XVIII

Stephen's paper was fixed for the second Saturday in March. Between Christmas and that date he had therefore an ample space of time wherein to perform preparative abstinences. His forty days were consumed in aimless solitary walks during which he forged out his sentences. In this manner he had his whole essay in his mind ᶜ from the first word to the last ᶜ before he had put any morsel of it on paper. In thinking or constructing the form of the essay he found himself much ᶜ hampered by the sitting posture.ᶜ His body disturbed him and he adapted the expedient of appeasing it by gentle promenading. Sometimes during his walks he lost the train of his thought and whenever the void of his mind seemed irreclaimable he forced order upon it by ejaculatory fervours. His morning walks were critical, his evening walks imaginative and whatever had seemed plausible in the evening was always rigorously examined in the light of day. These wanderings in the desert were reported from different points and Mr Daedalus once asked his son what the hell had brought him out to ᶜ Dolphin's Barn.ᶜ Stephen said he had [been] gone part of the way home with a fellow from the college whereupon Mr Daedalus remarked that the fellow from the college [must] should have gone all the way into the county Meath to live as his hand was in. Any acquaintances that were encountered during these walks were never allowed to intrude on the young man's meditations by commonplace conversation – a fact which they seemed to recognize in advance by a deferent salute. Stephen was therefore very much surprised one evening as he was walking past the Christian Brothers' School in North Richmond St to feel his arm seized from behind and to hear a voice say somewhat blatantly:

— Hello, Daedalus, old man, is that you?

Stephen turned round and saw a tall young man with many eruptions on his face dressed completely in heavy black. He stared for a few moments, trying to recall the face.

— Don't you remember me? I knew you at once.

— O, yes now I do, said Stephen. But you've changed.

— Think so?

— I wouldn't know you ... Are you ... in mourning?

Wells laughed.

— By Jove, that's a good one. Evidently ° you don't know your Church when you see it.°

— What? You don't mean to say ...?

— Fact, old man. I'm in Clonliffe at present. Been down in Balbriggan today on leave: the boss is very bad. Poor old chap!

— O, indeed!

— You're over in the Green now, Boland told me. Do you know him? He said you were at Belvedere with him.

— Is he in too? Yes I know him.

— He has a great opinion of you. He says you're a littérateur now.

Stephen smiled and did not know what subject to suggest next. He wondered how far this loud-voiced student intended to accompany him.

— See me down a bit of the way, will you? I've just come off the train at Amiens St. I'm making for dinner.

— Certainly.

So they walked on side by side.

— Well, and what have you been doing with yourself? Having a good time, I suppose? Down in Bray?

— Ah, the usual thing, said Stephen.

— I know: I know. After the esplanade girls, isn't that it? Silly game, old man, silly game! Get tired of it.

— You have, evidently.

— Should think so: time too ... Ever see any of the Clongowes fellows?

— Never one.

— That's the way. We all lose sight of each other after we leave. You remember Roth?

— Yes.

— Out in Australia now – bushranger or something. You're going in for literature, I suppose.

— I don't know really what I'm going in for.

— I know: I know. On the loose, isn't that it? ° I've been there myself.°

— Well, not exactly ... began Stephen.

— O, of course not! said Wells quickly with a loud laugh.

Passing down Jones's Road they saw a gaudy advertisement in strong colours for a melodramatic play. Wells asked Stephen had he read *Trilby*.

— Haven't you? Famous book, you know; style would suit you, I think. Of course it's a bit . . . blue.

— How is that?

— O, well, you know . . . Paris, you know . . . artists.

— O, is that the kind of book it is?

— Nothing very wrong in it that I could see. Still some people think it's a bit immoral.

— You haven't it in the library in Clonliffe?

— No, not likely . . . Don't I wish I was out of the show!

— Are you thinking of leaving?

— Next year – perhaps this year – I go to Paris for my theology.

— You won't be sorry, I suppose.

— You bet. Rotten show, this place. Food is not so bad but so dull, you know.

— Are there many students in it now?

— O, yes . . . I don't mix much with them, you know . . . There are a good lot.

— I suppose you'll be a parish priest one of these days.

— I hope so. You must come and see me when I am.

— Very good.

— When you're a great writer yourself – as the author of a second *Trilby* or something of that sort . . . Won't you come in?

— Is it allowed?

— O, with me . . . you come in, never mind.

The two young men went into the grounds of the college and along the circular carriage-drive. It was a damp evening and rather dark. In the uncertain light a few of the more adventurous were to be seen vigorously playing handball in a little side-alley, the smack of the wet ball against the concrete wall of the alley alternating with their lusty shouts. For the most part the students were walking in little groups through the ground, some with their berettas [*sic*] pushed far back to the nape of their necks and others holding their soutanes up as women do with their skirts when they cross a muddy street.

— Can you go with anyone you like? asked Stephen.

68

— ^c Companions are not allowed.^c You must join the first group you meet.

— Why didn't you go to the Jesuit order?

— Not likely, my boy. Sixteen years of noviciate and no chance of ever settling down. Here today, there tomorrow.

As Stephen looked at the big square block of masonry looming before them through the faint daylight, he re-entered again in thought the seminarist life which he had led for so many years, to the understanding of the narrow activities of which he could now in a moment bring the spirit of an acute sympathetic alien. He recognized at once the martial mind of the Irish Church in the style of this ecclesiastical barracks. He looked in vain at the faces and figures which passed him for a token of moral elevation: all were cowed without being humble, modish without being simple-mannered. Some of the students saluted Wells but got scanty thanks for the courtesy. Wells wished Stephen to gather that he despised his fellow-students and that it was not his fault if they regarded him as an important person. At the foot of the stone steps he turned to Stephen:

— I must go in to see the Dean for a minute. I'm afraid it's too late for me to show you round the show this evening . . .

— O, not at all. Another time.

— Well, will you wait for me. Stroll along there towards the chapel. I won't be a minute.

He nodded at Stephen for a temporary farewell and sprang up the steps. [Wells] Stephen wandered on towards the chapel meditatively kicking a white flat stone along the grey pebbly path. He was not likely to be deceived by Wells' words into an acceptance of that young man as a quite vicious person. He knew that Wells had exaggerated his airs in order to hide his internal sense of mortification at meeting one who had not forsaken the world, the flesh and the devil and he suspected that, if there were any tendency to oscillation in the soul of the free-spoken young student, the iron hand of the discipline of the Church would firmly intervene to restore equipoise. At the same time Stephen felt somewhat indignant that anyone should expect him to entrust spiritual difficulties to such a confessor or to receive with pious feelings any sacrament or benediction from the hands of the young students whom he saw walking through the grounds. It was not any personal pride which would prevent him but a recognition of the incompatibility of two natures, one trained to repressive enforcement of a creed, the other equipped with a vision the angle of which would never adjust itself for the reception of hallucinations and with an intelligence ᶜ which was as much in love with laughter as with combat.ᶜ

The mist of the evening had begun to thicken into slow fine rain and Stephen halted at the end of a narrow path beside a few laurel bushes, watching at the end of a leaf a tiny point of rain form and twinkle and hesitate and finally take the plunge into the sodden clay beneath. He wondered was it raining in Westmeath, [were the cattle standing together patiently in the shelter of the hedges]. He remembered seeing the cattle standing together patiently in the hedges and reeking in the rain. A little band of students passed at the other side of the laurel bushes: they were talking among themselves:

— But did you see Mrs Bergin?

— O, I saw her . . . with a black and white boa.

— And the two Miss Kennedys were there.

— Where?

— Right behind the Archbishop's Throne.

— O, I saw her – one of them. Hadn't she a grey hat with a bird in it?

— That was her! She's very lady-like, isn't she.

The little band went down the path. In a few minutes another little band passed behind the bushes. One student was talking and the others were listening.

— Yes and an astronomer too: that's why he had [built] that observatory built over there at the side of the palace. I heard a priest say once that the three greatest men in Europe were Gladstone, Bismarck (the great German statesman) and our own Archbishop – as all-round men. He knew him at Maynooth. He said that in Maynooth . . .

The speaker's words were lost in the crunch of the heavy boots on the gravel. The rain was spreading and increasing and the vagrant bands of students were all turning their steps towards the college. Stephen still waited at his post and at last saw Wells coming down the path quickly: he had changed his outdoor dress for a soutane. He was very apologetic and not quite so familiar in manner. Stephen wanted him to go in with the others but he insisted on seeing his visitor to the gate. They took a short cut down beside the wall and were soon opposite the lodge. The [gate] side-door was shut and Wells called out loudly to the lodge-woman to open it and let the gentleman out. Then he shook hands with Stephen and pressed him to come again. The lodge-woman opened the side-door and Wells looked out for a second or two almost enviously. Then he said:

— Well, goodbye, old man. Must run in now. Awfully glad to see you again – see any of the old Clongowes set, you know. Be good now: I must run. Goodbye.

As he tucked up his soutane high and ran awkwardly up the drive [and] he ᶜlooked a strange, almost criminal, fugitive in the dreary dusk.ᶜ Stephen's eyes followed the running figure for a moment: and as he passed through the door into the lamplit street he smiled at his own impulse of pity.[1]

[1] In the MS 'End of Second Episode of V' is written in red crayon here – an afterthought; the MS originally had no break or chapter division at this point.

XIX

He smiled because it seemed to him so unexpected a ripeness in himself – this pity – or rather this impulse of pity for he had no more than entertained it. But it was the actual achievement of his essay which had allowed him so mature a pleasure as the sensation of pity for another. Stephen had a thoroughgoing manner in many things: his essay was not in the least the exhibition of polite accomplishments. It was on the contrary very seriously intended to define his own position for himself. He could not persuade himself that, if he wrote round about his subject with facility or treated it from any standpoint of impression, good would come of it. On the other hand he was persuaded that no-one served the generation into which he had been born so well as he who offered it, whether in his art or in his life, the gift of certitude. The programme of the patriots filled him with very reasonable doubts; its articles could obtain no intellectual assent from him. He knew, moreover, that concordance with it would mean for him a submission of everything else in its interest and that he would thus be obliged to corrupt the springs of speculation at their very source. He refused therefore to set out for any task if he had first to prejudice his success by oaths to his patria and this refusal resulted in a theory of art which was at once severe and liberal. His Esthetic was in the main ᶜ applied Aquinas,ᶜ and he set it forth plainly with a naif air of discovering novelties. This he did partly to satisfy his own taste for enigmatic rôles and partly from a genuine predisposition in favour of all but the ᶜ premisses of scholasticism. He proclaimed at the outset that art was the human disposition of intelligible or sensible matter for an esthetic end, and he announced further that all such human dispositions must fall into the division of three distinct natural kinds, lyrical, epical and dramatic. Lyrical art, he said, is the art whereby the artist sets forth his image in immediate relation to himself; epical art is the art whereby the artist sets forth his image in immediate relation to himself and to others; and dramatic art is the art whereby the artist sets forth his image in immediate relations to others.ᶜ The various forms of art, such as music, sculpture, literature, do not offer this division with the same clearness and he concluded from this that those forms of art which offered the division most clearly were to be called the most excellent forms: and he was not greatly perturbed because he could not decide for himself whether a portrait was a work of epical art or not or whether it was possible for an architect to be a lyrical, epical or dramatic poet at will. Having by this simple process established the literary form of art as the most excellent he proceeded to examine it in favour of his theory, or, as he rendered it, to establish the relations which must subsist between the literary image, the work of art itself, and that energy which had imagined and fashioned it, that centre of conscious, re-acting, particular life, the artist.

The artist, he imagined, standing in the position of mediator between the world of his experience and the world of his dreams – ^c a mediator, consequently gifted with twin faculties, a selective faculty and a reproductive faculty.^c To equate these faculties was the secret of artistic success: the artist who could disentangle the subtle soul of the image from its mesh of defining circumstances most exactly and ^c re-embody ^c it in artistic circumstances chosen as the most exact for it in its new office, he was the supreme artist. This perfect coincidence of the two artistic faculties Stephen called poetry and he imagined the domain of an art to be cone-shaped. The term 'literature' now seemed to him a term of contempt and he used it to designate the vast middle region which lies between apex and base, between poetry and the chaos of unremembered writing. Its merit lay in its portrayal of externals; the realm of its princes was the realm of the manners and customs of societies – a spacious realm. But society is itself, he conceived, the complex body in which certain laws are involved and overwrapped and he therefore proclaimed as the realm of the poet the realm of these unalterable laws. Such a theory might easily have led its deviser to the acceptance of spiritual anarchy in literature had he not at the same time insisted on the classical style. A classical style, he said, is the syllogism of art, the only legitimate process from one world to another. Classicism is not the manner of any fixed age or of any fixed country: it is a constant state of the artistic mind. It is a temper of security and satisfaction and patience. The romantic temper, so often and so grievously misinterpreted and not more by others than by its own, is an insecure, unsatisfied, impatient temper which sees no fit abode here for its ideals and chooses therefore to behold them under insensible figures. As a result of this choice it comes to disregard certain limitations. Its figures are blown to wild adventures, lacking the gravity of solid bodies, and the mind that has conceived them ends by disowning them. The classical temper on the other hand, ever mindful of limitations, chooses rather to bend upon these present things and so to work upon them and fashion them that the quick intelligence may go beyond them to their meaning which is still unuttered. In this method the sane and joyful spirit issues forth and achieves imperishable perfection, nature assisting with her goodwill and thanks. ᶜFor so long as this place in nature is given us it is right that art should do no violence to the gift.ᶜ

Between these two conflicting schools the city of the arts had become marvellously unpeaceful. To many spectators the dispute had seemed a dispute about names, a battle in which the position of the standards could never be foretold for a minute. Add to this internecine warfare – the classical school fighting the materialism that must attend it, the romantic school struggling to preserve coherence – and behold from what ungentle manners criticism is bound to recognize the emergence of all achievement. The critic is he who is able, by means of the signs which the artist affords, to approach the temper which has made the work and to see what is well done therein and what it signifies. For him a song by Shakespeare which seems so free and living, as remote from any conscious purpose as rain that falls in a garden or as the lights of evening, discovers itself as the rhythmic speech of an emotion otherwise incommunicable, or at least not so fitly. But to approach the temper which has made art is an act of reverence before the performance of which many conventions must be first put off for certainly that inmost region will never yield its secret to one who is enmeshed with profanities.

Chief among these profanities Stephen set the antique principle that the end of art is to instruct, to elevate, and to amuse. 'I am unable to find even a trace of this Puritanic conception of the esthetic purpose in the definition which Aquinas has given of beauty,' he wrote 'or in anything which he has written concerning the beautiful. The qualifications he expects for beauty are in fact of so abstract and common a character that it is quite impossible for even the most violent partizan to use the Aquinatian theory with the object of attacking any work of art that we possess from the hand of any artist whatsoever.' This recognition of the beautiful in virtue of the most abstract relations afforded by an object to which the term could be applied so far from giving any support to a commandment of *Noli Tangere* was itself no more than a just sequence from the taking-off of all interdictions from the artist. The limits of decency suggest themselves somewhat too readily to the modern speculator and their effect is to encourage the profane mind to very futile jurisdiction. For it cannot be urged too strongly on the public mind that the tradition of art is with the artists and that even if they do not make it their invariable practice to outrage these limits of decency the public mind has no right to conclude therefrom that they do not arrogate for themselves an entire liberty to do so if they choose. It is as absurd, wrote the fiery-hearted revolutionary, for a criticism itself established upon homilies to prohibit the elective courses of the artist in his *revelation* of the beautiful as it would be for a police-magistrate to prohibit the sum of any two sides of a triangle from being together greater than the third side.

In fine the truth is not that the artist requires a document of licence from householders entitling him to proceed in this or that fashion but that every age must look for its sanction to its poets and philosophers. The poet is the intense centre of the life of his age to which he stands in a relation than which none can be more vital. He alone is capable of absorbing in himself the life that surrounds him and of flinging it abroad again amid planetary music. When the poetic phenomenon is signalled in the heavens, exclaimed this heaven-ascending essayist, it is time for the critics to verify their calculations in accordance with it. It is time for them to acknowledge that here the imagination has contemplated intensely the truth of the being of the visible world and that beauty, the splendour of truth, has been born. The age, though it bury itself fathoms deep in formulas and machinery has need of these realities which alone give and sustain life and it must await from those chosen centres of vivification the force to live, the security for life which can come to it only from them. Thus the spirit of man makes a continual affirmation.

Except for the eloquent and arrogant peroration Stephen's essay was a careful exposition of a carefully meditated theory of esthetic. When he had finished it he found it necessary to change the title from 'Drama and Life' to 'Art and Life' for he had occupied himself so much with securing the foundations that he had not left himself space enough to raise the complete structure. This strangely unpopular manifesto was traversed by the two brothers phrase by phrase and word by word and at last pronounced flawless at all points. It was then safely laid by until the time should come for its public appearance. Besides Maurice two other well-wishers had an advance view of it; these were Stephen's mother and his friend Madden. Madden had not asked for it directly but at the end of a conversation in which Stephen had recounted sarcastically his visit to Clonliffe College he had vaguely wondered what state of mind could produce such irreverences and Stephen had at once offered him the manuscript saying 'This is the first of my explosives.' The following evening Madden had returned the manuscript and praised the writing highly. Part of it had been too deep for him, he said, but he could see that it was beautifully written.

— You know Stevie, he said (Madden had a brother Stephen and he sometimes used this familiar form) you always told me I was a country *buachail*[1] and I can't understand you mystical fellows.

— Mystical? said Stephen.

— About the planets and the stars, you know. Some of the fellows in the League belong to the mystical set here. They'd understand quick enough.

— But there's nothing mystical in it I tell you. I have written it carefully . . .

— O, I can see you have. It's beautifully written. But I'm sure it will be above the heads of your audience.

— You don't mean to tell me, Madden, you think it's a 'flowery' composition!

— I know you've thought it out. But you are a poet, aren't you?

— I have . . . written verse . . . if that's what you mean.

— Do you know Hughes is a poet too?

— Hughes!

— Yes. He writes for our paper, you know. Would you like to see some of his poetry?

— Why, could you show me any?

— It so happens I have one in my pocket. There's one in this week's *Sword*[2] too. Here it is: read it.

[1] boy, bumpkin
[2] The name of this periodical was *An Claidheamh Solius* (The Sword of Light).

Stephen took the paper and read a piece of verse entitled *Mo Náire Tù* - (My shame art thou). There were four stanzas in the piece and each stanza ended with the Irish phrase - *Mo Náire Tù*, the last word, of course, rhyming to an English word in the corresponding line. The piece began:

> What! Shall the rippling tongue of Gaels
> Give way before the Saxon slang!

and in lines full of excited patriotism proceeded to pour scorn upon the Irishman who would not learn the ancient language of his native land. Stephen did not remark anything in the lines except the frequency of such contracted forms as 'e'en' 'ne'er' and 'thro'' instead of 'even' 'never' and 'through' and he handed back the paper to Madden without offering any comment on the verse.

— I suppose you don't like that because it's too Irish but you'll like this, I suppose, because it's that mystical, idealistic kind of writing you poets indulge in. Only you mustn't say I let you see . . .

— O, no.

Madden took from his inside pocket a sheet of foolscap folded in four on which was inscribed a piece of verse, consisting of four stanzas of eight lines each, entitled 'My Ideal'. Each stanza began with the words 'Art thou real?' The poem told of the poet's troubles in a 'vale of woe' and of the 'heart-throbs' which these troubles caused him. It told of 'weary nights', and 'anxious days' and of an 'unquenchable desire' for an excellence beyond that 'which earth can give'. After this mournful idealism the final stanza offered a certain consolatory, hypothetical alternative to the poet in his woes: it began somewhat hopefully:

> Art thou real, my Ideal?
> Wilt thou ever come to me
> In the soft and gentle twilight
> With your baby on your knee?

The [combined] effect of this apparition on Stephen was a long staining blush of anger. The tawdry lines, the futile change of number, the ludicrous waddling approach of Hughes's 'Ideal' weighed

77

down by an inexplicable infant combined to cause him a sharp agony in the sensitive region. Again he handed back the verse without saying a word of praise or of blame but he decided that attendance in Mr Hughes's class was no longer possible for him and he was foolish enough to regret having yielded to the impulse for sympathy from a friend.

When a demand for intelligent sympathy goes unanswered he [it] is a too stern disciplinarian who blames himself for having offered a dullard an opportunity to participate in the warmer movement of a more highly organized life. So Stephen regarded his loans of manuscripts as elaborate ᶜ flag-practices with phrases.ᶜ He did not consider his mother a dullard but the result of his second disappointment in the search for appreciation was that he was enabled to place the blame on the shoulders of others – not on his own: he had enough responsibilities thereon already, inherited and acquired. His mother had not asked to see the manuscript: she had continued to iron the clothes on the kitchen-table without the ᶜ least suspicion of the agitation in the mind of her son.ᶜ He had sat on three or four kitchen chairs, one after another, and had dangled his legs unsuccessfully from all free corners of the table. At last, unable to control his agitation, he asked her point-blank would she like him to read out his essay.

— O, yes, Stephen – if you don't mind my ironing a few things . . .
— No, I don't mind.

Stephen read out the essay to her slowly and emphatically and when he had finished reading she said it was very beautifully written but that as there were some things in it which she couldn't follow, would he mind reading it to her again and explaining some of it. He read it over again and allowed himself a long exposition of his theories ᶜ garnished with many crude striking allusions with which he hoped to drive it home the better.ᶜ His mother who had never suspected probably that 'beauty' could be anything more than a convention of the drawingroom or a natural antecedent to marriage and married life was surprised to see the extraordinary honour which her son conferred upon it. Beauty, to the mind of such a woman, was often a synonym for licentious ways and probably for this reason she was relieved to find that the excesses of this new worship were supervised by a recognized saintly authority. However as the essayist's recent habits were not very reassuring she decided to combine a discreet motherly solicitude with an interest, which without being open to the accusation of factitiousness was at first intended as a compliment. While she was nicely folding a handkerchief she said:

— What does Ibsen write, Stephen?

— Plays.

— I never heard of his name before. Is he alive at present?

— Yes, he is. But, you know, in Ireland people don't know much about what is going on out in Europe.

— He must be a great writer from what you say of him.

— Would you like to read some of his plays, mother. I have some.

— Yes. I would like to read the best one. What is the best one?

— I don't know . . . But do you really want to read Ibsen?

— I do, really.

— To see whether I am reading dangerous authors or not, is that why?

— No, Stephen, answered his mother with a brave prevarication. I think you're old enough now to know what is right and what is wrong without my dictating to you what you are to read.

— I think so too . . . But I'm surprised to hear you ask about Ibsen. I didn't imagine you took the least interest in these matters.

Mrs Daedalus pushed her iron smoothly over a white petticoat ᶜ in time to the current of her memory.ᶜ

— Well, of course, I don't speak about it but I'm not so indifferent ᴹ? . . . Before I married your father I used to read a great deal. I used to take an interest in all kinds of new plays.

— But since you married neither of you so much as bought a single book!

— Well, you see, Stephen, your father is not like you: he takes no interest in that sort of thing . . . When he was young he told me he used to spend all his time out after the hounds or rowing on the Lee. He went in for athletics.

— I suspect what he went in for, said Stephen irreverently. I know he doesn't care a jack straw about what I think or what I write.

— He wants to see you make your way, get on in life, said his mother defensively. That's his ambition. You shouldn't blame him for that.

— No, no, no. But it may not be my ambition. That kind of life I often loathe: I find it ugly and cowardly.

79

— Of course life isn't what I used to think it was when I was a young girl. That's why I would like to read some great writer, to see what ideal of life he has — amn't I right in saying 'ideal'?

— Yes, but . . . .

— Because sometimes — not that I grumble at the lot Almighty God has given me and I have more or less a happy life with your father — but sometimes I feel that I want to leave this actual life and enter another — for a time.

— But that is wrong: that is the great mistake everyone makes. Art is not an escape from life!

— No?

— You evidently weren't listening to what I said or else you didn't understand what I said. Art is not an escape from life. It's just the very opposite. Art, on the contrary, is the very central expression of life. An artist is not a fellow who dangles a mechanical heaven before the public. The priest does that. The artist affirms out of the fulness of his own life, he creates . . . Do you understand?

And so on. A day or two afterwards Stephen gave his mother a few of the plays to read. She read them with great interest and found Nora Helmer a charming character. Dr Stockmann she admired but her admiration was naturally checked by her son's light-heartedly blasphemous description of that stout burgher as 'Jesus in a frock-coat'. But the play which she preferred to all others was the *Wild Duck*. Of it she spoke readily and on her own initiative: it had moved her deeply. Stephen, to escape a charge of hotheadedness and partizanship, did not encourage her to an open record of her feelings.

— I hope you're not going to mention Little Nell in the *Old Curiosity Shop*.

— Of course I like Dickens too but I can see a great difference between Little Nell and that poor little creature — what is her name?

— Hedvig Ekdal?

— Hedvig, yes . . . It's so sad: it's terrible to read it even . . . I quite agree with you that Ibsen is a wonderful writer.

— Really?

— Yes, really. His plays have impressed me very much.

— Do you think he is immoral?

— Of course, you know, Stephen, he treats of subjects . . . of which I know very little myself . . . subjects . . .

— Subjects which, you think, should never be talked about?

— Well, that was the old people's idea but I don't know if it was right. I don't know if it is good for people to be entirely ignorant . . .

— Then why not treat them openly?

— I think it might do harm to some people – uneducated, unbalanced people. People's natures are so different. You perhaps . . .

— O, never mind me . . . Do you think these plays are unfit for people to read?

— No, I think they're magnificent plays indeed.

— And not immoral?

— I think that Ibsen . . . has an extraordinary knowledge of human nature . . . And I think that human nature is a very extraordinary thing sometimes.

Stephen had to be contented with this well-worn generality as he recognized in it a genuine sentiment. His mother, in fact, had so far evangelized herself that she undertook the duties of missioner to the heathen; that is to say, she offered some of the plays to her husband to read. He listened to her praises with a somewhat startled air, observing no feature of her face, his eyeglass screwed into an astonished eye and his mouth poised in naïf surprise. He was always interested in novelties, childishly interested and receptive, and this new name and the phenomena it had produced in his house were novelties for him. He made no attempt to discredit his wife's novel development but he resented both that she should have achieved it unaided by him and that she should be able thereby to act as intermediary between him and his son. He condemned as inopportune but not discredited his son's wayward researches into strange literature and, though a similar taste was not discoverable in him, he was prepared to commit that most pious of heroisms namely, the extension of one's sympathies late in life in deference to the advocacy of a junior. Following the custom of certain old-fashioned people who can never understand why their patronage or judgments should put men of letters into a rage he chose his play from the title. A metaphor is a vice that attracts the dull mind by reason of its aptness and repels the too serious mind by reason of its falsity and danger so that, after all, there is something to be said, nothing voluminous perhaps, but at least a word of concession for that class of society which in literature as in everything else goes always with its four feet on the ground. Mr Daedalus,

81

anyhow, suspected that *A Doll's House* would be a triviality in the manner of *Little Lord Fauntleroy* and, as he had never been even unofficially a member of that international society which collects and examines psychical phenomena, he decided that *Ghosts* would probably be some uninteresting story about a haunted house. He chose the *League of Youth* in which he hoped to find the reminiscences of like-minded roysterers and, after reading through two acts of provincial intrigue, abandoned the enterprise as tedious. He had promised himself arguing from the alienated attitudes and half-deferential half-words of pressmen at the mention of the name, a certain extravagance, perhaps an anomalous torridity of the North and [he] though the name beneath Ibsen's photograph never failed to reawaken his sense of wonder, the upright line of the 'b' running so strangely beside the initial letter as to suspend [one] the mind amid incertitudes for some oblivious instants, the final impression made upon him by the figure to which the name was affixed, a figure which he associated with a solicitor's or a stockbroker's office in Dame St, was an impression of [disappointment mixed] relief mixed with disappointment, the relief for his son's sake prevailing dutifully over his own slight but real disappointment. So that from neither of Stephen's parents did respectability get full allegiance.

A week before the date fixed for the reading of the paper Stephen consigned a small packet covered with neat characters into the Auditor's hands. McCann smacked his lips and put the manuscript into the inside pocket of his coat:

— I'll read this to-night and I'll see you here at the same hour tomorrow. I think I know all that is in it beforehand.

The next [evening] afternoon McCann reported:

— Well, I've read your paper.

— Well?

— Brilliantly written – a bit strong, it seems to me. However I gave it to the President this morning to read.

— What for?

— All the papers must be submitted to him first for approval, you know.

— Do you mean to say, said Stephen scornfully, that the President must approve of my paper before I can read it to your society!

— Yes. He's the Censor.

— What a valuable society!

— Why not?

— It's only child's play, man. You remind me of children in the nursery.

— Can't be helped. We must take what we can get.

— Why not put up the shutters at once?

— Well, it is valuable. It trains young men for public speaking — for the bar and the political platform.

— Mr Daniel could say as much for his charades.

— I daresay he could.

— So this Censor of yours is inspecting my essay?

— Well. He's liberal-minded . . .

— Ay.

While the two young men were holding this conversation on the steps of the Library, Whelan, the College orator[1] came up to them. This suave rotund young man, who was the Secretary of the Society, was reading for the Bar. His eyes regarded Stephen now with mild, envious horror and he forgot all his baggage from Attica:

— Your essay is tabu, Daedalus.

— Who said so?

— The Very Reverend Dr Dillon.

The delivery of this news was followed by a silence during which Whelan slowly moistened his lower lip with saliva from his tongue and McCann made ready to shrug his shoulders.

— Where is the damned old fool? said the essayist promptly.

Whelan blushed and pointed his thumb over his shoulder. Stephen in a moment was half across the quadrangle. McCann called after him:

— Where are you going?

Stephen halted but, discovering that he was too angry to trust himself to speak, he merely pointed in the direction of the College, and went forward quickly.

So after all his trouble, thinking out his essay and composing his periods, this old fogey was about to prohibit it! His indignation settled into a mood of politic contempt as he crossed the Green. The

[1] The words, 'offering him the grapes, "I never eat Muscatel grapes",' appear in pencil in the MS margin here, to be inserted after 'orator'. Joyce evidently forgot to alter the text to fit them.

clock in the hall of the College pointed to half past three as Stephen
addressed the ᶜ doddering ᶜ door-porter. He had to speak twice, the
second time with a distinct, separated enunciation, for the door-
porter was rather stupid and deaf:

— Can – I – see – the – President?

The President was not in his room: he was saying his office in the
garden. Stephen went out into the garden and went down towards the
ball-alley. A small figure wrapped in a loose Spanish-looking black
cloak presented its back to him near the far end of the side-walk.
The figure went on slowly to the end of the walk, halted there for a
few moments, and then turning about presented to him over the
edge of a breviary a neat round head covered with curly grey hair
and a very wrinkled face of an indescribable colour: the upper part
was the colour of putty and the lower part was shot with slate
colour. The President came slowly down the side-walk, in his
capacious cloak, noiselessly moving his grey lips as he said his office.
At the end of the walk he halted again and looked inquiringly at
Stephen. Stephen raised his cap and said 'Good evening, sir.' The
President answered with the smile which a pretty girl gives when she
receives some compliment which puzzles her – a 'winning' smile:

— What can I do for you? he asked in a [wonderfully] rich deep
calculated voice.

— I understand, said Stephen, that you wish to see me about my
essay – an essay I have written for the Debating Society.

— O, you are Mr Daedalus, said the President more seriously but
still agreeably.

— Perhaps I am disturbing . . .

— No, I have finished my office, said the President.

He [started] began to walk slowly down the path at such a pace as
implied invitation. Stephen kept therefore at his side.

— I admire the style of your paper, he said firmly, very much but I
do not approve at all of your theories. I am afraid I cannot allow you
to read your paper before the Society.

They walked on to the end of the path, without speaking. Then
Stephen said:

— Why, sir?

— I cannot encourage you to disseminate such theories among the
young men in this college.

84

—You think my theory of art is a false one?

—It is certainly not the theory of art which is respected in this college.

—I agree with that, said Stephen.

—On the contrary, it represents the sum-total of modern unrest and modern freethinking. The authors you quote as examples, those you seem to admire . . .

—Aquinas?

—Not Aquinas; I have to speak of him in a moment. But Ibsen, Maeterlinck . . . these atheistic writers . . .

—You do not like . . .

—I am surprised that any student of this college could find anything to admire in such writers, writers who usurp the name of poet, who openly profess their atheistic doctrines and fill the minds of their readers with all the garbage of modern society. That is not art.

—Even admitting the corruption you speak of I see nothing unlawful in an examination of corruption.

—Yes, it may be lawful—for the scientist, for the reformer . . .

—Why not for the poet too? Dante surely examines and upbraids society.

—Ah, yes, said the President explanatorily, with a moral purpose in view: Dante was a great poet.

—Ibsen is also a great poet.

—You cannot compare Dante and Ibsen.

—I am not doing so.

—Dante, the lofty upholder of beauty, the greatest of Italian poets, and Ibsen, the writer above and beyond all others, Ibsen and Zola, who seek to degrade their art, who pander to a corrupt taste . . .

—But *you* are comparing them!

—No, you cannot compare them. One has a high moral aim — he ennobles the human race: the other degrades it.

—The lack of a specific code of moral conventions does not degrade the poet, in my opinion.

—Ah, if he were to examine even the basest things, said the President with a suggestion of tolerance in store, [that] it would be different if he were to examine and then show men the way to purify themselves.

—That is for the Salvationists, said Stephen.

85

— Do you mean . . .

— I mean that Ibsen's account of modern society is as genuinely ironical as Newman's account of English Protestant morality and belief.

— That may be, said the President appeased by the conjunction.

— And as free from any missionary intention.

The President was silent.

— It is a question of temper. Newman could refrain from writing his *Apologia* for twenty years.

— But when he came out on him! said the President with a chuckle and an expressive incompletion of the phrase. Poor Kingsley!

— It is all a question of temper – one's attitude towards society whether one is poet or critic.

— O, yes.

— Ibsen has the temper of an archangel.

— It may be: but I have always believed that he was a fierce realist like Zola with some kind of a new doctrine to preach.

— You were mistaken, sir.

— This is the general opinion.

— A mistaken one.

— I understood he had some doctrine or other – a social doctrine, free living, and an artistic doctrine, unbridled licence – so much so that the public will not tolerate his plays on the stage and that you cannot name him even in mixed society.

— Where have you seen this?

— O, everywhere . . . in the papers.

— This is a serious argument, said Stephen reprovingly.

The President far from resenting this hardy statement seemed to bow to its justice: no-one could have a poorer opinion of the half-educated journalism of the present day than he had and he certainly would not allow a newspaper to dictate criticism to him. At the same time there was such a unanimity of opinion everywhere about Ibsen that he imagined . . .

— May I ask you if you have read much of his writing? asked Stephen.

— Well, no . . . I must say I . . .

— May I ask you if you have read even a single line?

— Well, no . . . I must admit . . .

— And surely you do not think it right to pass judgment on a writer a single line of whose writing you have never read?

— Yes, I must admit that.

Stephen hesitated after his first success. The President resumed:

— I am very interested in the enthusiasm you show for this writer. I have never had any opportunity to read Ibsen myself but I know that he enjoys a great reputation. What you say of him, I must confess, alters my views of him considerably. Some day perhaps I shall . . .

— I can lend you some of the plays if you like, sir, said Stephen with imprudent simplicity.

— Can you indeed?

Both paused for an instant: then –

— You will see that he is a great poet and a great artist, said Stephen.

— I shall be very interested, said the President with an amiable intention, to read some of his work for myself, I certainly shall.

Stephen had an impulse to say 'Excuse me for five minutes while I send a telegram to Christiania' but he resisted his impulse. During the interview he had occasion more than once to put severe shackles on this importunate devil within him whose appetite was on edge for the farcical. The President was beginning to exhibit the liberal side of his character, but with priestly cautiousness.

— Yes, I shall be most interested. Your opinions are somewhat strange. Do you intend to publish this essay?

— Publish it!

— I should not care for anyone to identify the ideas in your essay with the teaching in our college. We receive this college in trust.

— But you are not supposed to be responsible for everything a student in your college thinks or says.

— No, of course not . . . but, reading your essay and knowing you came from our college, people would suppose that we inculcated such ideas here.

— Surely a student of this college can pursue a special line of study if he chooses.

— It is just that which we always try to encourage in our students but your study, it seems to me, leads you to adopt very revolutionary . . . very revolutionary theories.

— If I were to publish tomorrow a very revolutionary pamphlet on the means of avoiding potato-blight would you consider yourself responsible for my theory?

— No, no, of course not . . . but then this is not a school of agriculture.

— Neither is it a school of dramaturgy, answered Stephen.

— Your argument is not so conclusive as it seems, said the President after a short pause. However I am glad to see that your attitude towards your subject is so genuinely serious. At the same time you must admit that this theory you have – if pushed to its logical conclusion – would emancipate the poet from all moral laws. I notice too that in your essay you allude satirically to what you call the 'antique' theory – the theory, namely, that the drama should have special ethical aims, that it should instruct, elevate and amuse. I suppose you mean Art for Art's sake.

— I have only pushed to its logical conclusion the definition Aquinas has given of the beautiful.

— Aquinas?

— *Pulcra sunt quae visa placent.* He seems to regard the beautiful as that which satisfies the esthetic appetite and nothing more – that the mere apprehension of which pleases . . .

— But he means the sublime – that which leads man upwards.

— His remark would apply to a Dutch painter's representation of a plate of onions.

— No, no; that which pleases the soul in a state of sanctification, the soul seeking its spiritual good.

— Aquinas' definition of the good is an unsafe basis of operations: it is very wide. He seems to me almost ironical in his treatment of the 'appetites'.

The President scratched his head a little dubiously –

— Of course Aquinas is an extraordinary mind, he murmured, the greatest doctor of the Church: but he requires immense interpretation. There are parts of Aquinas which no priest would think of announcing in the pulpit.

— But what if I, as an artist, refuse to accept the cautions which are considered necessary for those who are still in a state of original stupidity?

— I believe you are sincere but I will tell you this as an older human being than you are and as a man of some experience: the cult of beauty is difficult. Estheticism often begins well only to end in the vilest abominations of which . . .

— *Ad pulcritudinem tria requiruntur.*

— It is insidious, it creeps into the mind, little by little . . .

— *Integritas, consonantia, claritas.* There seems to me . . . to be effulgence in that theory instead of danger. The intelligent nature apprehends it at once.

— S. Thomas of course . . .

— Aquinas is certainly on the side of the capable artist. I hear no mention of instruction or elevation.

— To support Ibsenism on Aquinas seems to me somewhat paradoxical. Young men often substitute brilliant paradox for conviction.

— My conviction has led me nowhere; my theory states itself.

— Ah, you are a paradoxist, said the President smiling with gentle satisfaction. I can see that . . . And there is another thing — a question of taste perhaps rather than anything else – which makes me think your theory juvenile. You don't seem to understand the importance of the classical drama . . . Of course in his own line Ibsen also may be an admirable writer . . .

— But, allow me, sir, said Stephen. My entire esteem is for the classical temper in art. Surely you must remember that I said . . .

— So far as I can remember, said the President lifting to the pale sky a faintly smiling face on which memory endeavoured to bring a vacuous amiability to book, so far as I can remember you treated the Greek drama – the classical temper – very summarily indeed, with a kind of juvenile . . . impudence, shall I say?

— But the Greek drama is heroic, monstrous [*sic*]. Eschylus is not a classical writer!

— I told you you were a paradoxist, Mr Daedalus. You wish to upset centuries of literary criticism by a brilliant turn of speech, by a paradox.

— I use the word 'classical' in a certain sense, with a certain definite meaning, that is all.

— But you cannot use any terminology you like.

— I have not changed the terms. I have explained them. By 'classical' I mean the slow elaborate patience of the art of satisfaction. The heroic, the fabulous, I call romantic. Menander perhaps, I don't know . . .

— All the world recognizes Eschylus as a supreme classical dramatist.

— O, the world of professors whom he helps to feed . . .

— Competent critics, said the President severely, men of the highest culture. And even the public themselves can appreciate him. I have read, I think, in some . . . a newspaper, I think it was . . . that Irving, the great actor, Henry Irving produced one of his plays in London and that the London public flocked to see it.

— From curiosity. The London public will flock to see anything new or strange. If Irving were to give an imitation of a hard-boiled egg they would flock to see it.

The President received this absurdity with unflinching gravity and when he had come to the end of the path, he halted for a few instants before leading the way to the house.

— I do not predict much success for your advocacy in this country, he said generally. Our people have their faith and they are happy. They are faithful to their Church and the Church is sufficient for them. Even for the profane world these modern pessimistic writers are a little too . . . too much.

With his scornful mind scampering from Clonliffe College to Mullingar Stephen strove to make himself ready for some definite compact. The President had carefully brought the interview into the region of chattiness.

— Yes, we are happy. Even the English people have begun to see the folly of these morbid tragedies, these wretched unhappy, unhealthy tragedies. I read the other day that some playwright had to change the last act of his play because it ended in catastrophe – some sordid murder or suicide or death.

— Why not make death a capital offence? said Stephen. People are very timorous. It would be so much simpler to take the bull by the horns and have done with it.

When they reached the hall of the college the President stood at the foot of the staircase before going up to his room. Stephen waited silently:

— Begin to look at the bright side of things, Mr Daedalus. Art should be healthy first of all.

The President gathered in his soutane for the ascent with a slow hermaphroditic gesture:

— I must say you have defended your theory very well ... very well indeed. I do not agree with it, of course, but I can see you have thought it all out carefully beforehand. You have thought it out carefully?

— Yes, I have.

— It is very interesting – a little paradoxical at times and a little juvenile – but I have been very interested in it. I am sure too that when your studies have brought you further afield you will be able to amend it so as to – fit in more with recognized facts; I am sure you will be able to apply it better then – when your mind has undergone a course of ... regular ... training and you have a larger, wider sense of ... comparison ...

The President's indefinite manner of closing the interview had left some doubts in Stephen's mind; he was unable to decide whether the retreat upstairs was a breach of friendly relations or a politic confession of inability. However as no definite prohibition had been pronounced upon him he determined to proceed calmly on his way until he encountered a substantial check. When he met McCann again he smiled and waited to be questioned. His account of the interview went the rounds of the undergraduate classes and he was much amused to observe the startled expression of many pairs of eyes which, to judge from their open humiliated astonishment, appeared to behold in him characteristics of a moral Nelson. Maurice listened to his brother's account of his battle with recognized authority but he made no remark upon it. Stephen himself, in default of another's service, began to annotate the incident copiously expanding every suggestive phase of the interview. He consumed much imaginative fuel in this diverting chase of the presumable and his rapid changeful courses kindled in him a flame of discontent for Maurice's impassiveness:

— Are you listening to me at all? Do you know what I'm talking about?

— Yes, it's all right . . . You can read your paper, can't you?

— Yes, of course, I can . . . But what's up with you? Are you bored? Are you thinking of anything?

— Well . . . yes, I am.

— What?

— I have found out why I feel different this evening. Why, do you think?

— I don't know. Tell us.

— I have been walking [on] from the ball of my left foot. I usually walk from the ball of my right foot.

Stephen looked sideways at the speaker's solemn face to see if there were any signs thereon of a satirical mood but, finding only steadfast self-analysis, he said:

— Indeed? That's damned interesting.

On the Saturday night which had been fixed for the reading of the

paper Stephen found himself facing the benches in the Physics'
Theatre. While the minutes were being read out by the secretary
he had time to observe his father's eyeglass glimmering high up near
the window and he divined more than saw the burly form of Mr
Casey hard by that observant centre. He could not see his brother but
in the front benches he noticed Father Butt and McCann and two
other priests. The chairman was Mr Keane, the professor of English
composition. When the formal business was ended the chairman
called on the essayist to read his paper and Stephen stood up. He
waited until a compliment of discreet applause had subsided, and until
McCann's ᶜ energetic hands had given four resounding claps as a con-
cluding solo of welcomeᶜ. Then he read out his essay. He read it
quietly and distinctly, involving every hardihood of thought or expression in an envelope of low innocuous melody. He read it on
calmly to the end: his reading was never once interrupted with
applause: and when he had read out the final sentence in a tone of
metallic clearness he sat down.

The first single thought that emerged through a swift mood of
confusion was the bright conviction that he should never have
written his essay. While he was gloomily taking counsel with himself
as to whether he should fling the ᶜ manuscript at their heads ᶜ and
march home or remain as he was shading his face from the light of
the candles on the Chairman's table he became aware that the discussion on his paper had begun: this discovery surprised him. Whelan,
the orator of the College, was proposing a vote of thanks and wagging
his head in time to ornate phrases. Stephen wondered did anyone
else observe the infantile movements of the orator's mouth. He wished
that Whelan would shut his jaws with a clap so as to reveal the presence of solid teeth; the mere sound of the speech reminded him of the
noise Nurse Sarah used to make when she mashed Isabel's bread-and-
milk in the blue bowl which his mother now used to hold starch.
But he at once corrected himself for such a manner of criticism and
strove to listen to the words of the orator. Whelan was profusely
admiring: he felt (he said) during the reading of Mr Daedalus' essay
as though he had been listening to the discourse of angels and did not
know the language that they spoke. It was with some diffidence that
he ventured to criticize but it was evident that Mr Daedalus did not
understand the beauty of the Attic theatre. He pointed out that

Eschylus was an imperishable name and he predicted that the drama of the Greeks would outlive many civilizations. Stephen noticed that Whelan said 'yisterday' twice instead of 'yesterday' in imitation of Father Butt who was a South of England man and he speculated as to whether it was a Dominican preacher or a Jesuit preacher [that] who had given the orator his final phrase. 'Greek art' said Whelan 'is not for a time but for all times. It stands aloof, alone. It is ᶜ imperial, imperious and imperative.ᶜ'

McCann seconded the vote of thanks which had been so ably proposed by Mr Whelan and he desired to add his tribute to Mr Whelan's eloquent tribute to the essayist of the night. There were perhaps many things in the paper which Mr Daedalus had read to them with which he could not agree but he was not such a blind partizan of antiquity for antiquity's sake as Mr Whelan seemed to be. Modern ideas must find their expression: the modern world had to face pressing problems: and he considered that any writer who could call attention to those problems in a striking way was well worthy of every serious person's consideration. He considered that he was speaking for one and all of those present when he said that Mr Daedalus, by reading his frank and earnest essay that night, had conferred a benefit on the society.

The general diversion of the night began when these two opening speeches had ended. Stephen was subjected to the fires of six or seven hostile speakers. One speaker, a young man named Magee, said he was surprised that any paper which was conceived in a spirit so hostile to the spirit of religion itself – he did not know if Mr Daedalus understood the true purport of the theory he propounded – should find approval in their society. Who but the Church had sustained and fostered the artistic temper? Had not the drama owed its very birth to religion? That was indeed a poor theory which tried to bolster up the dull dramas of sinful intrigues and to decry the immortal masterpieces. Mr Magee said he did not know as much about Ibsen as Mr Daedalus did – nor did he want to know anything about him – but he knew that one of his plays was about the sanitary condition of a bathing-place. If this was drama he did not see why some Dublin Shakespeare should not pen an immortal work dealing with the new Main Drainage Scheme of the Dublin Corporation. This speech was the signal for a general attack. The essay was pronounced a jingle of meaningless words, a clever presentation of vicious principles in the guise of artistic theories, a reproduction of the decadent literary opinions of exhausted European capitals. The essayist was supposed to intend parts of his essay as efforts at practical joking: everyone knew that *Macbeth* would be famous when the unknown authors of whom Mr Daedalus was so fond were dead and forgotten. Ancient art loved to uphold the beautiful and the sublime: modern art might select other themes: but those who still preserved their minds uncontaminated by atheistic poisons would know which to choose. The climax of aggressiveness was reached when Hughes stood up. He declared in ringing Northern accents that the moral welfare of the Irish people was ^c menaced by such theories.^c They wanted no foreign filth. Mr Daedalus might read what authors he liked, of course, but the Irish people had their own glorious literature where they could always find fresh ideals to spur them on to new patriotic endeavours. Mr Daedalus was himself a renegade from the Nationalist ranks: he professed cosmopolitism. But a man that was of all countries was of no country — you must first have a nation before you have art. Mr Daedalus might do as he pleased, kneel at the shrine of Art (with a capital A), and rave about obscure authors. In spite of [his] any hypocritical use of the name of a great doctor of the Church Ireland would be on her guard against the insidious theory that art can be separated from morality. If they were to have art let it be moral art, art that elevated, above all, national art,

> Kindly Irish of the Irish,
> Neither Saxon nor Italian.

When the time had come for the Chairman to sum up and to put the motion before the house there was the usual pause. In this pause Father Butt rose and begged leave to say a few words. The benches applauded with excitement and settled themselves to hear a denunciation *ex cathedra*. Father Butt excused himself amid cries of 'No, no' for detaining his audience at such an advanced hour but he thought he should enter a word in favour of the much-abused essayist. He would be *advocatus diaboli* and he felt the uncomfortableness of his office all the more since one of the speakers had, not unjustly, described the language in which Mr Daedalus' essay had been couched as a language of angels. Mr Daedalus had contributed a very striking paper, a paper which had filled the house and entertained them by the lively discussion it had provoked. Of course everyone could not be of the same opinion in ° matters artistic.° Mr Daedalus admitted the conflict between romantics and classicals as the condition of all achievement and they had certainly proof that night that a conflict between antagonistic theories had been able to produce such distinct achievements as the essay itself, a remarkable piece of work, on the one hand and the memorable attack delivered by Mr Hughes, as leader of the opposition, on the other hand. He thought that one or two of the speakers had been unduly severe with the essayist but he was confident that the essayist was well able to take care of himself in the matter of argument. As for the theory itself Father Butt confessed that it was a new sensation for him to hear Thomas Aquinas quoted as an authority on esthetic philosophy. Esthetic philosophy was a modern branch and if it was anything at all, it was practical. Aquinas had treated slightly of the beautiful but always from a theoretic standpoint. To interpret his statements practically one needed a fuller knowledge than Mr Daedalus could have of his entire theology. At the same time he would not go so far as to say that Mr Daedalus had really, intentionally or unintentionally, misinterpreted Aquinas. But just as an act which may be good in itself may become bad by reason of circumstances so an object intrinsically beautiful may be vitiated by other considerations. Mr Daedalus had chosen to consider beauty intrinsically and to neglect these other considerations. But beauty also has its practical side. Mr Daedalus was a passionate admirer of the artistic and such people are not always the most practical people in the [wide] world. Father Butt then reminded his audience of the story of King Alfred and the old woman who was cooking cakes – of the theorist, that is, and of the practical person and concluded by expressing the hope that the essayist would emulate King Alfred and not be too severe on the practical persons who had criticized him.

The chairman in his summing-up speech complimented the essayist on his style but he said the essayist had evidently forgotten that art implied selection. He thought that the discussion on the paper had been very instructive and he was sure they were all thankful to Father Butt for his clear, concise criticism. Mr Daedalus had been somewhat severely handled but he thought that, considering the many excellences of his paper, he (the Chairman) was well justified in asking them to agree unanimously that the best thanks of this society [are] were due and [are] were hereby tendered to Mr Daedalus for his admirable and instructive paper! The vote of thanks was passed unanimously but without enthusiasm.

Stephen stood up and bowed. It was customary for the essayist of the night to avail himself of this occasion for replying to his critics but Stephen contented himself with acknowledging the vote of thanks. Some called on him for a speech but, when the Chairman had waited in vain for a few moments, the proceedings ran on rapidly to a close. In five minutes the Physics' Theatre was empty. Downstairs in the hall the young men were busy putting on their coats and lighting cigarettes. Stephen looked for his father and Maurice but could see them nowhere so he set out for home alone. At the corner of the Green he came up with a group of four young men, Madden, Cranly, a young medical student named Temple, and a clerk in the Custom-House. Madden caught Stephen's arm and said consolingly in private:

— Well, old man, I told you those fellows wouldn't understand it. I knew it was too good for them.

Stephen was touched by this show of friendship but he shook his head as if he wished to change the subject. Besides, he knew that Madden really understood very little of the paper and disapproved of what he understood. When Stephen came up with the four young men they were strolling very slowly, discussing a projected trip to Wicklow on Easter Monday. Stephen walked beside Madden at the edge of the footpath and thus the group advanced abreast along the wide footpath. Cranly in the centre was linking Madden and the clerk from the Custom-House. Stephen listened vaguely. Cranly was speaking (as was his custom when he walked with other gentlemen of leisure) in a language the base of which was Latin and the superstructure of which was composed of Irish, French and German:

— *Atque ad duas horas in Wicklowio venit.*

— *Damnum longum tempus prendit*, said the clerk from the Custom-House.

— *Quando* . . . no, I mean . . . *quo in* . . . *bateau* . . . *irons-nous?* asked Temple.

— *Quo in batello?* said Cranly, *in 'Regina Maris'.*

So after a little talk the young men agreed to take a trip to Wicklow on the *Sea-Queen*. Stephen was much relieved to listen to this conversation: in a few minutes the sting of his ᶜ disaster was no longer felt so acutely. Cranly at last observed Stephen walking at the edge of the path and said:

— *Ecce orator qui in malo humore est.*

— *Non sum*, said Stephen.

— *Credo ut estis*, said Cranly.

— *Minime.*

— *Credo ut vos sanguinarius mendax estis quia facies vestra mostrat* [sic] *ut vos in malo humore estis.*ᶜ

Madden who could not talk this language well led the group back to English. The clerk from the Custom-House seemed to have it on his conscience to express admiration for Stephen's style. He was a big stout young man with a lardy face and he carried an ᶜ umbrella.ᶜ He was several years [younger] older than any of his companions but he had decided to read for his degree in Mental and Moral Science. He was a constant companion of Cranly's and it was the latter's eloquence which had induced him to enter the night-classes in the college. Cranly spent a great part of his time persuading young men to ᶜ adopt different lines of life.ᶜ The clerk from the Custom-House was named O'Neill. He was a very amiable person, always laughing asthmatically at Cranly's serious fooling, but he was interested to hear of any occasion whereby he might improve himself mentally. He attended the Debating Society and the meetings of the College Sodality because he was thus brought into 'touch' with University life. He was a circumspect young man but he allowed Cranly to 'chaff' him about girls. Stephen tried to dissuade the company from alluding to his essay but O'Neill had accepted the occasion as one to be availed of. He asked Stephen questions such as are to be found in the pages of young ladies' confession-albums and Stephen thought that his mental heaven must greatly resemble a confectioner's shop. Temple was a raw Gipsy-looking youth with a shambling gait and a shambling manner of speaking. He was from the West of Ireland and he was known to be very revolutionary. When O'Neill had spoken for some time to Cranly, who had answered him more politely than Stephen, Temple after a few false starts got in a phrase:

— I think . . . was a bloody fine paper.

Cranly turned a vacant face in the direction of the speaker but [O'Neill] Temple continued:

— Made 'em sit up too.

— *Habesne bibitum?* asked Cranly.

— 'Scuse me, sir, said [O'Neill] Temple to Stephen across the intervening bodies, do you believe in Jesus . . . I don't believe in Jesus, he added.

Stephen laughed loudly at the tone of this statement and he continued when Temple began to shamble through a kind of apology:

— 'Course I don't know . . . if you believe in Jesus. I believe in Man . . . If you b'lieve in Jesus . . . of course . . . I oughtn't to say anything the first time I met you . . . Do you think that?

O'Neill preserved a solemn silence until Temple's speech had faded into indistinct mutterings; then he said, as if he were beginning an entirely new subject:

— I was very much interested in your paper and in the speeches too . . . What did you think of Hughes?

Stephen did not answer.

— Bloody cod, said Temple.

— I thought his speech was in very bad taste, said O'Neill sympathetically.

— *Bellam boccam habet,* said Cranly.

— Yes, I think he went too far, said Madden, but, you see, he gets carried away by his enthusiasm.

— *Patrioticus est.* ✓

— Yes, he is patriotic 'cus, said O'Neill laughing wheezily. But I thought Father Butt's speech very good, very clear and philosophical.

— Did you think that? cried Temple from the inside of the path, to Stephen . . . 'Scuse me . . . I wanted to know what he thought of Butt's speech, he explained at the same time to the other [four] three . . . Did you think . . . he was a bloody cod too?

Stephen could not help laughing at this novel form of address though Father Butt's speech had put him into anything but a charitable mood.

— It was just the kind of thing he gives us every day, said Madden. You know the style.

— His speech annoyed me, said Stephen curtly.

— Why was that? said Temple eagerly. Why was it he annoyed you?

Stephen made a grimace instead of answering:

— Bloody cod of a speech, said Temple . . . I'm a rationalist. I don't b'lieve in any religion.

— I think he meant part of his speech kindly, said Cranly slowly after a pause, turning his full face towards Stephen. Stephen answered his gaze, [and met] looking steadily into a pair of bright dark eyes, and at the moment when their eyes met he felt hope. There was nothing in the phrase to encourage; he doubted its justice very much: yet he knew that hope had touched him. He walked on beside the four young men, pondering. Cranly stopped before the window of a little huckster's shop in one of the mean streets through which they passed, staring fixedly at an old yellow copy of the *Daily Graphic* which was hanging sideways on the glass. The illustration was a winter scene. No–one said anything and as silence seemed about to set in permanently Madden asked him what he was looking at. Cranly looked at his questioner and then looked back again at the dirty picture, towards which he nodded his head heavily:

— What is . . . what is? asked Temple, who had been looking at some cold crubeens[1] in the next window.

Cranly turned his vacant face again towards his questioner and pointed to the picture, saying:

— *Feuc an eis super stradam . . . in Liverpoolio.*[2]

Stephen's family circle was now increased by Isabel's return from her convent. For some time she had been in delicate health and the nuns had recommended that she should have home care. She came home a few days after the famous day of Stephen's paper. Stephen was standing at the little front window that looked towards the mouth of the river when he saw his parents walking from the tram with a thin pale girl walking between them. Stephen's father did not like the prospect of another inhabitant in his house, particularly a daughter for whom he had little affection. He was annoyed that his daughter would not avail herself of the opportunity afforded her in

---

[1] Pig's feet.

[2] Gaelic, German and Latin: 'See the ice on the street . . . in Liverpool.' *Feuc* should be spelt *Feuch*.

the convent but his sense of public duty was real if spasmodic and he would by no means permit his wife to bring the girl home without his aid. The reflection that his daughter, instead of being a help to him would be a hindrance, and the suspicion that the burden of responsibility which he had piously imposed on his eldest son's shoulders was beginning to irk that young man troubled his vision of the future. He had a taste for contrasts, perhaps, which led him to expect industry and sobriety in his offspring [and] but it cannot be said that he desired any material re-exaltation. It was just this impalpable excellence which he wished his son to assert again in the teeth of circumstances which gained him a conditional pardon at Stephen's hands. But this slight thread of union between father and son had been worn away by the usages of daily life and, by reason of its tenuity and of the [failure] gradual rustiness which had begun to consume the upper station, it bore fewer and feebler messages along it.

Stephen's father was quite capable of talking himself into believing what he knew to be untrue. He knew that his own ruin had been his own handiwork but he had talked himself into believing that it was the handiwork of others. He had his son's distaste for responsibility without his son's courage. He was one of those illogical wiseacres with whom no evidence can outreason the first impression. His wife had fulfilled her duties to him with startling literalness and yet she had never been able to expiate the offence of her blood. Misunderstanding such as this, which is accepted as natural in higher social grades, is wrongly refused recognition in the burgher class where it is often found to issue in feuds of insatiable, narrow hatred. Mr Daedalus hated his wife's maiden name with a medieval intensity: it stank in his nostrils. His alliance therewith was the only sin of which, in the entire honesty of his cowardice, he could accuse himself. Now that he was making for the final decades of life with the painful consciousness of having diminished comfortable goods and of having accumulated uncomfortable habits he consoled and revenged himself by tirades so prolonged and so often repeated that he was in danger of becoming a monomaniac. The hearth at night was the sacred witness of these revenges, pondered, muttered, growled and execrated. The exception which his clemency had originally made in favour of his wife was soon out of mind and she began to irritate him by her dutiful symbolism. The great disappointment of his life was accentuated by a lesser and keener loss – the loss of a coveted fame. On account of a certain income and of certain sociable gifts Mr Daedalus had been accustomed to regard himself as the centre of a little world, the darling of a little society. This position he still strove to maintain but at the cost of a reckless liberality from which his household had to suffer both in deed and in spirit. He imagined that while he strove to retain this infatuating position his home affairs would, through the agency of a son whom he made no effort to understand, in some divine manner right themselves. This hope when indulged in would sometimes embitter his affection for a son whom he thereby acknowledged as superior but, now that he was led to suspect that his hope was fatuous, an embitterment of that affection seemed likely to fix itself permanently among his emotional landmarks. His son's notion of aristocracy was not the one which he could sympathize with and his son's silence during the domestic battles no longer seemed to him a conveyed compliment. He was, in fact, sufficiently acute to observe here a covert menace against castellar rights and he would not have been wrong if he had imagined that his son regarded [these] assistance at these tortuous and obscene monologues as the tribute exacted by a father for affording a wayward child a base of supplies . . .

Stephen did not consider his parents very seriously. In his opinion they had opened up misleading and unnatural relations between themselves and him and he considered their affection for him requited by a studious demeanour towards them and by a genuine goodwill to perform for them a great number of such material services as, in his present state of fierce idealism, he could look upon as trifles. The only material services he would refuse them were those which he judged to be spiritually dangerous and it is as well to admit that this exception all but nullified his charity for he had cultivated an independence of the soul which could brook very few subjections. Divine exemplars abetted him in this. The phrase which preachers elaborate into a commandment of obedience seemed to him meagre, ironical and inconclusive and the narrative of the life of Jesus did not in any way impress him [with] as the narrative of the life of one who was subject to others. When he had been a Roman Catholic in the proper sense of the term the figure of Jesus had always seemed to him too ᶜ remote and too passionless ᶜ and he had never uttered from his heart a single fervent prayer to the Redeemer: it was to Mary, as to a ᶜ weaker and more engaging vessel ᶜ of salvation, that he had entrusted his spiritual affairs. Now his enfranchisement from the dicipline of the Church seemed to be coincident with an [natural] instinctive return to the Founder thereof and this impulse would have led him perhaps to a consideration of the merits of Protestantism had not another natural impulse inclined him to bring even the self-contradictory and the absurd into order. He did not know, besides, whether the ᶜ haughtiness of the Papacy was not as derivable from Jesus himself as the reluctance ᶜ to be pressed beyond 'Amen: I say to you' for an account of anything but he was quite sure that behind the enigmatic utterances of Jesus there was a very much more definite conception than any which could be supposed [to] discoverable behind Protestant theology:

— Put this in your diary, he said to transcriptive Maurice. Protestant Orthodoxy is like Lanty McHale's dog: it goes a bit of the road with everyone.

— It seems to me that S. Paul trained that dog, said Maurice.

One day when Stephen had gone to the college by accident he found McCann standing in the hall holding a long testimonial. Another part of the testimonial was on the hall-table and nearly all the young men in the college were signing their names to it. McCann was speaking volubly to a little group and Stephen discovered that the testimonial was the tribute of Dublin University students to the Tsar of Russia. World-wide peace: solution of all disputes by arbitration: general disarming of the nations: these were the benefits for which the students were returning their thanks. On the hall table there were two photographs, one of the Tsar of Russia, the other of the Editor of the *Review of Reviews*: both of the photographs were signed by the famous couple. As McCann was standing sideways to the light Stephen amused himself in tracing a resemblance between him and the pacific Emperor whose photograph had been taken in profile. The Tsar's air of besotted Christ moved him to scorn and he turned for support to Cranly who was standing beside the door. Cranly wore a very dirty yellow straw hat of the shape of an inverted bucket in the shelter of which his face was composed to a glaucuous [sic] calm.

— Doesn't he look a wirrasthrue Jaysus? said Stephen pointing to the Tsar's photograph and using the Dublin version of the name as an effective common noun.

Cranly looked in the direction of McCann and replied, nodding his head:

— Wirrasthrue Jaysus and hairy Jaysus.

At that moment McCann caught sight of Stephen and signalled that he would be with him in a moment:

— Have you signed? asked Cranly.

— This thing? No – have you?

Cranly hesitated and then brought out a well deliberated 'Yes'.

— What for?

— What for?

— Ay.

— For . . . *Pax*.

Stephen looked up under the bucket-shaped hat but could read no expression on his neighbour's face. His eyes wandered up to the dinged vertex of the hat.

— In the name of God what do you wear that hat for? It's not so terribly hot, is it? he asked.

Cranly took off the hat slowly and gazed into its depths. After a little pause he pointed into it and said:

— *Viginti-uno-denarios.*

— Where? said Stephen.

— I bought it, said Cranly very impressively and very flatly, last summer in Wickla.

He looked back into the hat and said, ^c smiling with a sour affection: ^c

— It's not . . . too bloody bad . . . of a hat . . . d'ye know.

And he replaced it on his head slowly, murmuring to himself, from force of habit 'Viginti-uno-denarios'.

— *Sicut bucketus est,* said Stephen.

The subject was not discussed further. Cranly produced a little grey ball from one of his pockets and began to examine it carefully, indenting the surface at many points. Stephen was watching this operation when he heard McCann addressing him.

— I want you to sign this testimonial.

— What about?

— It's a testimonial of admiration for the courage displayed by the

Tsar of Russia in issuing a rescript to the Powers, advocating arbitration instead of war as a means of settling national disputes.

Stephen shook his head. Temple who had been wandering round the hall in search of sympathy came over at this moment and said to Stephen:

— Do you believe in peace?

No-one answered him.

— So you won't sign? said McCann.

Stephen shook his head again.

— Why not? said McCann sharply.

— If we must have a Jesus, answered Stephen, let us have a legitimate Jesus.

— By hell! said Temple laughing, that's good. Did you hear that? he said to Cranly and McCann both of whom he seemed to regard as very hard of hearing. D'you hear that? Legitima' Jesus!

— I presume then you approve of war and slaughter, said McCann.

— I did not make the world, said Stephen.

— By hell! said Temple to Cranly. I believe in universal brotherhood. 'Scuse me, he said, turning to McCann, do you believe in universal brotherhood?

McCann took no heed of the question but continued addressing Stephen. He began an argument in favour of peace which Temple listened to for a few moments, but, as he spoke with his back to Temple, that revolutionary young man who could not hear him very well began to wander round the hall again. Stephen did not argue with McCann but at a convenient pause he said:

— I have no intention of signing.

McCann halted and Cranly said, taking Stephen's arm:

— *Nos ad manum ballum jocabimus.*

— All right, said McCann promptly, as if he was accustomed to rebuffs, if you won't, you won't.

He went off to get more signatures for the Tsar while Cranly and Stephen went out into the garden. The ball-alley was deserted so they arranged a match of twenty, Cranly allowing Stephen seven points. Stephen had not had much practice at the game and so he was only seventeen when Cranly cried out 'Game Ball'. He lost the second game also. Cranly was a strong, accurate player but Stephen thought too heavy of foot to be a brilliant one. While they were playing

Madden came into the alley and sat down on an old box. He was much more excited than either of the players and kept kicking the box with his heels and crying out 'Now, Cranly! Now, Cranly!' 'Butt it, Stevie!' Cranly who had to serve the third game put the ball over the side of the alley into Lord Iveagh's grounds and the game had to wait while he went in search of it. Stephen sat down on his heels beside Madden and they both looked up at the figure of Cranly who was holding on to the netting and making signals to one of the gardeners from the top of the wall. Madden took out smoking materials:

— Are you and Cranly long here?

— Not long, said Stephen.

Madden began to stuff very coarse tobacco into his pipe:

— D'ye know what, Stevie?

— What?

— Hughes . . . doesn't like you . . . at all. I heard him speaking of you to someone.

— 'Someone' is vague.

— He doesn't like you at all.

— His enthusiasm carries him away, said Stephen.

On the evening of the Saturday before Palm Sunday Stephen found himself alone with Cranly. The two were leaning over the marble staircase of the Library, idly watching the people coming in and going out. The big windows in front of them were thrown [open] and the mild air [entered] came through: [them]

— Do you like the services of Holy Week? said Stephen.

— Yes, said Cranly.

— They are wonderful, said Stephen. Tenebrae – it's so damned childish to frighten us by knocking prayerbooks on a bench. Isn't it strange to see the Mass of the Presanctified – no lights or vestments, the altar naked, the door of the tabernacle gaping open, the priests lying prostrate on the altar steps?

— Yes, said Cranly.

— Don't you think the Reader who begins the mass is a strange person. No-one knows where he comes from: he has no connection with the mass. He comes out by himself and opens a book at the right hand side of the altar and when he has read the lesson he closes the book and goes away as he came. Isn't he strange?

— Yes, said Cranly.

— You know how his lesson begins? *Dixit enim Dominus:*[1] *in tribulatione sua consurgent ad me: venite et revertamur ad Dominum –*

He chanted the openings of the lesson in *mezza voce* and his voice went flowing down the staircase and round the circular hall, each tone coming back upon the ear enriched and softened.

— He pleads, said Stephen. He is what that chalk-faced chap was for me, *advocatus diaboli.* Jesus has no friend on Good Friday. Do you know what kind of a figure rises before me on Good Friday?

— What kind?

— An ugly little man who has taken into his body the sins of the world:[2] Something between Socrates and a Gnostic Christ – A Christ of the Dark Ages. That's what his mission of redemption has got for him: a crooked ugly body for which neither God nor man have pity. Jesus is on strange terms with that father of his. His father seems to me something of a snob. Do you notice that he never notices his son publicly but once – when Jesus is in full dress on the top of Thabor?

— I don't like Holy Thursday much, said Cranly.

— Neither do I. There are too many mammas and daughters going chapel-hunting. The chapel smells too much of flowers and hot candles and women. Besides girls praying put me off my stroke.

— Do you like Holy Saturday?

— The service is always too early but I like it.

— I like it.

— Yes, the Church seems to have thought the matter over and to be saying 'Well, after all, you see, it's morning now and he wasn't so dead as we thought he was.' The corpse has become a paschal candle with five grains of incense stuck in it instead of its five wounds. The three faithful Marys too who thought all was over on Friday have a candle each. The bells ring and the service is full of irrelevant alleluias.[3] It's rather a technical affair, blessing this, that and the other

[1] Corrected in red crayon to read: '*Haec dicit Dominus.*'

[2] Written in the margin in pencil is the phrase, 'The idea of the scape-goat in the Old Testament and of the Lamb of God in the New (Christ's own words).' This may have been meant to follow 'world'.

[3] This sentence and the two preceding it are written in pencil in the margin as later additions.

but it's cheerfully ceremonious.

— But you don't imagine the damned fools of people see anything in these services, do you?

— Do they not? said Stephen.

— Bah, said Cranly.

One of Cranly's friends came up the stairs while they were talking. He was a young man who was by day a clerk in Guinness's Brewery and by night a student of mental and moral philosophy in the night classes of the college. It was, of course, Cranly who had induced him to attend. This young man, who was named Glynn, was unable to keep his head steady as he suffered from inherited nervousness and his hands trembled very much whenever he tried to do anything with them. He spoke with nervous hesitations and seemed to obtain satisfaction only in the methodic stamp of his feet. He was a low-sized young man, with a nigger's face and the curly black head of a nigger. He usually carried an umbrella and his conversation was for the most part a translation of commonplaces into polysyllabic phrases. This habit he cultivated partly because it saved him from the inconvenience of cerebrating at the normal rate and perhaps because he considered it was the channel best fitted for his peculiar humour.

— Here is Professor Bloody-Big-Umbrella Glynn, said Cranly.

— Good evening, gentlemen, said Glynn, bowing.

— Good . . . evening, said Cranly vacantly. Well, yes . . . it is a good evening.

— I can see, said Glynn shaking a trembling forefinger in reproof, I can see that you are about to make obvious remarks.

On Spy Wednesday night Cranly and Stephen attended the office of Tenebrae in the Pro-Cathedral. They went round to the back of the altar and knelt behind the students from Clonliffe who were chanting the office. Stephen was right opposite Wells and he observed the great change which a surplice made in that young man's appearance. Stephen did not like the office which was gabbled over quickly. He said to Cranly that the chapel with its polished benches and incandescent lamps reminded him of an insurance office. Cranly arranged that on Good Friday they should attend the office in the Carmelite Church, Whitefriar's St where, he said, the office was much more homely. Cranly accompanied Stephen part of the way home and explained very minutely, using his large hands for the purpose, all the merits of Wicklow bacon.

— You are no Israelite, said Stephen, I see you eat the unclean animal.

Cranly replied that it was nonsense to consider the pig unclean because he ate dirty garbage and at the same time to consider the oyster, which fed chiefly on excrements, a delicacy. He believed that the pig was much maligned: he said there was a lot of money to be made out of pigs. He instanced all the Germans who made small fortunes in Dublin by opening pork-shops.

— I often thought seriously, he said stopping in his walk to give emphasis to his remark, of opening a pork-shop, d'ye know ... and putting *Kranliberg*[1] or some German name, d'ye know, over the door ... and makin' a flamin' fortune out of pig's meat.

— God bless us! said Stephen. What a terrible idea!

— Ay, said Cranly walking on heavily, a flamin' bloody fortune I'd make.

On Good Friday as Stephen was wandering aimlessly about the city he caught sight of a placard on a wall which announced that the Three Hours' Agony would be preached by the Very Reverend W. Dillon S.J. and the Very Reverend J. Campbell S.J. in the Jesuit Church, Gardiner St. Stephen felt very solitary and purposeless as he traversed empty street after empty street and, without being keenly aware of it, he began to proceed in the direction of Gardiner St. It was a warm sunless day and the city wore an air of sacred torpor. As he passed under S. George's Church he saw that it was already half past two; – he had been three hours wandering up and down the city. He entered the Church in Gardiner St and, passing by without honouring the table of the lay-brother who roused himself from a stupefied doze in expectation of silver, arrived in the right wing of the chapel. The chapel was crowded from altar to doors with a well-dressed multitude. Everywhere he saw the same flattered affection for the Jesuits who are in the habit of attaching to their order the souls of thousands of the insecurely respectable middle-class by offering them a refined asylum, an interested, a considerate confessional, a particular amiableness of manners which their spiritual adventures in no way entitled them to. Not very far from him in the

[1] Written in pencil in the margin are the words, 'a gentleman butcher'; there is no indication where they are to be inserted.

shelter of one of the pillars Stephen saw his father and two friends. His father had directed his eyeglass upon the distant choir and his face wore an expression of impressed piety. The choir was executing some florid tracery which was intended as an expression of mourning. The walk, the heat, the crush, the darkness of the chapel overcame Stephen and, leaning against the lintel of the door, he half closed his eyes and allowed his thoughts to drift. Rhymes began to make themselves in his head.

He perceived dimly that a white figure had ascended the pulpit and he heard a voice saying *Consummatum est*. He recognized the voice and he knew that Father Dillon was preaching on the Seventh Word. He took no trouble to hear the sermon but every few minutes he heard a new translation of the Word rolling over the congregation. 'It is ended' 'It is accomplished'. This sensation awoke him from his daydream and as the translations followed [each] one another more and more rapidly he found his gambling instinct on the alert. He wagered with himself as to what word the preacher would select. 'It is . . . accomplished' 'It is . . . consummated' 'It is . . . achieved'. In the few seconds which intervened between the first part and the second part of the phrase Stephen's mind performed feats of divining agility 'It is . . . finished' 'It is . . . completed' 'It is . . . concluded'. At last with a final burst of rhetoric Father Dillon cried out that it was over and the congregation began to pour itself out into the streets. Stephen was borne along in the crowd and everywhere about him he heard the same murmurs of admiration and saw the same expressions of satisfaction, discreet murmurs, subdued expressions. The special charges of the Jesuits were congratulating themselves and one another on a well-spent Good Friday.

To avoid his father Stephen slipped round towards the body of the chapel and waited in the central porch while the common people came shuffling and stumbling past him. Here also there was admiration, satisfaction. A young workman passed out with his wife and Stephen heard the words 'He knows his thayology, I tell ye.' Two women stopped beside the holy water font and after scraping their hands ^e vainly over ^e the bottom crossed themselves in a slovenly fashion with their dry hands. One of them sighed and drew her brown shawl about her:

— An' his language, said the other woman.

— Aw yis.

Here the other woman sighed in her turn and drew her shawl about her:

— On'y, said she, God bless the gintleman, he uses the words that you nor me can't intarprit.[1]

[1] After this, written in pencil, are the words: 'If I told them there is no water in the font to symbolize that when Christ has washed us in blood we have no need of other aspersions.'

XXI

Between Easter and the end of May Stephen's acquaintance with Cranly progressed night by night. As the time of the Summer Examinations was approaching Maurice and Stephen were both supposed to be hard at work. Maurice retired to his room carefully every evening after tea-time and Stephen repaired to the Library where he was supposed to be engaged in serious work. As a matter of fact he read little or nothing in the Library. He talked with Cranly by the hour either at a table, or, if removed by the librarian or by the indignant glances of students, standing at the top of the staircase. At ten o'clock when the library closed the two returned together through the central streets exchanging banalities with the other students.

It would seem at first somewhat strange and improbable that these two young men should have anything in common beyond an incurable desire for leisure. Stephen had begun to regard himself seriously as a literary artist: he professed scorn for the rabblement and contempt for authority. Cranly's chosen companions represented the rabblement in a stage of partial fermentation when it is midway between vat and flagon and Cranly seemed to please himself in the spectacle of this caricature of his own unreadiness. Anyhow towards rabblement and authority alike he behaved with submissive defence and Stephen would have been disposed to regard this too mature demeanour as a real sign of interior corruption had he not daily evidence that Cranly was willing to endanger his own fair name as a member of the Sodality and as a general lay-servant of the Church by association with one who was known to be contaminated. Cranly, however, might have wished the fathers to suppose that he went with the rebellious young artist with the secret purpose of leading him back again to good ways and, as if from a secret appreciation of his own fitness for such a task, he always enlarged and interpreted the doctrines of the Church side by side with Stephen's theories. Thus confronted, it was a trick of the pleader for orthodoxy to suggest a possible reconciliation between neighbours and to suggest [even] further that the Church would not be over hasty in condemning vagaries of architecture or even the use of pagan emblems and flourishes so long as her ground rent was paid quarterly in advance. These accommodating business terms, which would have seemed of suspicious piety to more simple souls, were not likely to startle two young men who were fond of tracing even moral phenomena back to the region of their primal cells. The moral doctrine of Catholicism [with] so cunningly lined and interwoven with a studious alloy of conscience was capable under the management of a nimble spirit of performing feats of extension and contraction. After a thousand such ° changes of form this elastic body was suddenly detected in a change of position and a point hitherto external was now seen to be well enclosed within it: and all this imperceptibly, while the eye was lulled by the mere exhibition of so many variations executed with a certain amoeboid instinct.°

As for artistic sympathies Cranly could hardly be said to offer these. He had all the rustic's affection for the prosaic things of the six days of the week and, in addition to this, he lacked the hypocritical taste which the rustic affects for the fine arts on the seventh day. In the Library he read nothing but the weekly illustrated papers. Sometimes he took a big book from the counter and carried it solemnly to his place where he opened it and studied the title-page and preface for an hour or so. Of fine literature he had, almost literally speaking, no knowledge. His acquaintance with English prose seemed to be limited to a hazy acquaintance with the beginning of *Nicholas Nickleby* and of English verse he had certainly read Wordsworth's poem which is called *Advice to a Father*. Both of these accomplishments he divulged to Stephen one day when he had been discovered reading with great attention the title-page of a book which was called *Diseases of the Ox*. He offered no comment on what he had read and simply stated the achievement not without wonder at his having achieved it. He had a straggling regiment of words at his command and he was thus enabled to express himself: but he spoke flatly and frequently made childish errors. ° He had a defiant manner of using technical and foreign terms as if he wished to suggest that for him they were mere conventions of language.° His receptiveness was not troubled by any nausea: he received everything that came in his way and it was purely instinctive of Stephen to perceive any special affinity in so indiscriminate a vessel. He was fond of leading a philosophical argument back to the machinery of the intellectual faculty itself and in mundane matters he did likewise, testing everything by its food value.

It was in favour of this young man that Stephen decided to break his commandment of reticence. Cranly, on his side, must have been above all the accidents of life if he had not suffered a slight commotion from such delicately insistent flattery. Stephen spoke to his impoverished ear out of the plenitude of an amassed vocabulary, and confronted the daring commonplaces of his companion's moods with a complex radiance of thought. Cranly seldom or never obtruded his presence upon these monologues. He listened to all, seemed to understand all, and seemed to think it was the duty of his supposititious character to listen [to] and understand. He never refused his ear. Stephen claimed it in and out of season as he felt the need for intelligent sympathy. They promenaded miles of the streets together, arm-in-arm. They halted in wet weather under spacious porches, desisting at the sight of some inviting triviality. They sat sometimes in the pit of a music-hall and one unfolded to the other the tapestry of his poetical aims while the band bawled to the comedian and the comedian bawled to the band. Cranly grew used to having sensations and impressions recorded and analysed before him at the very instant of their apparition. Such concentration upon oneself was unknown to [Cranly] him and he wondered at first with the joy of solitary possession at Stephen's ingenuous arrogance. This phenomenon, which called all his previous judgments to account, and opened out a new system of life at the last limit of [Cranly's] his world, rankled somewhat in [Cranly's] his mind. It irritated him also because he knew too well the large percentage of Christian sentiment which concealed itself under [a] his veneer of Stoicism to suspect himself of any talent for a similar extravagance. And yet, hearing the wholehearted young egoist pour out his pride and anger at his feet like some costly ointment, and benefiting by a liberality which seemed to keep nothing in reserve, much as he would have liked to hold himself aloof from such ties he felt himself gradually answering the appeal by a silent, perverse affection. He affected more brutality than was in his nature and, as if infected by his companion's arrogance, seemed to expect that the practice of aggressive criticism would be suspended in his case.

A licence which he allowed himself rather freely was that of impolite abstraction, so deep as to suggest great mental activity but issuing at last in some blunt actuality. If a [conversation] monologue which had set out from a triviality seemed to him likely to run on unduly he would receive it with a silence through which aversion was just discernible and at a lull bring his hammer down brutally on the poor original object. At times Stephen found this ultra-classical habit very unpalatable. One evening the monologue was interrupted time after time. Stephen had mentioned his sister's illness and had spread out a few leagues of theory on the subject of the tyranny of home. Cranly never actually broke in upon the oration but he continued inserting question after question whenever he had an opening. He asked Isabel's age, her symptoms, her doctor's name her treatment, her diet, her appearance, how her mother nursed her, whether they had sent for a priest or not, whether she had ever been sick before or not. Stephen answered all these questions and still Cranly was not satisfied. He continued his questions until the monologue had in all decency to be abandoned; and Stephen, thinking over his manner, was unable to decide whether such conduct was to be considered the sign of a deep interest in a human illness or the sign of irritated dissatisfaction with an inhuman theorist.

Stephen did not in the least shrink from applying the reproach to himself but he found himself honestly unable to admit its justice. His sister had become almost a stranger to him on account of the way in which she had been brought up. He had hardly spoken a hundred words to her since the time when they had been children together. He could not speak to her now except as to a stranger. She had acquiesced in the religion of her mother; she had accepted everything that had been proposed to her. If she lived she had exactly the temper for a Catholic wife of limited intelligence and of pious docility and if she died she was supposed to have earned for herself a place in the eternal heaven of Christians from which her two brothers were likely to be shut out. Calamities in this world are reported to sit lightly on the shoulders of the true Christian who can bide his time until the Creator institutes the kingdom of the good. Isabel's case moved Stephen's anger and commiseration but he saw at once how hopeless it was and how vain it would be for him to interfere. Her life had been and would always be a trembling walk before God. The slightest interchange of ideas between them must be either a condescension on his part or an attempt to corrupt. No consciousness of their nearness in blood troubled him with natural, unreasoning affection She was called his sister as his mother was called his mother but there had never been any proof of that relation offered him in their emotional attitude towards him, or any recognition of it permitted in his emotional attitude towards them. The Catholic husband and wife, the Catholic father and mother, are allowed to be natural at discretion but the same grace is not vouchsafed to Catholic children. They must preserve an unquestioning orderliness even at the risk of being upbraided as unnatural by the very preachers who ᶜ assert that nature is the possession of Satan.ᶜ Stephen had felt impulses of pity for his mother, for his father, for Isabel, for Wells also but he believed that he had done right in resisting them: he had first of all to save himself and he had no business trying to save others unless his experiment with himself justified him. Cranly had all but formulated serious charges against him, calling up by implication the picture of Isabel with her gradually wasting flame, her long dark hair and great wondering eyes, but Stephen stood up to the charges and answered in his heart that it was injustice to point a finger of reproach at him and that a vague inactive pity from those who upheld a system of mutual servile association towards those who accepted it was only a play upon emotions as characteristic of the egoist as of the man of sentiment. Isabel, moreover, did not seem to Stephen to be in any great danger. He told Cranly she was probably growing too fast; many girls were delicate at that age. He confessed that the subject tired him a little. Cranly stood still and looked at him fixedly:

— My dear man, said he, d'ye know what it is . . . You're an extraordinary . . . man.

A week before the examination Cranly explained to Stephen his plan for reading the ᶜ course in five days.ᶜ It was a carefully made plan, founded upon an intimate knowledge of examiners and examination papers. Cranly's plan was to study from ten in the morning until half past two in the afternoon, then from four to six, and then from half past seven to ten. Stephen declined to follow this plan as he imagined he had a fair chance of passing on what he called 'roundabout' knowledge but Cranly said that the plan was perfectly safe.

— I don't quite see that, said Stephen, how can you manage to pass – in Latin composition, say – after such a cursory run over it?

If you like I'll show you some things – not that I can write so marvellously . . .

Cranly meditated without seeming to observe the offer. Then he averred flatly that his plan would work:

— I'll take my dyin' bible, he said, I'll write them as good a thing, d'ye know, ay – as good a thing as they want. What do they know about Latin prose?

— Not much, I suppose, said Stephen, but they may not be quite ignorant of Latin grammar.

Cranly thought this over and then found his remedy:

— D'ye know what, he said, whenever I can't think of the grammar I'll bring in a piece out of Tacitus.

— Apropos of what?

— What the flamin' hell does it matter what it's apropos of?[1]

— Quite right, said Stephen.

Cranly's plan neither succeeded nor failed for the very good reason that it was never followed. The nights before the examination were spent sitting outside under the porch of the Library. The two young men gazed up into the tranquil sky and discussed how it was possible to live with the least amount of labour. Cranly suggested bees: he seemed to know the entire economy of bee-life and he did not seem as intolerant towards bees as towards men. Stephen said it would be a good arrangement if Cranly were to live on the labour of the bees and allow him (Stephen) to live on the united labours of the bees and of their keeper.

— 'I will watch from dawn to gloom
    The lake-reflected sun illume
    The yellow bees in the ivy bloom.'

— 'Illume'? said Cranly.

— You know the meaning of 'illume'?

— Who wrote that?

— Shelley.

— Illume – it's just the word, d'ye know, for autumn, deep gold colour.

— A spiritual interpretation of landscape is very rare. Some people

[1] Among Joyce's notes (Gorman, p. 137) under the heading 'Byrne' – i.e. Cranly – is listed: 'Brutal "bloody" "flamin'" '.

think they write spiritually if they make their scenery dim and cloudy.

— That bit you said now doesn't seem to me spiritual.

— Nor to me: but sometimes Shelley does not address the eye. He says 'many a lake-surrounded flute'. Does that strike your eye or your sense of colour?

— Shelley has a face that reminds me of a bird. What is it? 'The lake-surrounded sun illume'? . . .

— 'The lake-reflected sun illume
    The yellow bees in the ivy bloom.'

— What are you quoting? asked Glynn who had just come out of the Library after several hours of study.

Cranly surveyed him before answering:

— Shelley.

— O, Shelley? What was the quotation again?

Cranly nodded towards Stephen.

— What was the quotation? asked Glynn. Shelley is an old flame of mine.

Stephen repeated the lines and Glynn nodded his head nervously several times in approval.

— Beautiful poetry Shelley wrote, didn't he? So mystical.

— D'ye know what they call them yellow bees in Wickla? asked Cranly suddenly, turning to Glynn.

— No? what?

— Red-arsed bees.

Cranly laughed loudly at his own remark and struck his heels on the granite steps. Glynn, conscious of a false position, began to fumble with his umbrella and to search for one of his stock witticisms.

— But that is only, he said, if you will pardon the expression, that is only so to speak . . .

— 'The lake-surrounded sun illume
    The red-arsed bees in the ivy bloom' – it's every bit as good bloody poetry as Shelley's, said Cranly to Glynn. What do you think?

— It seems to me undeniable, said Glynn driving his unsteady umbrella before him as an emphasis, that the bees are in the bloom. Of that we may say that it is distinctly so.

The examination lasted five days. After the first two days Cranly did not even go through the form of entering the examination hall but after each paper he was to be seen outside the University going over all the questions carefully with his more diligent friends. He said that the papers were very easy and that anyone could pass them on a fair knowledge. He did not ask Stephen any particular questions but said merely 'I suppose you're through'. 'I expect so' said Stephen. McCann usually came to meet the students who had been under examination. He came partly because he considered it was part of his duty to show an interest in all that concerned the college, and partly because one of Mr Daniel's daughters was under examination. Stephen who did not care very much whether he succeeded or failed in the examination was very much amused observing the jealousies and nervous anxieties which tried to conceal themselves under airs of carelessness. Students who had studied hard all the year pretended to be in the same case as idlers and idle and diligent both appeared to submit to the examinations with great unwillingness. Those who were rivals did not speak to each other, being afraid to trust their eyes, but one questioned wandering acquaintances privily about the other's success. Their excitement was so genuine that even the excitement of sex failed to overcome it. The girl students were not the subject of the usual sniggers and jokes but were regarded with some aversion as sly enemies. Some of the young men eased their enmity and vindicated their superiority at the same time by saying that it was no wonder the women would do well seeing that they could study ten hours [all] a day all the year round. McCann, who acted as go-between, told them the gossip from the other camp and it was he who [had] spread the report that Landy would not get first class honours in English because Miss Reeves had written an essay of twenty pages on *The Use and Abuse of Ridicule*.

The examination ended on Tuesday. On Wednesday morning Stephen's mother seemed to be rather anxious. Stephen had not given his parents much satisfaction as to his conduct at the examination but he could not think that this was the cause of his mother's trouble: he waited, however, for the trouble to declare itself. His mother waited till the room was clear and then she said casually:

— You have not made your Easter duty yet, have you, Stephen? Stephen answered that he had not.

— It would be better for you to go to confession in the day-time. Tomorrow is Ascension Thursday and the chapels are sure to be crowded tonight by people who have left off making their Easter duty till the last moment. It's a wonder people wouldn't have more shame in them. Goodness knows they have time enough from Ash Wednesday without waiting till the stroke of twelve to go to the priest . . . I'm not speaking of you, Stephen. I know you have been studying for your examination. But people who have nothing to do . . .

Stephen made no answer to this but went on scraping diligently in his eggshell.

— I have made my Easter duty already – on Holy Thursday – but I'm going to the altar in the morning. I am making a novena and I want you to offer up your communion for a special intention of mine.

— What special intention?

— Well, dear, I'm very much concerned about Isabel . . . I don't know what to think . . .

Stephen stuck his spoon ° angrily ° through the bottom of the shell and asked was there any more tea.

— There's no more in the pot but I can boil some water in a minute.

— O, never mind.

— It won't be a jiffy.

Stephen allowed the water to be put on as it would [allow] give him time to put an end to the conversation. He was much annoyed that his mother should try to wheedle him into conformity by using his sister's health as an argument. He felt that such an attempt dishonoured him and freed from the last dissuasions of considerate piety. His mother put on the water and appeared to be less anxious as if she had expected a blunt refusal. She even ventured on the small talk of religious matrons.

— I must try and get in to town tomorrow in time for High Mass in Marlborough St. Tomorrow is a great feast-day in the Church.

— Why? asked Stephen smiling.

— The Ascension of Our Lord, answered his mother gravely.

— And why is that a great feast-day?

— Because it was on that day that he showed Himself Divine: he ascended into Heaven.

Stephen began to plaster butter over a crusty heel of the loaf while his features settled into definite hostility:

— Where did he go off?

— From Mount Olivet, answered his mother reddening under her eyes.

— Head first?

— What do you mean, Stephen?

— I mean he must have been rather giddy by the time he arrived. Why didn't he go by balloon?

— Stephen, are you trying to scoff at Our Lord? I really thought you had more intelligence than to use that kind of language: it's only what people who believe only in what they can see under their noses say. I'm surprised.

— Tell me, mother, said Stephen between mouthfuls, do you mean to tell me you believe that our friend went up off the mountain as they say he did?

— I do.

— I don't.

— What are you saying, Stephen?

— It's absurd: it's Barnum. He comes into the world God knows how, walks on the water, gets out of his grave and goes up off the Hill of Howth. What drivel is this?

— Stephen!

— I don't believe it: and it would be no credit if I did. It's no credit to me that I don't. It's drivel.

— The most learned doctors of the Church believe it and that's good enough for me.

— He can fast for forty days.

— God can do all things . . .

— There's a fellow in Capel St at present in a show who says he can eat glass and hard nails. He calls himself *The Human Ostrich*.

— Stephen, said his mother, I'm afraid you have lost your faith.

— I'm afraid so too, said Stephen.

Mrs Daedalus looked very discomposed and sat down helplessly on the nearest chair. Stephen fixed his attention on the water and when it was ready made himself another cup of tea.

— I little thought, said his mother, that it would come to this – that a child of mine would lose the faith.

— But you knew some time ago.

— How could I know?

121

— You knew.

— I suspected something was wrong but I never thought . . .

— And yet you wanted me to receive Holy Communion!

— Of course you cannot receive it now. But I thought you would make your Easter duty as you have done every year up till now. I do not know what led you astray unless it was those books you read. John, too, your uncle – he was led astray by books when he was young but – only for a time.

— Poor fellow! said Stephen.

— You were religiously brought up by the Jesuits, in a Catholic home . . .

— A very Catholic home!

— None of your people, neither your father's nor mine, have a drop of anything but Catholic blood in their veins.

— Well, I'll make a beginning in the family.

— This is the result of being left too much liberty. You do as you like and believe what you like.

— I don't believe, for example, that Jesus was the only man that ever had pure auburn hair.

— Well?

— Nor that he was the only man that was exactly six feet high, neither more nor less.

— Well?

— Well, you believe that. I heard you tell that years ago to our nurse in Bray – Do you remember nurse Sarah?

Mrs Daedalus defended the tradition in a half-hearted way.

— That is what they say.

— O, they say! They say a great deal.

— But you need not believe that if you don't want to.

— Thanks very much.

— All you are asked to believe in is the word of God. Think of the beautiful teachings of Our Lord. Think of your own life when you believed in those teachings. Weren't you better and happier then?

— It was good for me at the time, perhaps, but it is quite useless for me now.

— I know what is wrong with you – you suffer from the pride of the intellect. You forget that we are only worms of the earth. You think you can defy God because you have misused the talents he has given you.

— I think Jehovah gets too high a salary for judging motives. I want to retire him on the plea of old age.

Mrs Daedalus stood up.

— Stephen, you may use that kind of language with your companions whoever they are but I will not allow you to use it with me. Even your father, bad as he is supposed to be, does not speak such blasphemy as you do. I am afraid that you are a changed boy since you went to that University. I suppose you fell in with some of those students . . .

— Good Lord, mother, said Stephen, don't believe that. The students are awfully nice fellows. They love their religion: they wouldn't say boo to a goose. /3

— Wherever you've learnt it I will not allow you to use such language to me when you speak of holy things. Keep that for the street-corners at night.

— Very well, mother, said Stephen. But you began the conversation.

— I never thought I would see the day when a child of mine would lose the faith. God knows I didn't. I did my best for you to keep you in the right way.

Mrs Daedalus began to cry. Stephen, having eaten and drunk all within his province, rose and went towards the door:

— It's all the fault of those books and the company you keep. Out at all hours of the night instead of in your home, the proper place for you. I'll burn every one of them. I won't have them in the house to corrupt anyone else.

Stephen halted at the door and turned towards his mother who had now broken out into tears:

— If you were a genuine Roman Catholic, mother, you would burn me as well as the books.

— I knew no good would come of your going to that place. You are ruining yourself body and soul. Now your faith is gone!

— Mother, said Stephen from the threshold, I don't see what you're crying for. I'm young, healthy, happy. What is the crying for? . . . It's too silly . . .

Stephen went over to the Library that evening expressly to see

Cranly and [tell him of] narrate his latest conflict with orthodoxy. Cranly was standing under the Library porch announcing the results of the examinations beforehand. He was surrounded, as usual, by a little group among whom were his friend, the clerk from the Custom-House, and another bosom friend, a very grave-looking elderly student named Lynch. Lynch was of a very idle disposition and had allowed six or seven years to intervene between [his] leaving school and beginning a course in medicine at the College of Surgeons. He was much esteemed by his colleagues because he had a deep bass voice, never 'stood' any drinks in return for those which he accepted from others, and seldom uttered any remarks in return for those he listened to. He always kept both his ᶜ hands in his trousers' pockets when he walked and jutted out his chest in a manner ᶜ which was intended as a criticism of life. He spoke, however, to Cranly principally about women and for this reason Cranly had nicknamed him Nero. It was possible to accuse his mouth of a Neronic tendency but he destroyed the illusion of imperialism by wearing his cap very far back from a ᶜ shock forehead.ᶜ He had unbounded contempt for medical students and their ways and, if he had not absorbed so much Dublin into his mind, he would have been a lover of the fine arts. He was, in fact, very interested in the art of singing. [and] He used this interest to attempt an intimacy with Stephen and, his gravity covering a ᶜ shame-faced idealism,ᶜ he had already begun to feel through Cranly the influence of Stephen's vivifying disorderliness. His objection, singular enough in a lax character, to trite and meaningless execrations, to the ᶜ facile iniquities ᶜ of the lips, had resulted for him in two moments of inspiration. He ᶜ execrated in yellow ᶜ in protest against the sanguine adjective of uncertain etymology and, to describe the hymeneal tract, he had one invariable term. He called it *oracle* and all within the frontiers he called *oracular*. The term was considered distinguished in his circle and he was careful never to explain the process which had discovered it.

Stephen stood on one of the steps of the porch but Cranly did not honour him with any kind of welcome. Stephen inserted a few phrases into the conversation but his presence was still ᶜ unhonoured by Cranly.ᶜ He was not in the least daunted by this reception, much as he was puzzled by it, and waited quietly for his opportunity. Once he addressed Cranly directly, but got no answer. His mind began to ruminate upon this and at last his ruminations expressed themselves in a prolonged smile. While he was enjoying his smile he saw that Lynch was observing him. Lynch came down from the group and said 'Good evening'. He then took a packet of Woodbine cigarettes from his side pocket and offered one to Stephen, saying:

— Five a penny.

Stephen, who knew that Lynch was a very poor young man, accepted the cigarette appreciatively. They smoked in silence for some minutes and at length the group under the porch fell silent also:

— Have you a copy of your essay? said Lynch.

— Do you want it?

— I'd like to read it.

— I'll bring it to you tomorrow night, said Stephen going up the steps.

He went up to Cranly who was leaning against a pillar and gazing straight before him and touched him lightly on the shoulder:

— I want to speak to you, he said.

Cranly turned slowly round and looked at him. Then he asked:

— Now?

— Yes.

They walked together up along Kildare St without speaking. When they came to the Green Cranly said:

— I'm going home on Saturday. Will you come as far as Harcourt St Station? I want to see the hour the train goes at.

— All right.

In the station Cranly spent a great deal of time reading the time-tables and making abstruse calculations. Then he went up to the plat-form and watched for a long time the shunting of the engine of a goods train on to a passenger train. The engine was steaming and blowing a deafening whistle and rolling billows of thick smoke to-wards the roof of the station. Cranly said that the engine-driver came from his part of the country and that he was the son of a cobbler in Tinahely. The engine executed a series of indecisive movements and finally settled itself on to the train. The engine-driver stuck his head out through the side and gazed languidly along the train:

— I suppose you would call him sooty Jaysus, said Cranly.

— Cranly, said Stephen, I have left the Church.

Cranly took his arm at the word and they turned away from the platform and went down the staircase. As soon as they had emerged into the street he said encouragingly:

— You have left the Church?

Stephen went over the interview phrase by phrase.

— Then you do not believe any longer?

— I cannot believe.

— But you could at one time.

— I cannot now.

— You could now if you wanted to.

— Well, I don't want to.

— Are you sure you do not believe?

— Quite sure.

— Why do you not go to the altar?

— Because I do not believe.

— Would you make a sacrilegious communion?

— Why should I?

— For your mother's sake.

— I don't see why I should.

— Your mother will suffer very much. You say you do not believe. The Host for you is a piece of ordinary bread. Would you not eat a piece of ordinary bread to avoid causing your mother pain?

— I would in many cases.

— And why not in this case? Have you any reluctance to commit a sacrilege? If you do not believe you should not have any.

— Wait a minute, said Stephen. At present I have a reluctance to commit a sacrilege. I am a product of Catholicism. I was sold to Rome before my birth. Now I have broken my slavery but I cannot in a moment destroy every feeling in my nature. That takes time. However if it were a case of needs must – for my life, for instance – I would commit any enormity with the host.

— Many Catholics would do the same, said Cranly, if their lives were at stake.

— Believers?

— Ay, believers. So by your own showing you are a believer.

— It is not from fear that I refrain from committing a sacrilege.

— Why then?

— I see no reason for committing sacrilege.

— But you have always made your Easter Duty. Why do you

change? The thing for you is mockery, mummery.

— If I mum it is an act of submission, a public act of submission to the Church. I will not submit to the Church.

— Even so far as to mum?

— It is mumming with an intention. The outward show is nothing but it means a good deal.

— Again you are speaking like a Catholic. The host is nothing in outward show – a piece of bread.

— I admit: but all the same I insist on disobeying the Church. I will not submit any longer.

— But could you not be more diplomatic? Could you not rebel in your heart and yet conform out of contempt? You could be a rebel in spirit.

— That cannot be done for long by anyone who is sensitive. The Church knows the value of her services: her priest must hypno-tize himself every morning before the tabernacle. If I get up every morning, go to the looking-glass and say to myself 'You are the Son of God' at the end of twelve months I will want disciples.

— If you could make your religion pay like Christianity I would advise you to get up every morning and go to the looking-glass.

— That would be good for my vicars on earth but I would find crucifixion a personal inconvenience.

— But here in Ireland by following your new religion of unbelief you may be crucifying yourself like Jesus – only socially not physically.

— There is this difference. Jesus was good-humoured over it. I will die hard.

— How can you propose such a future to yourself and yet be afraid to trust yourself to perform even the simplest mumming in a Church? said Cranly.

— That is my business, said Stephen, tapping at his forehead.

When they had come to the Green they crossed the streets and began to walk round the enclosure inside the chains. A few mechanics and their sweethearts were sitting on the swinging-chains turning the shadows to account. The footpath was deserted except for the metallic image of a distant policeman who had been posted well in the gaslight as an admonition. When the two young men passed the college they both looked up at the same moment towards the dark windows.

127

— May I ask you why you left the Church? asked Cranly.

— I could not observe the precepts.

— Not even with grace?

— No.

— Jesus gives very simple precepts. The Church is severe.

— Jesus or the Church – it's all the same to me. I can't follow him. I must have liberty to do as I please.

— No man can do as he pleases.

— Morally.

— No, not morally either.

— You want me, said Stephen, to toe the line with those syco-phants and hypocrites in the college. I will never do so.

— No. I mentioned Jesus.

— Don't mention him. I have made it a common noun. They don't believe in him; they don't observe his precepts. In any case let us leave Jesus aside. My sight will only carry me as far as his lieutenant in Rome. It is quite useless. I will not be frightened into paying tribute in money or in thought.

— You told me – do you remember the evening we were standing at the top of the staircase talking about . . .

— Yes, yes, I remember, said Stephen who hated Cranly's ° method of remembering ° the past, what did I tell you?

— You told me the idea you had of Jesus on Good Friday, an ugly misshapen Jesus. Did it ever strike you that Jesus may have been a conscious impostor?

— I have never believed in his chastity – that is since I began to think about him. I am sure he [is] was no eunuch priest. His interest in loose women is too persistently humane. All the women associated with him are of dubious character.

— You don't think he was God?

— What a question! Explain it: explain the hypostatic union: tell me if the figure which ° that policeman worships ° as the Holy Ghost is intended for a spermatozoon with wings added. What a question! He makes general remarks on life, that's all I know: and I disagree with them.

— For example?

— For example . . . Look here, I cannot talk on this subject. I am not a scholar and I receive no pay as a minister of God. I want to live, do you understand. McCann wants air and food: I want them and a hell of a lot of other things too. I don't care whether I am right or wrong. There is always that risk in human affairs, I suppose. But even if I am wrong at least I shall not have to endure Father Butt's company for eternity.

Cranly laughed.

— Remember he would be glorified.

— Heaven for climate, isn't that it, and hell for society . . . the whole affair is too damn idiotic. Give it up. I am very young. When I have a beard to my middle I will study Hebrew and then write to you about it.

— Why are you so impatient with the Jesuits? asked Cranly.

Stephen did not answer and, when they arrived in the next region of light Cranly exclaimed:

— Your face is red!

— I feel it, said Stephen.

— Most people think you are self-restrained, said Cranly after a pause.

— So I am, said Stephen.

— Not on this subject. Why do you get so excited: I can't understand that. It is a thing for you to think out.

— I can think out things when I like. I have thought this affair out very carefully though you may not believe me when I tell you. But my escape excites me: I must talk as I do. I feel a flame in my face. I feel a wind rush through me.

— 'Like a mighty wind rushing', said Cranly.

— You urge me to postpone life – till when? Life is now – this is life: if I postpone it I may never live. To walk nobly on the surface of the earth, to express oneself without pretence, to acknowledge one's own humanity! You mustn't think I rhapsodize: I am quite serious. I speak from my soul.

— Soul?

— Yes: from my soul, my spiritual nature. Life is not a yawn. Philosophy, love, art will not disappear from my world because I no longer believe that by entertaining an emotion of desire for the tenth part of a second I prepare for myself an eternity of torture. I am happy.

— Can you say that?

— Jesus is sad. Why is he so sad? He is solitary ... I say, you must feel the truth of what I say. You are holding up the Church against me ...

— Allow me ...

— But what is the Church? It is not Jesus, the magnificent solitary with his inimitable abstinences. The Church is made by me and my like[1] – her services, legends, practices, paintings, music, traditions. These her artists gave her. They made her what she is. They accepted Aquinas' commentary on Aristotle as the Word of God and made her what she is.

— And why will you not help her to be so still – you as an artist?

— I see you recognize the truth of what I say though you won't admit it.

— The Church allows the individual conscience to have great ... ... in fact, if you believe ... believe, that is, said Cranly stamping each heavy foot on the words, honestly and truly ...

— Enough! said Stephen gripping his companion's arm. You need not defend me. I will take the odds as they are.

They paced along three sides of the Green in silence while the couples began to leave the chains and return meekly to their modest resting-places and after a while Cranly began to explain to Stephen how he too had felt a desire for life – a life of freedom and happiness – when he had been younger and how at that time he too had been about to leave the Church in search of happiness but that many considerations had restrained him.

[1] In the MS the words 'made by me and my like' are added in red crayon.

XXII

Cranly went to Wicklow at the end of the week leaving Stephen to find another auditor. Luckily Maurice was enjoying his holidays and though Stephen spent a great deal of his time roaming through the slums of the city while Maurice was out on the Bull the two brothers often met and discoursed. Stephen reported his long conversations with Cranly of which Maurice made full notes. The younger sceptic did not seem to share his brother's high opinion of Cranly though he said little. It was not from jealousy but rather from an over-estimate of Cranly's rusticity that Maurice allowed himself this prejudice. To be rustic, in his eyes, was to be a mass of cunning and stupid and cowardly habits. He had spoken with Cranly only once but he had often seen him. He gave it as his opinion that Cranly never thought until someone spoke to him and then he [gives] gave birth to some commonplace which he would have liked to have been able to disbelieve. Stephen thought this exaggerated [and] saying that Cranly was daringly commonplace, that he ° could talk like a pint,° and that it was possible to credit him with a certain perverse genius. Cranly's undue scepticism and his heavy feet moved Maurice ° to hit the rustic ° in him with a name. He called him Thomas Squaretoes[1] and he would not even admit that [Cranly] he had to a certain extent the grand manner. Cranly, in his opinion, went to Wicklow because it was necessary for him to ° play the god to an audience.° He will grow to dislike you, said the shrewd young heathen, when you begin to play the god to someone else. He will give you nothing in exchange for what you give him whether he has it or not because his [nature] character is naturally overbearing. He cannot possibly understand half of what you say to him and yet he would like to be thought the only one who could understand you. He wants to become more and more necessary to you until he can have you in his power. Be careful never to show any weakness to him when you are together. You can have him in your power so long as you hold the whip-hand.

[1] Among Joyce's notes (Gorman, p. 137), under the heading 'Byrne, (Cranly) is the name: 'Thomas Squaretoes'.

Stephen replied that he thought this was a very novel conception of friendship which could not be proved true or false by debate alone but that he was himself the conscious possessor of an intuitive instrument which might be trusted to register any enmity as soon as it appeared. He defended his friend and his friendship at the same time.

The summer was dull and warm. ᶜ Nearly every day Stephen wandered through the slums watching the sordid lives of the inhabitants. He read all the street-ballads which were stuck in the dusty windows of the Liberties. He read the racing names and prices scrawled in blue pencil outside the dingy tobacco-shops, the windows of which were adorned with scarlet police journals. He examined all the book-stalls which offered old directories and volumes of sermons and unheard-of treatises [for] at the rate of a penny each or three for twopence. He often posted himself opposite one of the factories in old Dublin at two o'clock to watch the hands coming out to dinner – ᶜ principally young boys and girls with colourless, expressionless faces, who seized the opportunity to be gallant in their way. He drifted in and out of interminable chapels in which an old man dozed on a bench or a clerk dusted the woodwork or an old woman prayed before the candle she had lighted. As he walked slowly through the maze of poor streets he stared proudly in return for the glances of stupid wonder that he received and watched from under his eyes the great cow-like trunks of police constables swing slowly round after him as he passed them. These wanderings filled him with deep-seated anger and whenever he encountered a burly black-vested priest taking a stroll of pleasant inspection through these warrens full of swarming and cringing believers he cursed the farce of Irish Catholicism: an island [whereof] the inhabitants of which entrust their wills and minds to others that they may ensure for themselves a life of spiritual paralysis, an island in which all the power and riches are in the keeping of those whose kingdom is not of this world, an island in which Caesar [professes] confesses Christ and Christ confesses Caesar that together they may wax fat upon a starveling rabblement which is bidden ironically to take to itself this consolation in hardship 'The Kingdom of God is within you'.

ᐳ This mood of indignation which was not guiltless of a certain superficiality was undoubtedly due to the excitement of release and it was hardly countenanced by him before he realized the dangers of being a demagogue. The attitude which was constitutional with him was a silent self-occupied, contemptuous manner and his intelligence, moreover, persuaded him that the tomahawk, as an effective instrument of warfare, had become obsolete. He acknowledged to himself in honest egoism that he could not take to heart the distress of a nation, the soul of which was antipathetic to his own, so bitterly as the indignity of a bad line of verse: but at the same time he was nothing in the world so little as an amateur artist. He wished to express his nature freely and fully for the benefit of a society which he would enrich and also for his own benefit, seeing that it was part of his life to do so. It was not part of his life to undertake an extensive alteration of society but he felt the need to express himself such an urgent need, such a real need, that he was determined no conventions of a society, however plausibly mingling pity with its tyranny, should be allowed to stand in his way, and though a taste for elegance and detail unfitted him for the part of demagogue, [in] from his general attitude he might have been supposed not unjustly an ally of the collectivist politicians, who are often very seriously upbraided by [believers] opponents who believe in Jehovahs, and decalogues and judgments [for] with sacrificing the reality to an abstraction.

That kind of Christianity which is called Catholicism seemed to him to stand in his way and forthwith he removed it. He had been brought up in the belief of the Roman supremacy and to cease to be a Catholic for him meant to cease to be a Christian. The idea that the power of an empire is weakest at its borders requires some modification for everyone knows that the Pope cannot govern Italy as he governs Ireland nor is the Tsar as terrible an engine to the tradesmen of S. Petersburg as he is to the little Russian of the Steppes. In fact in many cases the government of an empire is strongest at its borders and it is invariably strongest there in the case when its power at the centre is on the wane. The waves of the rise and fall of empires do not travel with the rapidity of waves of light and it will be perhaps a considerable time before Ireland will be able to understand that the Papacy is no longer going through a period of anabolism.[1] The bands of pilgrims who are shepherded safely across the continent by their Irish

---

[1] This word is underlined in pencil in the MS and misspelt 'anabilism'.

133

pastors must shame the jaded reactionaries of the eternal city by their stupefied intensity of worship in much the same way as the staring provincial newly arrived from Spain or Africa may have piqued the loyalty of some smiling Roman for whom [the his past had but] the future of his race was becoming uncertain as its past had already become obvious. Though it is evident on the one hand that this persistence of Catholic power in Ireland must intensify very greatly the loneliness of the Irish Catholic who voluntarily outlaws himself yet on the other hand the force which he must generate to propel himself out of so strong and intricate a tyranny may often be sufficient to place him beyond the region of re-attraction. It was, in fact, the very fervour of Stephen's former religious life which sharpened for him now the pains of his solitary position and at the same time hardened into a less pliable, a less appeasable enmity molten rages and glowing transports on which the emotions of helplessness and loneliness and despair had first acted as chilling influences.

The tables in the Library were deserted during the summer months and whenever Stephen wandered in there he found few faces that he knew. Cranly's friend [O'Neill] Glynn, the clerk from [the Custom-House] Guinness', was one of these familiar faces: he was very busy all the summer reading philosophical handbooks. Stephen had the misfortune to be captured one night by [O'Neill] Glynn, who at once attempted a conversation on the modern school of Irish writers – a subject of which Stephen knew nothing – and he had to listen to an inconstant stream of literary opinions. These opinions were not very interesting: Stephen, for instance, [was] grew rather weary of [O'Neill's] Glynn's telling him what beautiful poetry Byron and Shelley and Wordsworth and Coleridge and Keats and Tennyson wrote, and of hearing that Ruskin and Newman and Carlyle and Macaulay were the greatest modern English prose stylists. At last when [O'Neill] Glynn was about to begin an account of a literary paper which his sister had read to the Girls' Debating Society in Loreto Convent Stephen thought he was justified in putting a closure on the conversation, ᵉsomewhat in Cranly's manner, by asking [O'Neill] Glynn very pointedly ᵉ could he manage to get him a 'pass' to see the Brewery. The request was made in such a tone of subdued thirsty curiosity that [O'Neill] Glynn was too discouraged to continue his literary criticism and promised to do his best to get the 'pass'. Another reader in the Library who seemed to wish to be very friendly with Stephen was a young student named Moynihan who had been elected Auditor of the Literary and Historical Society for the following year. He had to read his inaugural address in November and he had chosen as his subject 'Modern Unbelief and Modern Democracy'. He was an extremely [small] ugly young man with a wide mouth which gave the idea that it was under his chin until the face was seen at close quarters, eyes of an over-washed olive green colour set viciously close together, and large rigid ears standing far apart. He took a most agitated interest in the success of his paper as he was going to be a solicitor and he relied on this inaugural address to make his name known. He had not yet developed the astuteness of the legal mind in as much as he imagined that Stephen shared his agitated interest concerning the inaugural address. Stephen came upon him one night while he was busily 'making-up' his subject. He had some bulky volumes by Lecky at his side and he was reading and making notes upon an article in the *Encyclopaedia Britannica* under the heading of 'Socialism'. He desisted from his labours when he saw Stephen and began to explain the preparations which the committee were making. He showed the letters which had been received from various public men who had been written to by the committee to know if they would speak. He showed the patterns of the cards of invitation which they had decided to have printed and he showed a copy of the notice which was to be sent to all the papers. Stephen who did not know Moynihan very well was surprised at all these confidences. Moynihan said he was sure Stephen would be the auditor who would be elected after him and added how much he had admired the style of Stephen's paper. After this he began to discuss his own and Stephen's prospects for the degree. He said German was more useful than Italian (though, of course, Italian was more beautiful as a language) and that he had always studied it for that reason. When Stephen rose to go Moynihan said he might as well go too and put up his books. He came along Nassau St to catch his tram for Palmerston Park and on the way, the night being wet and the streets black and glistening with rain, he united himself still more intimately with his successor-designate by little ejaculations and glances in the wake of a hospital nurse who wore brown stockings and pink petticoats. Stephen was not at all displeased by the spectacle which he had been quietly observing for a long time before Moynihan had caught sight of it but Moynihan's [ejaculatory desi] desirous ejaculations [also] reminded him of the clicking of a typewriting machine. Moynihan who by this time was on famous terms with him said he would like to know Italian on account of Boccaccio and the other Italian writers. He told Stephen that if he wanted to read something 'smutty' [that] the *Decameron* took the biscuit for 'smut'.

— I wish I was like you, he said, it must be ten times as bad in the original. I can't tell you now because here's my tram . . . but it takes the biscuit for downright . . . you know? . . . well, Tooraloo!

Mr Daedalus had not an acute sense of the rights of private property: he paid rent very rarely. To demand money for eatables seemed to him just but to expect people to pay for shelter the exorbitant sums which are demanded annually by houseowners in Dublin seemed to him unjust. He had now been a year in his house in Clontarf and for that year he had paid a quarter's rent. The writ which had been first served on him had ° contained a legal flaw ° and this fact enabled him to prolong his term of occupancy. Just now matters were drawing to a head and he was scouring the city for another house. A private message from a friend in the Sheriff's office gave him exactly five days of grace and every morning he brushed his silk hat very diligently and polished his eyeglass and went forth humming derisively to offer himself as a bait to landlords. The halldoor was often banged loudly on these occasions as the only possible close of an altercation. The results of the examination had awarded Stephen a mere pass and his father told him very confidentially that he had better look out for some kind of a doss because in a week's time they would all be out on the street. The funds in the house were very low for the new furniture had fetched very little after its transport piecemeal to a pawn-office. Tradesmen who had seen it depart had begun a game of knocking and ringing which was very often followed by the curious eyes of street-urchins. Isabel was lying upstairs in the backroom, day by day growing more wasted and querulous. The doctor came twice a week now and ordered her delicacies. Mrs Daedalus had to set her wits to work to provide even one substantial meal every day and she certainly had no time to spare between accomplishing this feat, appeasing the clamour at the hall-door, parrying her husband's ill-humour and attending on her dying daughter. As for her sons, one was a freethinker, the other surly. ᶜ Maurice ate dry bread, muttered maledictions against his father and his father's creditors, practised pushing a heavy flat stone in the garden ᶜ and raising and lowering a broken dumb-bell, and trudged to the Bull every day that the tide served. In the evening he wrote his diary or went out for a walk by himself. Stephen wandered about morning, noon and night. The two brothers were not often together [until after]. One dusky summer evening [when] they walked into each other very gravely at a corner and both burst out laughing: and after that they sometimes went for walks together in the evening and discussed the art of literature.

Stephen had lent his essay to Lynch as he had promised to do and this loan had led to a certain intimacy. Lynch had almost taken the final vows in the order of the discontented but Stephen's unapologetic egoism, his remorseless lack of sentiment for himself no less than for others, gave him pause. His taste for fine arts which had always seemed to him a taste which should be carefully hidden away, now began to encourage itself timidly. He was also very much relieved to find Stephen's estheticism united with a sane and conscienceless acceptance of the animal needs of young men for, being a shrewd animal himself, he had begun to ᶜ suspect from Stephen's zeal and loftiness of discourse at least an assertion of that incorrigible virginity which the Irish race ᶜ demands alike from any John who would baptize it or from any Joan who would set it free as the first heavenly proof of fitness for such high offices. Daniel's household had become so wearisome to Stephen that he had discontinued his Sunday visits there and had substituted rambles with Lynch through the city. They made their way with difficulty along the crowded streets where underpaid young men and flaunting girls were promenading in bands. After a few of these rambles Lynch had absorbed the new terms which expressed the new point of view and he began to feel that he was justifying the contempt to which the spectacle of Dublin manners had always moved him. Many times they stopped to confer in scrupulous slang with the foolish virgins of the city, whose souls were almost terrified out of their naughty intentions by the profundity of the tones of the elder of the young men, and Lynch, sunning himself in a companionship which was so alert and liberal, so free from a taint of secret competition or patronage, began tQ wonder how he could ever have thought Stephen an affected young man. Everyone, he thought now, who has a character to preserve must have a manner to preserve it with.

One evening as Stephen was coming down the Library staircase after idling away a half-hour at [a dictionary of music] a medical treatise on singing, he heard a dress brushing the steps behind him. The dress belonged to Emma Clery who, of course, was very much surprised at seeing Stephen. She had just been working at some old Irish and now she was going home: her father didn't like her to stay in the Library until ten o'clock as she had no escort. The night was so fine that she thought she would not take the tram. Stephen asked her might he not see her home. They stood under the porch for a few minutes, talking. Stephen took out a cigarette and lit it but at once knocked off the lighted end [very] meditatively and put the cigarette back into his case: her eyes were very bright.

They went up Kildare St and when they came to the corner of the Green she crossed the road and they continued to walk, but not quite so quickly, along the gravel ° path beside the chains. The chains bore their nightly burden ° of amorousness. He offered her his arm which she took, leaning appreciably upon it. They talked gossip. She discussed the likelihood of McCann's marrying the eldest of Mr Daniel's daughters. She seemed to think it very amusing that McCann should have a desire for matrimony but she added quite seriously that Annie Daniel was certainly a nice girl. A feminine voice called out from the dusky region of the couples 'Don't!'

— 'Don't', said Emma. Isn't that Mr Punch's advice to young men who are about to marry . . . I hear you are quite a woman-hater now, Stephen.

— Wouldn't that be a change?

— And I heard you read a dreadful paper in the college – all kinds of ideas in it. Isn't that so?

— Please don't mention that paper.

— But I'm sure you're a woman-hater. You've got so stand-offish, you know, so reserved. Perhaps you don't like ladies' company?

Stephen pressed her arm a little by way of a disclaimer.

— Are you a believer in the emancipation of women too? she asked.

— To be sure! said Stephen.

— Well, I'm glad to hear you say that, at any rate. I didn't think you were in favour of women.

— O, I am very liberal – like Father Dillon – he is very liberal-minded.

— Yes? Isn't he? she said in a puzzled manner . . . Why do you never go to Daniel's now?

— I . . . don't know.

— What do you do with yourself on Sunday evenings?

— I . . . stay at home, said Stephen.

— You must be morose when you're at home.

— Not I. I'm as happy as if the divil had me.

— I want to hear you sing again.

— O, thanks . . . Some time, perhaps . . .

— Why don't you study music? Have your voice trained?

— Strange to say I was reading a book on singing tonight. It is called . . .

— I am sure you would make a success with your voice, she said quickly, evidently afraid to allow him control of the conversation . . . Have you ever heard Father Moran sing?

— No. Has he a good voice?

— O, very nice: he sings with such taste. He's an awfully nice man, don't you think?

— Very nice indeed. Do you go to confession to him?

She leaned a little more appreciably on his arm and said:

— Now, don't be bold, Stephen.

— I wish you would go to confession to me, Emma, said Stephen from his heart.

— That's a dreadful thing to say . . . Why would you like that?

— To hear your sins.

— Stephen!

— To hear you murmur them into my ear and say you were sorry and would never [do] commit them again and ask me to forgive you. And I would forgive you and make you promise to commit them every time you liked and say 'God bless you, my dear child.'

— O, for shame, Stephen! Such a way to talk of the sacraments!

Stephen had expected that she would blush but her cheek maintained its innocence and her eyes grew brighter and brighter.

— You'd get tired of that too.

— Do you think so? said Stephen making an effort not to be surprised at such an intelligent remark.

— You'd be a dreadful flirt, I'm sure. You get tired of everything so quickly – just the way you did in the Gaelic League.

— People should not think of the end in the beginning of flirtations, should they?

— Perhaps not.

When they came to the corner of her terrace she stopped and said:

— Thanks ever so much.

— Thank *you*.

— Well, you must reform, won't you, and come next Sunday to Daniel's.

— If you expressly . . .

— Yes, I insist.

— Very good, Emma. In that case, I'll go.

— Mind. I expect you to obey me.

— Very good.

— Thanks again for your kindness coming across with me. *Au revoir!*[1]

— Good night.

He waited till he had seen her enter the fourth garden of the terrace. She did not turn her head to see if he was watching but he was not cast down because he knew she had a trick of seeing things without using her eyes frankly.

Of course when Lynch heard of this incident he rubbed his hands together and prophesied. By his advice Stephen went to Daniel's on the following Sunday. The old horsehair sofa was there, the picture of the Sacred Heart was there, she was there. The prodigal was welcomed. She spoke to him very little during the evening and seemed to be in deep conversation with Hughes. who had lately been honoured by an invitation. She was dressed in cream colour and the great mass of her hair lay heavily upon her cream-coloured neck. She asked him to sing and when he had sung a song of Dowland's she asked him would he not sing them an Irish song. Stephen glanced

[1] There is a pencilled note opposite this phrase: 'Should be in Irish'. The handwriting of this note is not that of the MS. Is it that of Joyce's brother Stanislaus (the Maurice of the text)? He was with Joyce in Trieste when the MS was written.

from her eyes to Hughes's face and sat down again at the piano. He sang her one of the few Irish melodies which he knew, 'My love was born in the North Countree'. When his song was over she applauded loudly and so did Hughes.

— I love the Irish music, she said a few minutes afterwards, inclining herself towards him with an air of oblivion, it is so soul-stirring.

Stephen said nothing. He remembered almost every word she had said from the first time he had met her and he strove to recall any word which revealed the presence of a spiritual principle in her worthy of so significant a name as soul. He submitted himself to the perfumes of her body and strove to locate a spiritual principle in it: but he could not. She seemed to conform to the Catholic belief, to obey the commandments and the precepts. By all outward signs he was compelled to esteem her holy. But he could not so stultify himself as to misread the gleam in her eyes as holy or to interpret the [motions] rise and fall of her bosom as a movement of a sacred intention. He thought of his own [fervid religiousness] spendthrift religiousness and airs of the cloister, he remembered having astonished a labourer in a wood near Malahide by an ecstasy of oriental posture and no more than half-conscious under the influence of her charm he wondered whether the God of the Roman Catholics would put him into hell because he had failed to understand that most marketable goodness which makes it possible to give comfortable assent to propositions without in the least ordering one's life in accordance with them and had failed to appreciate the digestive value of the sacraments. — ⸦|ᖇ

Among the guests was an elder brother of Mrs Daniel's, Father Healy. He had just come back from the United States of America where he had been for seven years collecting money to build a chapel near Enniscorthy. He was being fêted on his home-coming. He sat in the armchair which Mr Daniel insisted on giving him and joined the tips of his fingers lightly together and smiled on the company. He was a little fat white priest whose body reminded one of a new tennis-ball and as he sat in his chair with one leg thrown smartly over the other he kept agitating quickly a fat little foot which was encased in a fat little creaky leather shoe. He spoke with a ᶜjudicious American accent ᶜ and when he spoke the room was all ears. He was greatly interested in the new Gaelic revival and in the new literary movement in

Ireland. He paid particular attention to McCann and to Stephen, asking both of them many questions. He agreed with McCann that Gladstone was the greatest man of the nineteenth century and then Mr Daniel, who was glowing with pride at the honour he was paying so honourable a guest, told a dignified story of Gladstone and Sir Ashmead Bartlett and deepened his voice to reproduce the oratory of the grand old man. During the charades [he] Father Healy kept asking Mr Daniel to repeat to him the witticisms of the players and very often he shook laughing when Mr Daniel had told him what a player had said. He let no opportunity for increasing his knowledge of the interior life of the University escape him and every allusion was beaten out into an unmistakable flatness before he nodded a head in satisfaction. Attacking Stephen on the literary side he began a monologue on the writings of John Boyle O'Reilly but finding Stephen too polite he began to depreciate an exclusively literary training for young men. Stephen thereupon began to tell him of the alley in the college and of the hand-ball tournament and all with discreet earnestness.

— I am sure now, said Father Healy putting his head shrewdly on one side and looking genially at the youth, I am sure you would make a good player. You're just the build.

— O, no, said Stephen longing for Cranly's presence, I'm a poor player.

— So you say, said Father Healy laughing, so you say.

— Really, said Stephen, smiling at this clever detection of [the] his merits as a handball-player and at the recollection of Cranly's execrations at his play.

At last Father Healy began to yawn a little and this was taken as a signal for handing round cups of milk and slices of bread and butter to the young men and women, none of whom took anything stronger. Hughes, indeed, was so frugal that he declined to eat or drink anything at all whereat Stephen was somewhat disappointed as he could have had a good view of the idealist. McCann who represented the practical view of life ate rather noisily and asked for jam. This remark made Father Healy, who had never heard it before, laugh very heartily and made the others smile but Hughes and Stephen looked at each other very gravely across the ° uninhabited ° tablecloth. The young women were all sitting at one end of the table and the young men at the other end with the result that one end of the table was very lively and the other end very serious. Stephen after having failed to engage in conversation a maiden aunt of the family who had fulfilled her office by bringing in two tumblers of punch, one for Father Healy and the other for Mr Daniel, retired silently to the piano where he began to strum old airs and hum them to himself until someone at the table said 'Do sing us something' and then he left the piano and returned to the horsehair sofa.

Her eyes were very bright. Stephen's way through self-examinations had worn him out so much that he could not but long to repose himself in the neighbourhood of her beauty. He remembered the first mood of monstrous dissatisfaction which had overcome him on his entrance into Dublin life and how it was her beauty that had appeased him. Now she seemed to offer him rest. He wondered did she understand him or sympathize with him and was the vulgarity of her manners only a condescension of one who was consciously playing the game. He knew that it was not for such an image that he had constructed a theory of art and life and a garland of verse and yet if he could have been sure of her he would have held his art and verses lightly enough. The longing for a mad night of love came upon him, a desperate willingness to cast his soul away, his life and his art, and to bury them all with her under fathoms of ᵉ lust-laden slumber. The ugly artificiality of the lives over which Father Healy was comfortably presiding struck this outrageous instant out of him and he went on repeating to himself a line from Dante for no other reason except that it contained the angry disyllable 'frode'. Surely, he thought, I have as much right to use the word as ever Dante had. The spirits of Moynihan and O'Neill and Glynn seemed to him worthy of some blowing about round the verges of a hell which would be a caricature of Dante's. The spirits of the patriotic and religious enthusiasts seemed to him fit to inhabit the fraudulent circles where hidden in hives of immaculate ice they might work their bodies to the due pitch of frenzy. The spirits of the tame sodalists, unsullied and undeserving, he would petrify amid a ring of Jesuits in the circle of foolish and grotesque virginities and ascend above them and their baffled icons to where his Emma, with no detail of her earthly form or vesture abated, invoked him from a Mohammadan paradise.

At the door he had to resign her to others and see her depart with insignificant courtesies and as he came home alone he led his mood through mazes of doubts and misgivings. After that evening he did not see her for a little time as home affairs were rather engrossing. His father's days of grace were exciting days. It seemed likely that the family would not have where to lay its heads when at the eleventh hour Mr Daedalus found a roof with a friend from the North of Ireland who was traveller for an ironmonger. Mr Wilkinson was in possession of an old-fashioned house containing perhaps fifteen rooms of which he was nominally a tenant but, the landlord, an old miser without kith or kin in the world, having died very opportunely, Mr Wilkinson's tenancy was untroubled by considerations of time or money. Mr Daedalus was allowed a set of apartments in this dilapidated mansion for a small weekly payment and on the night before the day fixed for his legal eviction he moved his camp by night. The little furniture which remained to them was carried on a ° float ° and Stephen and his brother and his mother and his father carried the ancestral portraits themselves as the draymen had drunk a good deal more than was good for them. It was a clear night of late summer freshened with cold as they walked in a body beside the sea-wall. Isabel had been removed earlier in the day and put in Mrs Wilkinson's charge. Mr Daedalus was a long way in front with Maurice and in high spirits with his successful manœuvre. Stephen followed with his mother and even she was light-hearted. The tide was lapping softly [at] by the wall, being at the full, and through the clear air Stephen heard his father's voice like a muffled flute singing a love-song. He made his mother stop to listen and they both leaned on the heavy picture-frames and listened:

> Shall carry my heart to thee
> Shall carry my heart to thee
> And the breath of the balmy night
> Shall carry my heart to thee

In Mr Wilkinson's house there was a lofty drawing-room panelled in oak entirely bare of furniture except for a piano. During the winter Mr Wilkinson had been paid seven shillings a week by a dancing club for the use of the room on Tuesdays and Fridays but now he used the lower end of the room as a place of general storage for hardware samples. He was a tall one-eyed man with a silent manner and a great power of holding his drink. He had a deep appreciation of his guest whom he never addressed without the prefix ᶜ 'Mr'.ᶜ He was married to a tall woman as silent as himself who read a great many novelettes and hung half her body out of the windows while her two young children entangled themselves in ᶜ pieces of wire-netting and coils ᶜ of gas-pipes. She had a long white face and she laughed at everything. Mr Daedalus and Mr Wilkinson went to town every morning together and often came back together and, during the day, Mrs Wilkinson hung out of the windows or talked with messenger boys and milkmen while Mrs Daedalus sat by Isabel's bedside. There could be no doubt now that the girl was in a bad way. Her eyes were piteously enlarged and her voice had become hollow: she sat half propped-up by pillows in the bed all day, her damp-looking hair hanging in wisps about her face, turning over the pages of an illustrated book. She began to whimper when she was told to eat or when anyone left her bedside. She showed very [few] little animation except when the piano was playing in the room below and then she made them leave the bedroom door open and closed her eyes. Money was still scarce and still the doctor ordered her delicacies. The lingering nature of her illness had spread a hopeless apathy about the household and, though she herself was little more than a child, she must have been aware of this. Stephen alone with persistent kindness preserved his usual manner of selfish cheerfulness and ᶜ strove to stir a fire out of her embers ᶜ of life. He even exaggerated and his mother reproved him for being so noisy. He could not go into his sister and say to her 'Live! live!' but he tried to touch her soul in the shrillness of a whistle or the vibration of a note. Whenever he went into the room he asked questions with an indifferent air as if her illness was of no importance and once or twice he could have assured himself that the eyes that looked at him from the bed had guessed his meaning.

The summer closed in sultry weather. Cranly was still in Wicklow and Lynch had begun to study for an examination in October. Stephen was too concerned with himself to talk much with his brother. In a few days Maurice was to return to school, that event having been delayed a fortnight on account of what he himself called the 'boot and clothes' complaint. Mr Wilkinson's household dragged out day after day, Mrs Wilkinson hanging herself out of the windows and Mrs Daedalus watching her daughter. Very often Mr Wilkinson brought his guest home after a day's carouse and the two would sit in the kitchen for the rest of the night talking politics loudly. When Stephen turned the corner of the avenue he could often hear his father's voice shouting or his father's [voice] fist banging the table. When he came in the two disputants would ask him for his opinion but he always ate what supper there was without remark and [went up] retired to his room and as he went up the stairs he could hear his father say to Mr Wilkinson 'Queer chap, you know, queer chap!' and he could imagine the heavy stare of Mr Wilkinson's eyes.[1]

Stephen was very lonely. As at the beginning of the summer so now: he wandered vaguely through the streets. Emma had gone away to the Isles of Aran with a Gaelic party. He was hardly unhappy and yet not happy. His moods were still waited upon and courted and set down in phrases of prose and verse: and when the soles of his feet were too tired [or] his mood ° too dim ° a memory or too timid a hope, he would wander into the long lofty dusty drawing-room and sit at the piano ° while the sunless dusk enwrapped him.° He could feel about him and above him the hopeless house and the decay of leaves and in his soul the one bright insistent star of joy trembling at her wane. The chords that floated towards the cobwebs and rubbish and floated vainly to the dust-strewn windows were the meaningless voices of his perturbation and all they could do was flow in meaningless succession through all the chambers of sentience. He breathed an air of tombs.

Even the value of his own life came into doubt with him. He laid a finger upon every falsehood it contained: [an] egoism which proceeded bravely before men to be frighted by the least challenge of the conscience, freedom which would dress the world anew in [the] vestments and usages begotten of enslavement, mastery of an art understood by few which owed its very delicacy to a physical decrepitude, itself the brand and sign of vulgar ardours. Cemeteries revealed their ineffectual records to him, ° records of the lives of all those who with good grace or bad grace had accepted an obvious divinity. The vision of all those failures, and the vision, far more pitiful, of congenital lives, shuffling onwards amid yawn and howl,

---

[1] In pencil in the margin is written 'eye'.

146

beset him with evil: and evil, in the similitude of a distorted ritual, called to his soul to commit fornication with her.

One evening he sat [silent] at his piano while the dusk enfolded him. The dismal sunset lingered still upon the window-panes in a smoulder of rusty fires. Above him and about him hung the shadow of decay, the decay of leaves and flowers, the decay of hope. He desisted from his chords and waited, bending upon the keyboard in silence: and his soul commingled itself with the assailing, inarticulate dusk. A form which he knew for his mother's appeared far down in the room, standing in the doorway.[c] In the gloom her excited face was crimson. A voice which he remembered as his mother's, a voice of a terrified human being, called his name. The form at the piano answered:

— Yes?

— Do you know anything about the body? . . .

He heard his mother's voice addressing him excitedly like the voice of a messenger in a play:

— What ought I do? There's some matter coming away from the hole in Isabel's . . . stomach . . . Did you ever hear of that happening?

— I don't know, he answered trying to make sense of her words, trying to say them again to himself.

— Ought I send for the doctor . . . Did you ever hear of that? . . . What ought I do?

— I don't know . . . What hole?

— The hole . . . the hole we all have . . . here.

XXIII

Stephen was present in the room when his sister died. As soon as her mother had been alarmed the priest was sent for. He was a diminutive man who carried his head mostly on his right shoulder and spoke in a lisping voice which was not very easily heard. He heard the girl's confession and went away saying 'Leave it to God: He knows best: leave it to God'. The doctor came with Mr Daedalus on a car, examined the girl and asked had she seen a priest. He went away saying that while there was life there was hope but she was very low: he would call in the morning. Isabel died a little after midnight. Her father who was not quite sober walked about the room on tiptoe, cried in little fits every time his daughter showed a change and kept on saying 'That's right, duckey: take that now' whenever her mother forced her to swallow a little champagne and then nodded his head until he began to cry afresh. He kept telling everyone to keep her spirits up. Maurice sat down by the empty fireplace and gazed in the grate. Stephen sat at the head of the bed and held his sister's hand, her mother bending over her offering her the glass and kissing her and praying. Isabel seemed to Stephen to have grown very old: her face had become a woman's face. Her eyes turned constantly between the two figures nearest to her as if to say she had been wronged in being given life and, at Stephen's word, she gulped down whatever was offered to her. When she could swallow no more her mother said to her 'You are going home, dear, now. You are going to heaven where we will all meet again. Don't you know? . . . Yes, dear . . . Heaven, with God' and the child fixed her great eyes on her mother's face while her bosom began to heave loudly beneath the bedclothes.

Stephen felt very acutely the futility of his sister's life. He would have done many things for her and, though she was almost a stranger to him he was sorry to see her lying dead. Life seemed to him a gift; the statement 'I am alive' seemed to him to contain a satisfactory certainty and many other things, held up as indubitable, seemed to him uncertain. His sister had enjoyed little more than the fact of life, few or none of its privileges. The supposition of an allwise God calling a soul home whenever it seemed good to Him could not redeem in his eyes the futility of her life. The wasted body that lay before him had existed by sufferance: the spirit that dwelt therein had literally never dared to live and had not learned anything by an abstention which it had not willed for itself. She had not been anything herself and for that reason had not attached anything to herself or herself to anything. When they were children together people had spoken of 'Stephen and Maurice' and her name had been added by an afterthought. Even her name, a certain lifeless name, had held her apart from the plays of life. Stephen remembered the voices of children crying with glee and venom:

Stephen, the Reephen, the Rix-Dix Deephen

but it was always with half-hearted glee and shamefaced venom that they called out her name:

Isabel, the Risabel, the Rix-Dix Disabel.

Isabel's death was the occasion of bringing to the house many of Mrs Daedalus' relatives. They knocked a little timidly at the halldoor and though they were very retiring in manner their host convicted them – the females, at least – privately of making a cunning use of their eyes. The males he received in the long empty drawingroom in which an early fire had been lit. During the two nights of the girl's wake a big company assembled in the drawingroom: they did not smoke but they drank and told stories. [Every] The morning after the table looked like a marine-store so crowded was it with empty bottles, black and green. Isabel's two brothers assisted at this wake. The discussions were often general. One of the boys' uncles was a very shock-headed asthmatic man who had been in his youth rather indiscreet with his landlady's daughter and the family had been scarcely appeased by a tardy marriage. One of Mr Daedalus' friends, a clerk in the Police Courts, told the company of the task which a friend of his in the Castle had in examining prohibited books:

— Such filth, he said, You'd wonder how any man would have the face to print it.

— When I was a boy, said Uncle John in a very flat accent, and had more of a taste for reading than now and much less money I used to go to a bookshop near Patrick's Close. One day I went there to buy a copy of the *Colleen Bawn*. The man asked me in and he showed me a book . . .

— I know, I know, said the clerk from the Police Courts.

— Such a book to put into the hands of a young lad! Such ideas to put in his head! Scandalous!

Maurice let a moment of respectful approval pass and then he asked:

— Did you buy the book, Uncle John?

Everyone seemed inclined to laugh but Uncle John grew very red and angry and went on:

— They should be prosecuted for putting such books on sale. Children should be kept in their places.

Standing beside the closed piano on the morning of the funeral Stephen heard the coffin bumping down the crooked staircase. The mourners followed it out and seated themselves in the four carriages. Stephen and Maurice carried the three wreaths into the mourning coach. The hearse made for Glasnevin Cemetery at a smart trot. At the cemetery gates six hearses were drawn up. The funeral which had drawn up immediately before Isabel's was a funeral of someone of the poor class. The mourners, who were huddled in sixes on outside cars, were just scrambling down from the cars as Mr Daedalus and his fellow-mourners drove up. The first funeral went in through the gates where a little crowd of loungers and officials were grouped. Stephen watched them pass in. Two of them who were late pushed their way viciously through the crowd. ᶜ A girl, one hand catching the woman's skirt, ran a pace in advance. The girl's face was the face of a fish, discoloured and oblique-eyed; the woman's face was square and pinched, the face of a bargainer. The girl, her mouth distorted, looked up at the woman to see if it was time to cry: ᶜ the woman, settling a flat bonnet, hurried on towards the mortuary chapel.

At the mortuary chapel Mr Daedalus and his friends had to wait until the poor mourners had first been served. In a few minutes the service was over and Isabel's coffin was carried up and laid on the bier. The mourners scattered in the seats and knelt timidly on their handkerchiefs. A priest with a great toad-like belly balanced to one side came out of the sacristy, followed by an altar boy. He read the service rapidly in a croaking voice and shook the aspergill drowsily over the coffin, the boy piping responses at intervals. When he had read the service he closed the book, crossed himself, and made back for the sacristy at a swinging [gate] gait. Labourers came in and bore out the coffin to a barrow and pushed it along the gravel-path. The superintendent of the cemetery shook hands with Mr Daedalus at the door of the chapel and followed the funeral slowly. The coffin slid evenly into the grave and the grave-diggers began to shovel in the earth. At the sound of the first clods Mr Daedalus began to sob and one of his friends came to his side and held his arm.

When the grave had been covered in the grave-diggers laid their shovels upon it and crossed themselves. The wreaths were put on the grave and after a pause for prayer the mourning party returned through the trim alleys of the cemetery. The unnatural tension of condolence had been somewhat relieved and the talk was becoming practical again. They got into the carriages and drove back along the Glasnevin Road. At Dunphy's corner the carriage drew up behind the carriages of other funerals. In the bar Mr Wilkins stood the party the first drink: the drivers of the carriages were called in and they stood by the door in a clump and rubbed their coat-sleeves across their bony battered-looking faces until they were asked to name their drink. They all chose pints and indeed their own bodily tenements were not unlike hardly used pewter measures. The mourners drank small specials for the most part. Stephen, when asked what he would drink, answered at once:

— A pint.

His father ceased talking and began to regard him with great attention but, Stephen feeling too cold-hearted to be abashed, received his pint very seriously and drank it off in a long draught. While his head was beneath the tankard he was conscious of his startled father and he felt the savour of the bitter clay of the graveyard sharp in his throat.

The inexpressively mean way in which his sister had been buried inclined Stephen to consider rather seriously the claims of water and fire to be the last homes of dead bodies. The entire apparatus of the State seemed to him at fault from its first to its last operation. No young man can contemplate the fact of death with extreme satisfaction and no young man, specialized by fate or her step-sister chance for an organ of sensitiveness and intellectiveness, can contemplate the network of falsities and trivialities which make up the funeral of a dead burgher without extreme disgust. For some days after the funeral Stephen, clothed in second-hand clothes of ᶜ two shades ᶜ of black, had to receive sympathies. Many of these sympathies proceeded from casual friends of the family. Nearly all the men said 'And how is the poor mother bearing it?' and nearly all the women said 'It's a great trial for your poor mother': and the sympathies were always uttered in the same listless unconvincing monotone. McCann was also sympathetic. He came over to Stephen while that young man was looking into a haberdasher's window at some ties and wondering why the Chinese chose yellow[1] as a colour of mourning. He shook hands briskly with Stephen:

— I was sorry to hear of the death of your sister . . . sorry we didn't know in time . . . to have been at the funeral.

Stephen released his hand gradually and said:

— O, she was very young . . . a girl.

McCann released his hand at the same rate of release, and said:

— Still . . . it hurts.

The acme of unconvincingness seemed to Stephen to have been reached at that moment.

The second year of Stephen's University life opened early in October. His godfather had made no comment on the result of the first year but Stephen was told that this opportunity would be the last given him. He chose Italian as his optional subject, partly from a desire to read Dante seriously, and partly to escape the crush of French and German lectures. No-one else in the college studied Italian and every second morning he came to the college at ten o'clock and went up to Father Artifoni's bedroom. Father Artifoni was an intelligent little *moro*, who came from Bergamo, a town in Lombardy. He had clean ively eyes and a thick full mouth. Every morning when Stephen rapped at his door [he] there was the noise of chairs being disarranged before the 'Avanti!' The little priest never read in the sitting posture and the noise which Stephen heard was the noise of an improvised lectern returning to its constituent parts, namely, two cane chairs and a stiff blotting-pad. The Italian lessons often extended beyond the hour and much less grammar and literature was discussed than

[1] This word is crossed out, and 'white' substituted in red crayon.

philosophy. The teacher probably knew the doubtful reputation of his pupil but for this very reason he adopted a language of ingenuous piety, not that he was himself Jesuit enough to lack ingenuousness but that he was Italian enough to enjoy a game of belief and unbelief. He reproved his pupil once for an admiring allusion to the author of *The Triumphant Beast*.

— You know, he said, the writer, Bruno, was a terrible heretic.

— Yes, said Stephen, and he was terribly burned.

But the teacher was a poor inquisitor.[1] He told Stephen very slyly that when he and his clerical companions attended public lectures in the University the lecturer was shrewd enough to add a trifle of salt to his criticisms. Father Artifoni accepted the salt with a relish. He was unlike many of the citizens of the third Italy in his want of affection for the English and he was inclined to be lenient towards the audacities of his pupil, which, he supposed, must have been the outcome of too fervid Irishism. He was unable to associate audacity of thought with any temper but that of the irredentist.

Father Artifoni had to admit one day to Stephen that the most reprehensible moment of human delight in as much as it had given pleasure to a human being was good in the sight of God. The conversation had been about an Italian novel. A priest in the house had read the novel and condemned it to the dinner-table. It was bad, he said. Stephen urged that it had given him at least esthetic pleasure and that, for that reason, it could be said to be good:

— Father Byrne does not think so.

— But God?

— For God it might be . . . good.

— Then I prefer to side against Father Byrne.

They argued very acutely of the beautiful and the good. Stephen wished to amend or to clarify scholastic terminology: a contrast between the good and the beautiful was not necessary. Aquinas had defined the good as that towards the possession of which an appetite tended, the desirable. But the true and the beautiful were desirable, were the highest, most persistent orders of the desirable, truth being desired by the intellectual [appeased] appetite which was appeased

[1] The MS has 'inquisitioner'. The word 'inquisitor' is written in the margin in Stanislaus' (?) hand.

by the most satisfying relations of the intelligible, beauty being desired by the esthetic appetite which was appeased by the most satisfying relations of the sensible. Father Artifoni admired very much the wholehearted manner in which Stephen vivified philosophic generalizations and encouraged the young man to write a treatise on esthetic. It must have been a surprise for him to find in such latitudes a young man who could not conceive a divorce between art and nature, and that not for reasons of climate or temperament but for intellectual reasons. For Stephen art was neither a copy nor an imitation of nature: the artistic process was a natural process. In all his talk about artistic perfection it was impossible to detect an artificial accent. To talk about the perfection of one's art was not for him to talk about something agreed upon as sublime but in reality no more than a sublime convention but rather to talk a veritably sublime process of one's nature which had a right to examination and open discussion.

It was exactly this vivid interest which kept him away from such places of uncomely dalliance as the debating society and the warmly cushioned sodality. Mr Moynihan's inaugural address was held in the Aula Maxima in November. The President took the chair, surrounded by his professors. The platform was given up to notabilities and the body of the hall to the irregular intellectuals who go from address to address during the winter season and never miss attendance at the theatre when the play is not played in English. The end of the hall was packed with the students of the college. Nine-tenths of them were very serious and nine-tenths of the remainder were serious at intervals. Before the paper was read Whelan received from the president a gold medal for oratory, and one of Mr Daniel's sons a silver medal for oratory. Mr Moynihan was in evening dress and the front of his hair was curled. [The president clapped him] When he stood up to read his paper the president clapped him and then the hall clapped. Moynihan's paper showed that the true consoler of the afflicted was not the self-seeking demagogue with his ignorance and lax morality but the Church and that the true way to better the lot of the working classes was not by teaching them to disbelieve in a spiritual and material order, working together in harmony, but by teaching them to follow in humility the life of One who was the friend of all humanity, great and lowly, rich and poor, just and unjust, lettered and unlettered, of One who though above all other men was Himself the meekest of men. Moynihan alluded also to the strange death of a French atheistic writer and implied that Emmanuel had chosen to revenge himself on the unhappy gentleman by privily tampering with his gas-stove.

Among the speakers who followed Moynihan were a County Court Judge and a retired colonel of reactionary sympathies. All the speakers praised the work done by the Jesuits in training the youth of Ireland for the higher walks of life. The essayist of the night was adduced as an example. From his post beside Cranly in an angle of the hall Stephen glanced along the ranks of students. The faces which were now composed to seriousness all bore the same stamp of Jesuit training. For the most part they were free from the more blatant crudities of youth; they were not without a certain inoffensive ᶜ genuine distaste for the vices of youth.ᶜ¹ They admired Gladstone, physical science and the tragedies of Shakespeare: and they believed in the adjustment of Catholic teaching to everyday needs, in the Church diplomatic. Without displaying an English desire for an aristocracy of substance they held violent measures to be unseemly and in their relations among themselves and towards their superiors they displayed a nervous and (whenever there was question of authority) a very English liberalism. They respected spiritual and temporal authorities, the spiritual authorities of Catholicism and of patriotism, and the temporal authorities of the hierarchy and the government. The memory of Terence MacManus was not less revered by them than the memory of Cardinal Cullen.² If the call to a larger and nobler life

¹ The words 'Requires modification' are written in the margin here, in Stanislaus' (?) hand.

² Terence MacManus (1823?–1860) was a revolutionary Irish patriot who was tried for treason and sentenced to death. But the sentence was commuted to transportation for life, and he was shipped to Van Dieman's Land. In 1850 he escaped to San Francisco, where he died in poverty. His body was brought to Ireland in 1861 and buried in Glasnevin cemetery amid nationalist demonstrations. These demonstrations were opposed by Cardinal Cullen (1803–1878), the first Irishman to be made a cardinal. He was an ultramontane of a rigid type, with strong feelings against Fenianism. He is said to be the author of the final form of words used to define papal infallibility. He was the founder of Stephen Daedalus's University.

ever came to visit them they heard it with secret gladness but always they decided to defer their lives until a favourable moment because they felt unready. They listened to all the speakers attentively and applauded whenever there was an allusion to the President, to Ireland or to the faith. Temple shambled into the hall in the middle of the proceedings and introduced a friend of his to Stephen:

— 'Scuse me, this is Fitz, decent fellow. He admires you. 'Scuse me for introducing him, decent fellow.

Stephen shook hands with Fitz, a grey-headed young man with a puzzled flushed face. Fitz and Temple stood against the wall for support as they were both a little unsteady. Fitz began to doze quietly.

— He's a revolutionist, said Temple to Stephen and Cranly. D'ye know what, Cranly, I believe you're a revolutionist too. Are you a revolutionist . . . Ah, by hell, you don't like answering that . . . I'm a revolutionist.

At this moment a speaker was applauded for mentioning the name of John Henry Newman.

— Who is he, said Temple to everyone near him, who's this chap?

— Colonel Russell.

— O, is this Colonel . . . What did he say? What was it he said?

Nobody answered him so he shambled through a few more incoherent questions and at last, unable to satisfy himself as to the Colonel's way of thinking, called out 'Hurrah for the Mad Mullah' and then asked Cranly did he not think the Colonel was a 'bloody cod'.

Stephen studied even less regularly during the second year than he had done during the first. He attended lectures oftener but he seldom went to the Library to read. The *Vita Nuova* of Dante suggested to him that he should make his scattered love-verses into a perfect wreath and he explained to Cranly at great length the difficulties of the verse-maker. His love-verses gave him pleasure: he wrote them at long intervals and when he wrote it was always a mature and reasoned emotion which urged him. But in his expressions of love he found himself compelled to use what he called the feudal terminology and as he could not use it with the same faith and purpose as animated the feudal poets themselves he was compelled to express his love a little ironically. This suggestion of relativity, he said, mingling itself with so immune a passion is a modern note: we cannot swear or expect eternal fealty because we recognize too accurately the limits of every human energy. It is not possible for the modern lover to think the universe an assistant at his love-affair and modern love, losing somewhat of its fierceness, gains also somewhat in amiableness. Cranly would not hear of this: for him a distinction between ancient and modern was a trick of words because he had in his own mind reduced past and present to a level of studious ignobility. Stephen tried to sustain against him that though humanity may not change beyond recognition during the short eras known as the ages of man yet these ages are the preys of different ideas in accordance with which every activity, even the least, which they engender is conceived and directed. The distinction, he argued, between the feudal spirit and the spirit of humanity at present is not a phrase of the men of letters. Cranly, like many cynical romanticists, held that the civil life affected in no way the individual life and that it was possible for men to preserve ancient superstitions and prejudices in the midst of a machinery of modernity just as it was possible for men to live in the medley of machines a life of conformity and yet to be in his heart a rebel against the order he upheld: human nature was a constant quantity. As for the scheme of making a wreath of songs in praise of love he thought that if such a passion really existed it was incapable of being expressed.

— We are not likely to know whether it exists or not if no man tries to express it, said Stephen. We have nothing to test it by.

— What can you test it by? said Cranly. [Jesus] The Church says the test of friendship is to see if a man will lay down his life for a friend.

— You do not believe that, surely?

— No; bloody fools of people will die for different things. McCann, for instance, would die out of sheer obstinacy.

— Renan says a man is a martyr only for things of which he is not quite sure.

— Men die for two sticks put crosswise even in this modern age. What is a cross but two common sticks?

— Love, said Stephen, is a name, if you like, for something inexpressible ... but no, I won't admit that ... I believe it might be a test of love to see what exchanges it offers. What do people give when they love?

— A wedding breakfast, said Cranly.

— Their bodies, isn't it: that, at the very least. It is something to give one's body even for hire.

— Then you think that women who give their bodies for hire, as you say, love the people they give them to?

— When we love, we give. In a way they love too. We give something, a tall hat or a book of music or one's time and labour or one's body, in exchange for love.

— I'd a damn sight sooner them women gave me a tall hat than their bodies.

— A matter of taste. You may like tall hats. I don't.

— My dear man, said Cranly, you know next to nothing about human nature.

— I know a few elementary things and I express them in words. I feel emotions and I express them in rhyming lines. Song is the simple rhythmic liberation of an emotion. Love can express itself in part through song.

— You idealize everything.

— You make me think of Hughes when you say that.

— You imagine that people are capable of all these . . . all this beautiful imaginary business. They're not. Look at the girls you see every day. Do you think they would understand what you say about love?

— I don't know really, said Stephen. I do not idealize the girls I see every day. I regard them as marsupials.[1] . . . But still I must express my nature.

— Write the verses, anyway, said Cranly.

— I feel rain, said Stephen stopping under a branch and waiting for the fall of raindrops.

Cranly stood beside him and watched his pose with an expression of bitter satisfaction on his face.

During his wanderings Stephen came on an old library in the midst of those sluttish streets which are called old Dublin. The

[1] Among Joyce's notes (Gorman, p. 136), is the phrase, 'The marsupials'.

library had been founded by Archbishop Marsh and though it was open to the public few people seemed aware of its existence. The librarian, [was] delighted at the prospect of a reader, showed Stephen niches and nooks inhabited by dusty brown volumes. Stephen went there a few times in the week to read old Italian books of the Trecento. He had begun to be interested in Franciscan literature. He appreciated not without pitiful feelings the legend of the mild heresiarch of Assisi. He knew, by instinct, that S. Francis' love-chains would not hold him very long but the Italian was very quaint. Elias and Joachim also relieved the naïf history. He had found on one of the carts of books near the river an unpublished book containing two stories by W. B. Yeats. One of these stories was called *The Tables of the Law* and in it was mentioned the fabulous preface which Joachim, abbot of Flora, is said to have prefixed to his Eternal Gospel. This discovery, coming so aptly upon his own researches, induced him to follow his Franciscan studies with vigour. He went every Sunday evening to the church of the Capuchins whither he had once carried the disgraceful burden of his sins to be eased of it. He was not offended by the processions of artizans and labourers round the church and the sermons of the priests were grateful to him inasmuch as the speakers did not seem inclined to make much use of their rhetorical and elocutionary training nor anxious to reveal themselves, in theory, at least, men of the world. He thought, in an Assisan mood, that these men might be nearer to his purpose than others: and one evening while talking with a Capuchin, he had over and over to restrain an impulse which urged him to take the priest by the arm, lead him up and down the chapel-yard and deliver himself boldly of the whole story of the *Tables of the Law*, every word of which he remembered. Considering Stephen's general attitude towards the Church, there was certainly a profound infection in such an impulse which it needed great efforts of his intelligent partner to correct. He satisfied himself by leading Lynch round the enclosure of Stephen's Green and making that young man very awkward by reciting Mr Yeats's story with careful animation. Lynch said he didn't know what the story was about but, afterwards, when safely secluded in a 'snug' he said that the recitation had given him immense pleasure.

— These monks are worthy men, said Stephen.

— Full, round men, said Lynch.

— Worthy men. I went a few days ago to their library. I had great trouble getting in: all the monks came out of different corners to spy at me. Father [Abbot] Guardian asked me what I wanted. Then he brought me in and gave himself a great deal of trouble going over books. Mind you, he was a fat priest and he had just dined so he really was good-natured.

— Good worthy man.

— He didn't know in the least what I wanted or why I wanted it but he went up one page and down the next with his finger looking for the name and puffing and humming to himself 'Jacopone, Jacopone, Jacopone, Jacopone'. Haven't I a sense of rhythm, eh?

Stephen was still a lover of the deformations wrought by dusk. Late autumn and winter in Dublin are always seasons of damp gloomy weather. He went through the streets at night intoning phrases to himself. He repeated often the story of *The Tables of the Law* and the story of the *Adoration of the Magi*. The atmosphere of these stories was heavy with incense and omens and the figures of the monk-errants, Ahern and Michael Robartes strode through it with great strides. Their speeches were like the enigmas of a disdainful Jesus; their morality was infrahuman or superhuman: the ritual they laid such store by was so incoherent and heterogeneous, so strange a mixture of trivialities and sacred practices that it could be recognized as the ritual of men who had received from the hands of high priests, [who had been] anciently guilty of some arrogance of the spirit, a confused and dehumanized tradition, a mysterious ordination. Civilization may be said indeed to be the creation of its outlaws but the least protest against the existing order is made by the outlaws whose creed and manner of life is not renewable even so far as to be reactionary. These inhabit a church apart; they lift their thuribles wearily before their deserted altars; they live beyond the region of mortality, having chosen to fulfil the law of their being. A young man like Stephen in such a season of damp and unrest [had] has no pains to believe in the reality of their existence. They lean pitifully [above] towards the earth, like vapours, desirous of sin, remembering the pride of their origin, calling to others to come to them. Stephen was fondest of repeating to himself this beautiful passage from *The*

Tables of the Law: Why do you fly from our torches which were made out of the wood of the trees under which Christ wept in the gardens of Gethsemane? Why do you fly from our torches which were made of sweet wood after it had vanished from the world and come to us who made it of old tunes with our breath?

A certain extravagance began to tinge his life. He was aware that though he was nominally in amity with the order of society into which he had been born, he would not be able to continue so. The life of an errant seemed to him far less ignoble than the life of one who had accepted the tyranny of the mediocre because the cost of being exceptional was too high. The young generation which he saw growing up about him regarded his manifestations of spiritual activity as something more than unseemly and he knew that, under their air of fearful amiableness, the representatives of authority cherished the hope that his unguided nature would bring him into such a lamentable conflict with actuality that they would one day have the pleasure of receiving him officially into some hospital or asylum. This would have been no unusual end for the high emprise of youth often [leads] brings one to premature senility and [De Nerval's] a poet's boldness [was] is certainly proved an ill keeper of promises when it induces him to lead a lobster by a bright blue ribbon along the footpath reserved for the citizens. He felt acutely the insidious dangers which conceal themselves under the guise of extravagance but he was convinced also that a dull discharge of duties, neither understood nor congenial, was far more dangerous and far less satisfactory.

— The Church believes that in every act a man does he seeks some good, said Cranly. The public man wants to make money. Whelan wants to become a County Court judge, that girl I saw you talking to yesterday . . .

— Miss Clery?

— She wants a man and a little house to live in. The missioner wants to make heathens [into] Christian, the librarian of the National Library wants to make the Dublin people [into] students and readers. [What good] I understand the good which these men seek but what do you seek?

— The Church differentiates between the good which this man

seeks and the good which I seek. There is a *bonum simpliciter*. The men you mention seek a good of that kind because they are impelled by [direct] passions which are direct even if they are menial: lust, ambition, gluttony. I seek a *bonum arduum*.

— It might be a *bonum* very much *simpliciter*. I don't think you know, said Cranly.

XXIV

About this time there was some agitation in the political world concerning the working of the Royal University. It was proposed to institute a commission to examine into the matter. The Jesuits were accused of working the machine for their own ends without a just sense of impartiality. To parry the charge of obscurantism a monthly review was started under the editorship of McCann. The new editor was in high spirits over this event.

— I have got nearly all the 'copy' for the first number, he said to Stephen. I'm sure it will be a success. I want you to write us something for the second number — but something we can understand. Condescend a little. You can't say we are such barbarians now: we have a paper of our own. We can express our views. You will write us something, won't you? We have an article by Hughes in this month.

— Of course there is a censor? said Stephen.

— Well, said McCann, the person who originated the idea of the paper in the first instance was Father Cummins.

— The director of your sodality?

— Yes. He originated the idea so you see he acts as a kind of sponsor to us.

— He is the Censor then?

— He has discretionary powers but he is not at all narrow-minded. You needn't be afraid of him.

— I see. And tell me, will I be paid?

— I thought you were an idealist, said McCann.

— Good luck to the paper, said Stephen waving his hand in adieu.

The first number of McCann's paper contained a long article by Hughes on *The Future of the Celt*. It contained also an article in Irish by Glynn's sister and an editorial article by McCann in which was narrated the history of the inception of the paper. The article began 'It was a happy thought of the director of our sodality to unite the various elements of our college life by affording them the opportunity of interchanging ideas and criticisms through the medium of a University magazine. Thanks to the zeal and enterprise of Father Cummins the initial difficulties have been surmounted and we make our bow to the public in the expectation that the public will give us a hearing'. The paper also contained several pages of notes from various sporting and intellectual societies in which celebrities were chaffed under the thin disguise of their Latinized surnames. The 'Medical Memoes' which were signed 'H₂O' [and] consisted of several congratulatory paragraphs about medicoes who had passed their final examinations and a few complimentary paragraphs about the genial professors of the medical school. The paper also contained some verses: *The Female Fellow* (a swallow-flight of song) which were signed 'Toga Girilis'.

Stephen was shown the new review in the Library by Cranly who seemed to have read it from the first line to the last. Cranly took his friend from one item to another with great persistence, paying no heed to Stephen's exclamations of impatience. At the 'Medical Memoes' Stephen execrated with such smothered fervour that Cranly began to laugh between the pages of the paper and a red-faced priest who was sitting opposite stared indignantly across his copy of *The Tablet*. In the porch of the Library were a little knot of young men and a little knot of young women, all provided with copies of the new review. All were laughing and talking, making the rain an excuse for lingering under shelter. McCann, brisk and heated with his cycling-cap sideways on his head, went to and fro between the groups. When he saw Stephen he approached with an air of expectancy.

— Well? Have you seen . . . ?

— It is a great day for Ireland, said Stephen, seizing the Editor's hand and shaking it gravely.

— Well . . . it is something, said McCann with a suffused forehead.

Stephen leaned against one of the stone pillars and regarded the farther group. She stood in a ring of her companions, laughing and talking with them. The anger with which the new review had filled him gradually ebbed away and he chose to contemplate the spectacle which she and her companions offered him. As on his entrance into the grounds of Clonliffe College a ᶜ sudden sympathy arose out of a sudden reminiscence, a reminiscent sympathy toward a [sheltered] protected seminarist life the very virtues of which seemed to be set provokingly before the wild gaze of the world, so provokingly that only the strength of walls and watch dogs held them in a little circle of modish and timid ways. Though their affectations often lacked grace and their vulgarity wanted only lungs to be strident the rain brought him charity. The babble of the young students reached him as if from a distance, in broken pulsations, and lifting his eyes he saw the high rain-clouds retreating across the rain-swept country. The quick light shower was over, tarrying, a cluster of diamonds, among the shrubs of the quadrangle where an exhalation ascended from the blackened earth. The company in the colonnade was leaving shelter, with many a doubting glance, with a prattle of trim boots, a pretty rescue of petticoats, under umbrellas, a light armoury, upheld at cunning angles. He saw them returning to the convent – demure corridors and simple dormitories, a quiet rosary of hours – while the rain-clouds retreated towards the west and the babble of the young men reached him in regular pulsations. He saw far away amid a flat rain-swept country a high plain building with windows that filtered the obscure daylight. Three hundred boys, noisy and hungry, sat at long tables eating beef fringed with green fat like blubber and junks of white damp bread and one young boy, leaning upon his elbows, opened and closed the flaps of his ears while the noise of the diners reached him rhythmically as the wild gabble of animals.

— There should be an art of gesture, said Stephen one night to Cranly.

— Yes?

— Of course I don't mean art of gesture in the sense that the elocution professor understands the word. For him a gesture is an emphasis. I mean a rhythm. You know the song 'Come unto these yellow sands'?

— No.

— This is it, said the youth making a graceful anapaestic gesture with each arm. That's the rhythm, do you see?

— Yes.

— I would like to go out into Grafton St some day and make gestures in the middle of the street.

— I'd like to see that.

— There is no reason why life should lose all grace and nobility even though Columbus discovered America. I will live a free and noble life.

— Yes?

— My art will proceed from a free and noble source. It is too troublesome for me to adopt the manners of these slaves. I refuse to be terrorized into stupidity. Do you believe that one line of verse can immortalize a man?

— Why not one word?

— 'Sitio' is a classical cry. Try [and] to improve on it.

— Do you think that Jesus when he hung on the cross appreciated what you would call the rhythm of that remark? Do you think that Shakespeare when he wrote a song went out into the street to make gestures for the people?

— It is evident that Jesus was unable to illustrate his remark by a correspondingly magnificent gesture but I do not imagine he uttered it in a matter-of-fact voice. Jesus had a very pure tragic manner: his conduct during his trial was admirable. Do you imagine the Church could have erected such elaborately artistic sacraments about his legend unless the original figure had been one of a certain tragic majesty?

— And Shakespeare . . . ?

— I don't believe he wanted to go out into the street but I am sure he appreciated his own music. I don't believe that beauty is fortuitous. A man might think for seven years at intervals and all at once write a quatrain which would immortalize him seemingly without thought or care – seemingly. Then the groundling will say: 'O, he could write poetry': and if I ask 'How was that?' the groundling will answer 'Well, he just wrote it, that's all'.

— In my opinion you imagine all this about rhythm and gesture. A poet according to you, is a terribly mixed-up fellow.

— The reason you say that is because you have never seen a poet in action before.

— How do you know that?

— You think my theorizing very high-flown and fantastical, don't you?

— Yes, I do.

— Well, I tell you you think me fantastical simply because I am modern.

— My dear man, that's rubbish. You're always talking about 'modern'. Have you any idea of the age of the earth? You ° say you're emancipated ^{c} but, in my opinion, you haven't got beyond the first book of Genesis yet. There is no such thing as 'modern' or 'ancient': it's all the same.

— What's all the same?

— Ancient and modern.

— O, yes, I know, everything is the same as everything else. Of course I know the word 'modern' is only a word. But when I use it I use it with a certain meaning . . .

— What do you mean, for instance?

— The modern spirit is vivisective. Vivisection itself is the most modern process one can conceive. The ancient spirit accepted phenomena with a bad grace. The ancient method investigated law with the lantern of justice, morality with the lantern of revelation, art with the lantern of tradition. But all these lanterns have magical properties: they transform and disfigure. The modern method examines its territory by the light of day. Italy has added a science to civilization by putting out the lantern of justice and considering the criminal in [action] production and in action. All modern political and religious criticism dispenses with presumptive States, [and] presumptive Redeemers and Churches. [and] It examines the entire community in action and reconstructs the spectacle of redemption. If you were an esthetic philosopher you would take note of all my vagaries because here you have the spectacle of the esthetic instinct in action. The philosophic college should spare a detective for me.

— I suppose you know that Aristotle founded the science of biology.

— I would not say a word against Aristotle for the world but I think his spirit would hardly do itself justice in treating of the 'inexact' sciences.

— I wonder what Aristotle would have thought of you as a poet?

— I'm damned if I would apologize to him at all. Let him examine me if he is able. Can you imagine a handsome lady saying 'O, excuse me, my dear Mr Aristotle, for being so beautiful'?

— He was a very wise man.

— Yes but I do not think he is the special patron of those who proclaim the usefulness of a stationary march.

— What do you mean?

— Have you noticed what a false and unreal sound abstract terms have on the lips of those ancients in the college? You see what talk they have now about their new paper. McCann is supposed to lead them out of captivity. Doesn't that paper of theirs make you say to yourself 'O Lord, I'm glad I had no hand in this'? The toy life which the Jesuits permit these docile young men to live is what I call a stationary march. The marionette life which the Jesuit himself lives as a dispenser of illumination and rectitude is another variety of the stationary march. And yet both these classes of puppets think that Aristotle has apologized for them before the eyes of the world. Kindly remember the monstrous legend upon which all their life is regulated – how Aristotelian it is! Kindly remember the minute bylaws they have for estimating the exact amount of salvation in any good work – what an Aristotelian invention!

A week or so before Christmas Stephen was standing one night in the porch of the Library when Emma came out. She stopped to talk with him. She was dressed cosily in warm tweeds and the long even coils of her white boa presented her smiling face to the wintry air. Any young man of reasonable sanity, seeing so happy and so glowing a figure in a cheerless landscape, would have longed to take it in his arms. She wore a little brown fur cap which made her look like a Christmas doll and her incorrigible eyes seemed to say 'Wouldn't you like to fondle me?' She began to chatter at once. She knew the girl that had written *The Female Fellow* – an awfully smart girl at that kind of thing. They had a magazine in her convent too; she wrote 'skits' for it.

— By the way I hear dreadful things about you.

— How is that?

— Everyone says you have dreadful ideas, that you read dreadful books. You're a mystic or something. Do you know what I heard a girl say?

— No. What?

— That you didn't believe in God.

They were walking along the Green inside the chains and as she said this she gave more of her body's warmth to him and her eyes looked at him with an expression of solicitude. Stephen looked into them steadfastly.

— Never mind God, Emma, he said. You interest me much more than that old gentleman does.

— What gentleman? said Emma frankly.

— The middle-aged gentleman with the aviary – Jehovah the Second.

— You must not say such things to me, I told you that before.

— Very good, Emma. I see you are afraid you will lose the faith. But you needn't be afraid of my influence.

They walked from the Green as far as the South Circular Road without an attempt at further conversation. At every step that they took Stephen's resolution to leave her and see no more of her became more deeply rooted. Even as a diversion her company was slightly degrading to his sense of dignity. As they passed under the tall trees of the Mall she slackened her pace and, when safe from the lights of the bridge, halted deliberately. Stephen was very much surprised as the hour and the place made their position equivocal and, though she had chosen the broad shadow of the trees to halt in, she had committed this audacity in sight of her own house. They listened for a moment to the quiet flowing of the water and saw the tram begin to crawl off the apex of the bridge.

— Do I interest you so much as that? she said, speaking at last in a rich significant voice.

— Of course you do, said Stephen trying to match her tone. I know that you are alive and human.

— But so many people are alive.

— You are a woman, Emma.

— Would you call me a woman now? Don't you think I am still a girl?

Stephen's gaze traversed the provoking territory for a few moments during which her half-closed eyes suffered the trespass without remonstrating.

— No, Emma, he said. You are not a girl any longer.

— But you are not a man, are you? she said quickly for pride and youth and desire were beginning to inflame her cheek even in the shadow.

— I am a hobbledehoy, said Stephen.

She leaned a little more towards him and the same expression of tender solicitude appeared in her eyes. The warmth of her body seemed to flow into his and without a moment's hesitation he put his hand into his pocket and began to finger out his coins.

— I must be going in, she said.

— Good night, said Stephen smiling.

When she had gone in he went along by the canal bank, still in the shadow of the leafless trees, humming to himself the chant of the Good Friday gospel. He thought of what he had said to Cranly that when people love they give and he said aloud 'I will never speak to her again'. As he came near the lower bridge a woman emerged from the shadows and said 'Good night, love'. Stephen stood still and looked at her. ° She was an undersized woman and even in that chilly season her clothes gave off an odour of ancient sweats. A black straw hat was set rakishly [upon] above her glazed face. She asked him to come for a little walk. Stephen did not speak to her but, still humming the chant of the passion, transferred his coins to her hand and continued on his way.° He heard her benedictions at his back as he walked and he began to wonder which was better from the literary point of view: Renan's account of the death of Jesus or the account given by the evangelists. He had once heard a preacher allude in horrified piety to the theory put forward by some literary agent of the devil that Jesus was a maniac. The woman in the black straw hat would never believe that Jesus was a maniac and Stephen shared her opinion. He is certainly a great exemplar for bachelors, he said to himself, but he is a little too careful of himself for a divine person. The woman in the black straw hat has never heard of the name of Buddha but Buddha's character seems to have been superior to that of Jesus with respect to unaffected sanctity. I wonder how she would like that story of Yasodhara's kissing Buddha after his illumination and penance. Renan's Jesus is a trifle Buddhistic but the fierce eaters and drinkers of the western world would never worship such a figure. Blood will have blood. There are some people in this island who sing a hymn called 'Washed in the blood of the Lamb' by way of easing the religious impulse. Perhaps it's a question of [impulse] diet but I would prefer to wash in ricewater. Yeow! what a notion! A blood-bath to cleanse the spiritual body of all its sinful sweats ... The sense of decorum makes that woman wear a black straw hat in mid-winter. She said to me 'Good night, love'. The greatest lover of all time could not say more than that. Think of it 'Good night, love'. Mustn't the devil be annoyed to hear her described as an evil creature?

— I am not going to see her any more, said Stephen a few nights later to Lynch.

— That is a great mistake, said Lynch expanding his chest.

— It's only waste of time. I'll never get what I want from her.

— And what do you want from her?

— Love.

— Eh?

— Love.

Lynch halted abruptly, saying:

— Look here, I have fourpence . . .

— *You* have?

— Let us go in somewhere. But if I give you a drink you must promise not to say that any more.

— Say what?

— That word.

— 'Love' is it?

— Let us go in here.

When they were sitting in the squalid gloom of a tavern Stephen began to rock his [chair] stool from leg to leg meditatively.

— I see I have educated you too much, my good Lynch?

— But that was an atrocity, said Lynch enjoying the luxury of entertaining and rebuking his companion.

— You do not believe me?

— Of course not.

Stephen concerned himself with his pewter measure for a little time.

— Of course, he said at last, I would take something less if she would give it to me.

— O, I know you would.

— Would you like me to seduce her?

— Very much. It would be very interesting.

— Ah, it wouldn't be possible!

Lynch laughed.

— The sorrow-stricken tone you say that in. I wish McCann could hear you.

— You know, Lynch, said Stephen, we may as well acknowledge openly and freely. We must have women.

— Yes I agree. We must have women.

— Jesus said 'Whoso looketh upon a woman to lust after her hath already committed adultery with her in his heart:' but he did not condemn 'adultery'. Besides it is impossible not to commit 'adultery'.

— Quite impossible.

— Consequently if I see a woman inclined for oracle I go to her: if she has no inclination I stay away.

— But that girl has an inclination for oracle.

— That's the tantalizing part of it: I know she has. It's very unfair of her to tantalize me. I must go to where I am sure of my ground.

— But that costs money; and besides it is dangerous. You may get a dose that will last you your life. I wonder you have not got it before this.

— Ah, yes, isn't it a nuisance. And yet I must go somewhere . . . She is a human being, you know. I can't say I consider harlots as human beings. *Scortum* and *moechus* are both neuter nouns.

— Of course a human being would be much better. But you could get her, if you liked.

— How?

— In marriage.

— I'm glad you reminded me of that, said Stephen. I was almost forgetting it.

— You may be sure she doesn't forget it, said Lynch, or let anyone else forget it either.

Stephen sighed.

— You remember in *The Adoration of the Magi* – 'When the immortals wish to overthrow the things that are today and to bring the things that were yesterday they have no-one to help them except one whom the things that are today have cast out.'

— Yes.

— Who have I to help me except the woman in the black straw hat? And yet I wish to bring to the world the spiritual renewal which the poet brings to it . . . No, I have decided. I will not see her any more.

— The woman in the black straw hat?

— No, the virgin.

— Still I think you are making a mistake, said Lynch, finishing his pint.

One raw misty morning after Christmas Stephen was reading

Oreste in Father Artifoni's bedroom. He asked questions mechanically and listened to answers mechanically. He devised the following question and answer for the pseudo-classical catechism:

Question – What great truth do we learn from the *Libation-Pourers* of Eschylus?

Answer – We learn from the *Libation-Pourers* of Eschylus that in ancient Greece brothers and sisters took the same size in boots.

He looked wearily from the wretched Italian binding of his book towards the desolate gardens of S. Stephen's Green. Above him and beneath him and around him in little dark dusty rooms the intellectual heart of Ireland was throbbing – young men were engaged in the pursuit of learning. Above and beneath and around him were posted Jesuits to guide the young men amid the perilous ways of knowledge. The hand of Jesuit authority was laid firmly upon that intellectual heart and if, at times, it bore too heavily thereon what a little cross was that! The young men were sensible that such severity had its reasons. They understood it as an evidence of watchful care and interest, assured that in their future lives this care would continue, this interest be maintained: the exercise of authority might be sometimes (rarely) questionable, its intention, never. Who, therefore, readier than these young men to acknowledge gratefully the sallies of some genial professor or the surliness of some door-porter? Who more solicitous to cherish in every way and to advance in person the honour of Alma Mater?

The mortifying atmosphere of the college crept about Stephen's heart. For his part he was at the difficult age, dispossessed and necessitous, sensible of all that was ignoble in such manners, who in reverie, at least, had been acquainted with nobility. As a remedy for so untoward a malady an earnest Jesuit [had some days before] was to prescribe a clerkship in Guinness's: and doubtless the clerk-designate of a brewery would not have had scorn and pity only for an admirable community had it not been that he desired, in the language of the schoolmen, an arduous good. Impossible that he should find his soul's sufficient good in societies for the encouragement of thought among laymen, or any other than bodily solace in the warm sodality, in the company of those foolish and grotesque virginities! Impossible that a temperament ever trembling towards ecstasy should submit to acquiesce, that a soul should decree servitude for its portion over which the image of beauty had fallen as a mantle.

The deadly chill of the atmosphere of the college paralysed Stephen's heart. In a stupor of powerlessness he reviewed the plague of Catholicism. He seemed to see the vermin begotten in the catacombs in an age of sickness and cruelty issuing forth upon the plains and mountains of Europe.[1] Like the plague of locusts described in Callista they seemed to choke the rivers and fill the valleys up. They obscured the sun. Contempt of [the body] human nature, weakness, nervous tremblings, fear of day and joy, distrust of man and life, hemiplegia of the will, beset[2] the body burdened and disaffected in its members by its black tyrannous lice. Exultation of the mind before joyful beauty, exultation of the body in free confederate labours, every natural impulse towards health and wisdom and happiness had been corroded by the pest of these vermin. The spectacle of the world in thrall filled him with the fire of courage. He, at least, though living at the farthest remove from the centre of European culture, marooned on an island in the ocean, though inheriting a will broken by doubt and a soul the steadfastness of whose hate became as weak as water in siren arms, would live his own life according to what he recognized as the voice of a new humanity, active, unafraid and unashamed.

He followed his Italian lesson mechanically, feeling the unintermittent deadliness of the atmosphere of the college in his throat and lungs, obscuring his eyes and obfuscating his brain. The little iron watch on the table had barely passed the half hour: eleven o'clock seemed so far off. He had to open his Machiavelli and read out a paragraph until the teacher's ear was satisfied. The dingy chronicle fell piecemeal from his lips, dull wooden words. From time to time he glanced up from the page to see the thick mouth of the priest correct his slovenly 'o's now with a sudden harsh ejaculation of the vowel sound, now with a slow mute protrusion of the lips. The little iron watch ticked on for another five minutes. Then the teacher began

[1] Among Joyce's notes (Gorman, p. 135) is the phrase, 'Catacombs and vermin'.

[2] Scrawled in red crayon across this sentence and the next is the word 'Gogarty'.

to correct the exercise. ° Stephen gazed wearily out of the window, across the mist-laden gardens. The air was webbed with water vapours and all the flower-beds and walks confronted the grey of the sky with a truculent sodden brown. Mackintoshes and overcoats came along the walks or down the steps of the monument under their umbrellas or surmounted by a muffled human head.° The footpath inside the chains where Stephen had so often walked with his friends at night glistened like a grey mirror. Stephen watched the feet pass along the polished surface: he wondered if it was his moments of excessive vitality which cast back by revulsion on such hours of despair. He felt that he was looking at the world with Cranly's eyes and still he continued gazing along the footpath.

— You cannot say, said the teacher running his pencil under a phrase. It is not Italian.

Stephen withdrew his eyes from the window suddenly and stood up:

— Will you please excuse me, sir. I am sorry I forgot to tell you that today I must go away earlier . . . I am afraid I shall be late, he added looking at the watch. Will you excuse me?

— You have an appointment now?

— Yes, I nearly forgot. You must excuse me for today . . .

— Certainly, certainly. You can go now.

— Thanks. I am afraid I . . .

— Certainly, certainly.

With a flying hand for the banisters he ran down the stairs, taking five steps at a time. He struggled into his raincoat in the hall and emerged panting and half-dressed on to the front steps. He ran out into the middle of the muddy roadway and peered through the dull light towards the eastern side of the square. He walked on swiftly in the middle of the road with his eyes fixed on the same point and then came in again on the footpath and began to run. When he reached the corner of Earlsfort Terrace he stopped running and turning to the right walked on again swiftly. Outside of the University he came alongside of the object which he had been pursuing.

— Good morning!

— Stephen! . . . Have you been running?

— Yes.

— Where are you going to?

— I saw you from the window.

— What window?

— In the college. Where are you going?

— I am going to Leeson Park.

— This way, said Stephen taking her arm.

She seemed as if she were about to resent such an act in broad daylight but after a quick glance of remonstrance allowed him to escort her. Stephen held her arm tightly to his side and discomposed her somewhat by speaking very close to her face. Her face was glistening with mist and it had begun to glow in answer to his excited and passionate manner.

— Where did you see me?

— I was in the window at my Italian lesson with Father Artifoni. I saw you come through the Green and cross the road.

— Did you?

— So I jumped up at once and asked him to excuse me as I had to keep an appointment and flew downstairs and out after you.

The colour had begun to deepen very much on her cheek and it was plain that she was trying to appear quite at her ease. At first she had been flattered but now she was becoming a little nervous. She laughed nervously when he told her [why] that he had run out after her.

— Goodness! Why did you do that?

Stephen did not answer but he pressed her arm fiercely to his side. At the end of the terrace she turned into a side street instinctively. Here she walked more slowly. The street was very quiet and they both lowered their voices.

— How did you know it was I? she said. You must have good sight.

— I was gazing out of the window, he answered, looking at the sky and the Green. Lord God! I felt so full of despair. Sometimes I am taken that way! I live such a strange life – without help or sympathy from anyone. Sometimes I am afraid of myself. I call those people in the college not men but vegetables . . . Then while I was cursing my own character I saw you.

— Yes? she said looking at the disorderly figure beside her out of her large oval eyes.

— You know I was delighted to see you. I had to jump up and rush out. I couldn't have sat there another minute . . . I said, Here is a human creature at last . . . I can't tell you how delighted I was.

— You strange boy! she said. You mustn't go running about like that: You must have more sense.

— Emma! cried Stephen, don't start talking to me like that today. I know you want to be very sensible. But you and I – we are both young, aren't we?

— Yes, Stephen.

— Very good, then. If we're young we feel happy. We feel full of desire.

— Desire?

— Do you know when I saw you . . .

— Yes, how did you know me?

— I knew the stride.

— Stride!

— Do you know Emma, even from my window I could see your hips moving inside your waterproof? I saw a young woman walking proudly through the decayed city. Yes, that's the way you walk: You're proud of being young and proud of being a woman. Do you know when I caught sight of you from my window – do you know what I felt?[1]

There was no use in her essaying indifference now. Her cheeks were covered with a persistent flush and her eyes shone like gems. She gazed straight before her and her breath began to be agitated. They stood together in the deserted street and he continued speaking, a certain ingenuous disattachment guiding his excited passion.

— I felt that I longed to hold you in my arms – your body. I longed for you to take me in your arms. That's all . . . Then I thought I would run after you and say that to you . . . Just to live one night together, Emma, and then to say goodbye in the morning and never to see each other again! There is no such thing as love in the world: only people are young . . .

She tried to take her arm away from his and murmured as if she were repeating from memory:

— You are mad, Stephen.

Stephen let go her arm and took her hand in his, saying:

— Goodbye, Emma . . . I felt that I wanted to say that to you for

[1] Written across this paragraph in red crayon are the words 'pride of the flesh'.

my own sake but if I stand here in this stupid street beside you for much longer I shall begin to say more . . . You say I am mad because I do not bargain with you or say I love you or swear to you. But I believe you hear my words and understand me, don't you?

— I don't understand you indeed, she answered with a touch of anger.

— I will give you a chance, said Stephen, pressing her hand close in his two hands. Tonight when you are going to bed remember me and go to your window. I will be in the garden. Open the window and call my name and ask me to come in. Then come down and let me in. We will live one night together – one night, Emma, alone together and in the morning we will say goodbye.

— Let go my hand, please, she said pulling her hand away from him. If I had known [if] it was for this mad talk . . . You must not speak to me any more, she said moving on a pace or two and plucking her waterproof out of his reach. Who do you think I am that you can speak to me like that?

— It is no insult, said Stephen colouring suddenly as the reverse of the image struck him, for a man to ask a woman what I have asked you. You are annoyed at something else not at that.

— You are mad, I think, she said, brushing past him swiftly without taking any notice of his salute. She did not go quickly enough, however, to hide the tears that were in her eyes and he, surprised to see them and wondering at their cause, forgot to say the goodbye that was on his lips. As he watched her walk onward swiftly with her head slightly bowed he seemed to feel her soul and his falling asunder swiftly and for ever after an instant of all but union.

XXV

Lynch chuckled very much over this adventure.[1] He said it was the most original attempt at seduction of which he had ever heard, so original that . . .

— You know, he said, I must tell you that to the ordinary intelligence . . .

— To you, that is?

— To the ordinary intelligence it looks as if you had taken leave of your senses for the time being.

Stephen stared fixedly at his toes: they were sitting on a bench in the Green.

— It was the best I could do, he said.

— A very bad best, in my opinion. No girl with an ounce of brains would listen to you. That's not the way to go about it, man. You run out suddenly after her, come up sweating and puffing and say 'Let us lie together'. Did you mean it as a joke?

— No, I was quite serious. I thought she might . . . In fact I don't know what I thought. I saw her, as I told you, and I ran after her and said what was in my mind. We are friends for a long time . . . Now it seems I have acted like a lunatic.

— O, no, said Lynch, expanding his chest, not like a lunatic but you went about the affair so strangely.

— If I had run after her and proposed to her, proposed marriage that is, you would not say I had acted strangely.

— [No, no] Even in that case . . .

— No, no, don't deceive yourself, you would not. You would find an excuse for me.

— Well, you see, there is something relatively sane about marriage, isn't there?

— For a man of your ordinary intelligence there may be: not for me. Have you ever read the Form of Solemnization of Marriage in the Book of Common Prayer?

[1] Written in pencil on the margin of this page is the sentence: 'Stephen wished to avenge himself on Irish women who, he says, are the cause of all the moral suicide in the island.'

— Never.

— You should then. Your everyday life is Protestant: you show yourself a Catholic only when you discuss. Well, to me that ceremony is not acceptable: it is not so sane as you imagine. A man who swears before the world to love a woman till death part him and her is sane neither in the opinion of the philosopher who understands what mutability is nor in the opinion of the man of the world who understands that it is safer to be a witness than an actor in such affairs. A man who swears to do something which it is not in his power to do is not accounted a sane man. For my part I do not believe that there was ever a moment of passion so fierce and energetic that it warranted a man in saying 'I could love you for ever' to the adored object. Please understand the importance of Goethe . . .

— Still marriage is a custom. To follow a custom is a mark of sanity.

— It is a mark of ordinariness. I admit that many ordinary people are sane just as I know that many ordinary people have delusions. But a capacity for being deceived by others or by oneself cannot be said to constitute the essential part of sanity. It is rather a question whether a man does encourage an insane condition in himself by deceiving himself voluntarily or allowing himself to be deceived by others voluntarily.

— Anyhow your move was not diplomatic.

— We all know that, said Stephen standing up, but all genuine diplomacy is with a view to some particularly excellent plum. What plum do you think Cranly is likely to gain by a diplomacy which is highly meritorious in itself? What plum would I be likely to get by proposing a diplomatic marriage except a partner 'to behold my chaste conversation, coupled with fear' – eh?

— The juice of the fruit, answered Lynch standing up in his turn and looking very thirsty and tired.

— The woman herself, you mean?

— Exactly.

Stephen walked along the path without saying anything for about twenty yards: then he said:

— I like a woman to give herself. I like to receive . . . These people count it a sin to sell holy things for money. But surely what they call the temple of the Holy Ghost should not be bargained for!

Isn't that simony?

— You want to sell your verses, don't you, said Lynch abruptly, and to a public you say you despise?

— I do not want to sell my poetical mind to the public. I expect reward from the public for my verses because I believe my verses are to be numbered among the spiritual assets of the State. That is not a simoniacal exchange. I do not sell what Glynn calls the divine afflatus: I do not swear to love, honour and obey the public until my dying day – do I? A woman's body is a corporal asset of the State: ᶜ if she traffic with it she must sell it either as a harlot or as a married woman or as a working celibate or as a mistress. But a woman is (incidentally) a human being and a human being's love and freedom is not a spiritual asset of the State. Can the State buy and sell electricity? It is not possible. Simony is monstrous because it revolts our notion of what is humanly possible. A human being can exert freedom to produce or accept or love to procreate or to satisfy. Love gives and freedom takes.ᶜ The woman in the black straw hat gave something before she sold her body to the State; Emma will sell herself to the State but give nothing.

— You know even if you had proposed to buy her decently – for State purposes – said Lynch, kicking his toes moodily at the gravel, she would not have sold at the price.

— You think not. Not even if I . . .

— Not likely, said the other definitely. What a damn fool she is! Stephen blushed ingenuously:

— You have such a nice way of putting things, he said.

The next time Stephen met Emma in the street she did not salute him. He did not tell the incident to anyone but Lynch. From Cranly he expected scant sympathy and he was deterred from speaking of it to Maurice because he had still the elder brother's wish to appear successful. The conversation with Lynch had revealed to him with distressing effect the commonplace side of the adventure. He asked himself seriously and often had he expected that she would have answered 'Yes' to his proposal. His mind, he thought, must have been somewhat unbalanced that morning. And yet when he reconsidered his own defence of his conduct he found it just. The economic aspect of the affair did not present itself to him very vividly and, indeed, was only vivid enough to make him deplore the fact that the solution of moral problems should be so hopelessly entangled with merely material considerations. He was not sufficiently doctrinaire to wish to have his theory put to the test by a general [revulsion] revolution of society but he could not believe that his theory was utterly impracticable. The Roman Catholic notion that a man should be unswervingly continent from his boyhood and then be permitted to achieve his male nature, having first satisfied the Church as to his orthodoxy, financial condition, [and] prospects and general intentions, and having sworn before witnesses to love his wife for ever whether he loved her or not and to beget children for the kingdom of heaven in such manner as the Church approved of – this notion seemed to him by no means satisfactory.

During the train of these reflections the Church sent an embassy of nimble pleaders into his ears. These ambassadors were of all grades and of all types of culture. They addressed every side of his nature in turn. He was a young man with a doubtful future and an unusual character: this was the first salient fact. The ambassadors met it without undue pretence or haste. They stated that it was in their power to make smooth many of the ways which promised to be rough and, by diminishing the hardships of the material nature, to allow the unusual character scope and ease to develop and approve itself. He had deplored the entanglement of merely material considerations in a problem of morals and here, at least, was a warrant that if he chose to give ear to the pleadings of the embassy the moral problem in his case would be set on the road of solving itself free from minor and unworthier cares. He had what he called a 'modern' reluctance to give pledges: no pledges were required. If at the end of five years he still persevered in his obduracy of heart he could still seize upon his individual liberty without fear of being called oath-breaker therefor. The practice of due consideration was an old one and a wise one. He himself was the greatest sceptic concerning the perfervid enthusiasms of the patriots. As an artist he had nothing but contempt for a work which had arisen out of any but the most stable mood of the mind. Was it possible that he would exercise less rigour on his life than he desired to exercise on his art? How could he be guilty of such foolishness, of such cynical subordination of the actual to the abstract, if he honestly believed that an institution is to be accounted valuable in proportion to its nearness to some actual human need or energy and that the epithet 'vivisective' should be applied to the modern spirit as distinguished from the ancient or category-burdened spirit. He desired for himself the life of an artist. Well! And he feared that the Church would obstruct his desire. But, during the formulation of his artistic creed, had he not found item after item upheld for him in advance by the greatest and most orthodox doctor of the Church and was it anything but vanity which urged him to seek out the thorny crown of the heretic while the entire theory, in accordance with which his entire artistic life was shaped, arose most conveniently for his purpose out of the mass of Catholic theology? He could not accept wholeheartedly the offers of Protestant belief: he knew that the liberty it boasted of was often only the liberty to be slovenly in thought and amorphous in ritual. No-one, not the most rabid enemy of the Church, could accuse it of being slovenly in thought: the subtlety of its disquisitions had become a byword with demagogues. No-one again could accuse the Church of being amorphous in ritual. The Puritan, the Calvinist, the Lutheran were inimical to art and to exuberant beauty: the Catholic was the friend of him who professed to interpret or divulge the beautiful. Could he assert that his own aristocratic intelligence and passion for a supremely satisfying order in all the fervours of artistic creation were not purely Catholic qualities? The ambassadors did not labour this point.

Besides, they said, it is a mark of the modern spirit to be shy in the presence of all absolute statements. However sure you may be now of the reasonableness of your convictions you cannot be sure that you will always think them reasonable. If you sincerely regard a pledge as an infringement of human liberty you cannot pledge yourself against following a reactionary impulse which is certain to overtake you some day. You cannot leave out of sight the possibility that your views of the world will change to such an extent that you will regard all interference with the course of affairs as the part of such [who] as can still be deluded by hope. In that case what will have become of your life? You will have wasted it in efforts to save people who have neither inclination nor aptitude for freedom. You believe in an aristocracy: believe also in eminence of the aristocratic class and in the order of society which secures that eminence. Do you imagine that manners will become less ignoble, intellectual and artistic endeavour less conditioned, if the ignorant, enthusiastic, spiritual slovens whom we have subjected subject us? Not one of those slovens understands your aims as an artist or wants your sympathy: we, on the contrary, understand your aims and often are in sympathy with them and we solicit your support and consider your comradeship an honour. You are fond of saying that the Absolute is dead. If that be so it is possible that we are all wrong and if once you accept that as a possibility what remains for you but an intellectual disdain. With us you can exercise your contemptuous faculties when you are recognized as one of the patrician order and you will not even be obliged to grant a truce to the very doctrines, the success of which in the world has secured you your patricianship. Make one with us. Your life will be insured from grosser troubles, your art will be ° safeguarded against the intrusions of revolutionary notions which no artist of whom history tells us has ever made himself champion. Make one with us, on equal terms. In temper and in mind you are still a Catholic. Catholicism is in your blood.° Living in an age which professes to have discovered evolution, can you be fatuous enough to think that simply by being wrong-headed you can recreate entirely your mind and temper or can clear your blood of what you may call the Catholic infection? A revolution such as you desire is not brought about by violence but gradually: and, within the Church you have an opportunity of beginning your revolution in a rational manner. You can sow the seeds in the careful furrows entrusted to you and if your seed is good it will prosper. But by going into the unnecessary wilderness and scattering your seed broadcast on all soils what harvest will you have? Everything seems to urge you to a course of moderation, of forbearance, and the purified will can surely display itself quite as well in acceptance as in rejection. The trees do not resent autumn nor does any exemplary thing in nature resent its limitations. Neither then do you resent the limitations of compromise.

These pleadings which Stephen so punctiliously heard out were supplemented by Cranly's influence. Neither of the young men [were] was studying for [their] his examination and they spent their evenings as usual in aimless walking and talking. Their walks and talks led nowhere because whenever anything definite threatened to make its appearance in their talk Cranly promptly sought the company of some of his chosen companions. The billiard-room of the Adelphi

Hotel was now a favourite resort of the two friends. After ten o'clock every night they went into the billiard-room. It was a big room well furnished with ill-kept inelegant tables and poorly furnished with players. Cranly played protracted matches with one or other of his companions while Stephen sat on the seat that ran alongside the table. A game of fifty cost sixpence which was duly paid by each of the players in equal parts, Cranly producing ᶜ his threepence very deliberately from a leather heart-shaped purse. The players sometimes sent their balls on to the floor and ᶜ Cranly occasionally swore at his flamin' cue. There was a bar attached to the billiard-room. In the bar was a stout barmaid who wore badly-made stays, served bottles of stout with her head on one side, and conversed in an English accent with her customers about the theatrical companies of the different theatres. Her customers were young men who carried their hats sideways far back on their heads and walked with their feet far apart. Their trousers were usually turned up high above their tan boots. One of the regular customers at this bar (though he did not mix with the young gentlemen mentioned above) was a friend of Cranly's, a young man who was a clerk in the Agricultural Board Office. He was a bandy-legged little man who spoke very little when he was sober but very much when he was drunk. When he was sober he was very orderly but his tipsiness, signalled by a dark-coloured ooze upon his pock-marked face, was boastful and disorderly. One night he engaged in a fierce argument about Tim Healy with a thickset medical student who had a taste for the art of self-defence. The argument was nearly entirely one-sided inasmuch as the medical student's contributions were derisive laughs and such remarks as 'Is he handy with the mitts?' 'Can he put up his props?' 'Is he a good man with the mitts?' At last the clerk from the Agricultural Board Office called the medical student a dirty name whereupon the medical student immediately knocked down all the drinks on the counter in his efforts to 'smash' the offender. The barmaid ran screaming for the proprietor, the medical student was soothed and restrained by considerate friends and the offender was escorted out by Cranly and Stephen and a few others. At first he lamented that his new cuffs were stained with porter and expressed a great desire to go back and fight it out but, dissuaded by Cranly, he began to tell Stephen in an indistinct undertone that he had

185

got the highest marks in Pure Mathematics ever given in the degree examination.[1] He advised Stephen to go to London to write for the papers and said he could put him in the right way to get on. When Cranly had begun a conversation with the others concerning the interrupted game of billiards Stephen's companion again announced that he had got the highest marks ever given in the degree in Pure Mathematics.

Stephen continued making his book of verses in spite of these distracting influences. He had come to the conclusion that nature had designed him for a man of letters and therefore he determined that, in spite of all influences, he would do as nature counselled. He had begun to consider Cranly a bad influence. Cranly's method in argument was to reduce all things to their food values (though he himself was the most impractical of theorists) and Stephen's conception of art fared very badly from such a method. Stephen held the test of food values an extreme one and one which in its utter materialism suggested a declination from the heights of romanticism. He knew that Cranly's materialism was only skin-deep and he surmised that Cranly chose to express himself in language and conduct of direct ugliness simply because his fear of ridicule and more than diplomatic wish to be well with men urged him to refrain from beauty of any kind. He fancied moreover that he detected in Cranly's attitude towards him a certain hostility, arising out of a thwarted desire to imitate. Cranly was fond of ridiculing Stephen to his bar companions and though this was supposed to be no more than banter Stephen found touches of seriousness in it. Stephen refused to close with this trivial falsehood of his friend and continued to [disclose] share all the secrets of his bosom as if he had not observed any change. He no longer, however, sought his friend's opinion or allowed the sour dissatisfaction of his friend's moods to weigh with him. He was egoistically determined that nothing material, no favour [of] or reverse of fortune, no bond of association or impulse or tradition should hinder him from working out the enigma of his position in his own way. He avoided his father sedulously because he now regarded his father's presumptions as the most deadly part of a tyranny, internal and external, which he deter-

[1] Among Joyce's notes printed by Gorman (p. 135) is the phrase – in quotation marks – 'I got the highest marks in mathematics of any man that ever went in.'

mined to combat with might and main. He argued no further with his mother, persuaded that he could have no satisfactory commerce with her so long as she chose to set the shadow of a clergyman between her nature and his. His mother told him one day that she had spoken of him to her confessor and asked his spiritual advice. Stephen turned to her and remonstrated hotly with her for doing such a thing.

— It is a nice thing, he said, that you go and discuss me behind my back. Have you not your own nature to guide you, your own sense of what is right, without going to some Father Jack-in-the-Box to ask him to guide you?

— Priests know a great deal of the world, said his mother.

— And what did he advise you to do?

— He said if there were any young children in the house he would advise me to get[1] out away from there as quickly as I could.

— Very nice! said Stephen angrily. That's a pretty thing for you to come and say to a son of yours!

— I am simply telling you what the priest advised me to do, said his mother quietly.

— These fellows, said Stephen, know nothing of the world. You might as well say that a rat in a sewer knew the world. Anyway you won't repeat what I say to your confessor in future because I won't say anything. And the next time he asks you 'What is that mistaken young man, that unfortunate boy, doing?' you can answer 'I don't know, father. I asked him and he said I was to tell the priest he was making a torpedo'.

The general attitude of women towards religion puzzled and often maddened Stephen. His nature was incapable of achieving such an attitude of insincerity or stupidity. By brooding constantly upon this he ended by anathemizing [sic] Emma as the most deceptive and cowardly of marsupials. He discovered that it was a menial fear and no spirit of chastity which had prevented her from granting his request. Her eyes, he thought, just look strange when upraised to some holy image and her lips when poised for the reception of the host. He cursed her burgher cowardice and her beauty and he said to himself that though her eyes might cajole the half-witted God of the Roman Catholics they would not cajole him. In every stray

<hr />

[1] 'You' or 'them' omitted?

image of the streets he saw her soul manifest itself and every such manifestation renewed the intensity of his disapproval. It did not strike him that the attitude of women towards holy things really implied a more genuine emancipation than his own and he condemned them out of a purely suppositious [*sic*] conscience. He exaggerated their iniquities and evil influence and returned them their antipathy in full measure. He toyed also with a theory of dualism which would symbolize the twin eternities of spirit and nature in the twin eternities of male and female and even thought of explaining the audacities of his verse as symbolical allusions. It was hard for him to compel his head to preserve the strict temperature of classicism. More than he had ever done before he longed for the season to lift and for spring – the misty Irish spring – to be over and gone. He was passing through Eccles' St one evening, one misty evening, with all these thoughts dancing the dance of unrest in his brain when a trivial incident set him composing some ardent verses which he entitled a 'Vilanelle of the Temptress'. A young lady was standing on the steps of one of those brown brick houses which seem the very incarnation of Irish paralysis. A young gentleman was leaning on the rusty railings of the area. Stephen as he passed on his quest heard the following fragment of colloquy out of which he received an impression keen enough to afflict his sensitiveness very severely.

The Young Lady – (drawling discreetly) . . . O, yes . . . I was . . . at the . . . cha . . . pel . . .
The Young Gentleman – (inaudibly) . . . I . . . (again inaudibly) . . . I . . .
The Young Lady – (softly) . . . O . . . but you're . . . ve . . . ry . . . wick . . . ed . . .

This triviality made him think of collecting many such moments together in a book of epiphanies. By an epiphany he meant a sudden spiritual manifestation, whether in the vulgarity of speech or of gesture or in a memorable phase of the mind itself. He believed that it was for the man of letters to record these epiphanies with extreme care, seeing that they themselves are the most delicate and evanescent of moments. He told Cranly that the clock of the Ballast Office was capable of an epiphany. Cranly questioned the inscrutable dial of the Ballast Office with his no less inscrutable countenance.

— Yes, said Stephen. I will pass it time after time, allude to it, refer to it, catch a glimpse of it. It is only an item in the catalogue of Dublin's street furniture. Then all at once I see it and I know at once what it is: epiphany.

— What?

— Imagine my glimpses at that clock as the gropings of a spiritual eye which seeks to adjust its vision to an exact focus. The moment the focus is reached the object is epiphanized. It is just in this epiphany that I find the third, the supreme quality of beauty.

— Yes? said Cranly absently.

— No esthetic theory, pursued Stephen relentlessly, is of any value which investigates with the aid of the lantern of tradition. What we symbolize in black the Chinaman may symbolize in yellow: each has his own tradition. Greek beauty laughs at Coptic beauty and the American Indian derides them both. It is almost impossible to reconcile all tradition whereas it is by no means impossible to find the justification of every form of beauty which has been adored on the earth by an examination into the mechanism of esthetic apprehension whether it be dressed in red, white, yellow or black. We have no reason for thinking that the Chinaman has a different system of digestion from that which we have though our diets are quite dissimilar. The apprehensive faculty must be scrutinized in action.

— Yes . . .

— You know what Aquinas says: The three things requisite for beauty are, integrity, a wholeness, symmetry and radiance. Some day I will expand that sentence into a treatise. Consider the performance of your own mind when confronted with any object, hypothetically beautiful. Your mind to apprehend that object divides the entire universe into two parts, the object, and the void which is not the object. To apprehend it you must lift it away from everything else: and then you perceive that it is one integral thing, that is *a* thing. You recognize its integrity. Isn't that so?

— And then?

— That is the first quality of beauty: it is declared in a simple sudden synthesis of the faculty which apprehends. What then? Analysis then. The mind considers the object in whole and in part, in relation to itself and to other objects, examines the balance of its parts, contemplates the form of the object, traverses every cranny of the structure. So the mind receives the impression of the symmetry of the object. The mind recognizes that the object is in the strict sense of the word, a *thing*, a definitely constituted entity. You see?

— Let us turn back, said Cranly.

They had reached the corner of Grafton St and as the footpath was overcrowded they turned back northwards. Cranly had an inclination to watch the antics of a drunkard who had been ejected from a bar in Suffolk St but Stephen took his arm summarily and led him away.

— Now for the third quality. For a long time I couldn't make out what Aquinas meant. He uses a figurative word (a very unusual thing for him) but I have solved it. *Claritas* is *quidditas*. After the analysis which discovers the second quality the mind makes the only logically possible synthesis and discovers the third quality. This is the moment which I call epiphany. First we recognize that the object is *one* integral thing, then we recognize that it is an organized composite structure, a *thing* in fact: finally, when the relation of the parts is exquisite, when the parts are adjusted to the special point, we recognize that it is *that* thing which it is. Its soul, its whatness, leaps to us from the vestment of its appearance. The soul of the commonest object, the structure of which is so adjusted, seems to us radiant. The object achieves its epiphany.

Having finished his argument Stephen walked on in silence. He felt Cranly's hostility and he accused himself of having cheapened the eternal images of beauty. For the first time, too, he felt slightly awkward in his friend's company and to restore a mood of flippant familiarity he glanced up at the clock of the Ballast Office and smiled:

— It has not epiphanized yet, he said.

Cranly stared stolidly down the river and held his peace for a few minutes during which the expounder of the new esthetic repeated his theory to himself all over again. A clock at the far side of the bridge chimed and simultaneously Cranly's thin lips parted for speech:

— I wonder, he said . . .

— What?

Cranly continued to stare towards the mouth of the Liffey like a man in a trance. Stephen waited for the sentence to be finished and then he said again 'What?' Cranly then faced about suddenly and said with flat emphasis:

— ᶜ I wonder did that bloody boat, the *Sea-Queen* ever start? ᶜ¹

Stephen had now completed a series of hymns in honour of extravagant beauty and these he published privately in a manuscript edition of one copy. His last interview with Cranly had been so unsatisfactory that he hesitated to show the manuscript to him. He kept the manuscript by him and its presence tormented him. He wanted to show it to his parents but the examination was approaching and he knew that their sympathy would be incomplete. He wanted to show it to Maurice but he was conscious that his brother resented having been forsaken for plebeian companions. He wanted to show it to Lynch but he dreaded the physical labour of urging that torpid young man into a condition of receptiveness. He even thought for a moment of McCann and Madden. He saw Madden rarely; the salute which the young patriot gave him on those rare occasions was not unlike the salute which [one] a friend who has failed gives to a friend who has succeeded. Madden spent the greater part of his day in Cooney's tobacco-shop, sampling and discussing *camáns*, smoking very heavy tobacco and speaking Irish with [one] newly arrived provincials. McCann was still busily occupied in editing his magazine [for] to which he had himself contributed an article entitled 'Rationalism in Practice'. In this article he expressed the hope that mankind in the not too distant future would use mineral, [as] instead of animal [and] or vegetable diet. The tone of the editor's writing had become much more orthodox than his speech had been wont to be. In the report of the general meeting of the College Sodality which occupied a column and a half of the College magazine it was stated that Mr McCann, in a forcible speech, had [suggested] made many valuable suggestions for the working of the society on a more practical basis. Stephen was surprised at this and when one day, [when Mc] walking through Nassau St with Cranly, he encountered the editor striding vigorously towards the Library he said to Cranly:

— What is Bonny Dundee at?

— How – at?

— I mean . . . this sodality business he's mixing himself up in. He can't be stupid enough to think he can use the sodality for any good purpose.

¹ Among Joyce's notes (Gorman, p. 137), under the heading 'Byrne' (Cranly) is the phrase, 'Did that bloody boat the Seaqueen ever start?'

Cranly eyed Stephen quizzically but, after considering the matter, decided to make no remark.

The examination resulted in Cranly's being 'stuck' again and in Stephen's securing a low pass. Stephen did not think it necessary to take the results of these examinations very bitterly to heart inasmuch as he [judged] knew that Father Artifoni, who had presented himself for the matriculation examination, had been awarded higher marks for his English paper than for his Italian paper, having been tested in the latter language by a polyglot examiner who examined in French, Italian, Arabic, [Jewish] Hebrew, Spanish and German. Stephen sympathized with his teacher who was ingenuous enough to express his astonishment. One evening during the examinations Stephen was talking to Cranly under the arcade of the University when Emma passed them. Cranly raised his ancient straw hat (which he had once more resurrected) and Stephen followed suit. In reply she bowed very politely across Stephen at his friend. Cranly replaced his hat and proceeded to meditate in the shade of it for a few minutes.

— Why did she do that?' he said.

— An invitation, perhaps, said Stephen.

Cranly stared continuously at the air through which she had passed: and Stephen said smilingly:

— Perhaps she meant it as an invitation.

— Perhaps.

— You're incomplete without a woman, said Stephen.

— Only she's so flamin' fat, said Cranly, d'ye know ...

Stephen kept silent. He was not pleased that anyone else should speak against her and he did not smile when Cranly took his arm saying 'Let us eke go' which [he] was always intended as an ᶜ old English expression ᶜ inviting departure. Stephen had long ago debated with himself the advisability of telling Cranly that the expression should be amended but Cranly's persistent emphasis of the word 'eke' acted as a deterrent.

The announcement of the result of the examination led to a domestic squabble. Mr Daedalus ransacked his vocabulary in search of abusive terms and ended by asking Stephen what were his plans for the future.

— I have no plans.

— Well then the sooner you clear out the better. You've been having us I see. However with the help of God and His Holy Mother

I'll write to Mullingar the first thing in the morning. There's no use in your godfather wasting any more of his money on you.

— Simon, said Mrs Daedalus, you always go to the fair with the story. Can't you be reasonable?

— Reasonable be damned. Don't I know the set he has got into – lousy-looking patriots and that football chap in the knickerbockers. To tell you the God's truth, Stephen, I thought you'd have more pride than to associate with such *canaille*.

— I don't think Stephen has done so badly in his examination: he hasn't failed and after all . . .

— She will put in her word, you know, said Mr Daedalus to his son. That's a little hereditary habit. Her family, you know, by God they know anything you can ask them down to the making of the mainspring of a watch. Fact.

— You oughtn't to run away with the story, Simon. Many fathers would be glad to have such a son.

— You needn't interfere between me and my son. We understand each other. I'm not saying anything to him; but I want to know what he has been doing for twelve months.

Stephen continued tapping the blade of his knife on the edge of his plate.

— What have you been doing?

— Thinking.

— Thinking? Is that all?

— And writing a little.

— Hm. I see. Wasting your time, in fact.

— I don't consider it waste of time to think.

— Hm. I see. You see I know these Bohemian chaps, these poets, who don't consider it waste of time to think. But at the same time they're damn glad to borrow an odd shilling now and then to buy chops with. How will you like thinking when you have no chops? Can't you go for something definite, some good appointment in a government office and then, by Christ, you can think as much as you like. Study for some first-class appointment, there are plenty of them, and you can write at your leisure. Unless, perhaps, you would prefer to be a loafer eating orange-peels and sleeping in the Park.

Stephen made no reply. When the harangue had been repeated five or six times he got up and went out. He went over to the

Library to look for Cranly and, not finding him in the reading-room or in the porch, went to the Adelphi Hotel. It was a Saturday night and the rooms were crowded with clerks. [and] The clerk from the Agricultural Board Office was sitting in the corner of the bar with his hat pushed well back from his forehead and at once Stephen recognized the dark ooze which was threatening to emerge upon his heated face. He was occupied in twirling his moustache in the crook of his index finger, and in glancing between the barmaid's face and the label of his bottle of stout. The billiard-room was very noisy: all the tables were engaged and the balls hopped on to the floor every minute or so. Some of the players played in their shirt-sleeves.

Cranly was sitting stolidly on the seat that ran alongside the tables, watching a game [of]. Stephen sat beside him in silence, also watching the game. It was a three-handed game. An elderly clerk, evidently in a patronizing mood, was playing two of his junior colleagues. The elderly clerk was a tall stout man who wore gilt spectacles on a face like a red shrivelled apple. He was in his shirt-sleeves and he played and spoke so briskly as to suggest that he was drilling rather than playing. The young clerks were both clean-shaven. One of them was a thickset young man who played doggedly without speaking, the other was an effervescent young man with white eyebrows and a nervous manner. Cranly and Stephen watched the game progress, creep from point to point. The heavy young man put his ball on to the floor three times in succession and the scoring was so slow that the marker came and stood by the table as a reminder that the twenty minutes had passed. The players chalked their cues oftener than before and, seeing that they were in earnest about finishing the game, the marker did not say anything about the time. But his presence acted upon them. The elderly clerk jerked his cue at his ball, making a bad stroke, and stood back from the table blinking his eyes and saying 'Missed that time'. The effervescent young clerk hurried to his ball, made a bad stroke and, looking along his cue, said 'Ah!'. The dogged young man shot his ball straight into the top pocket, a fact which the marker registered at once on the broken marking-board. The elderly clerk peered for a few critical seconds over the rim of his glasses, made another bad stroke and, at once proceeding to chalk his cue, [briskly], said briefly and sharply to the effervescent young man 'Come on now, White. Hurry up now.'

The hopeless pretence of those three lives before him, their un-redeemable servility, made the back of Stephen's eyes feel burning hot. He laid his [arm] hand on Cranly's shoulder and said impetu-ously:

— We must go out at once. I can't stand it any longer.

They crossed the room together and Stephen said:

— If I had remained another minute I think I would have begun to cry.

— Yes, it is bloody awful, said Cranly.

— O, hopeless! hopeless! said Stephen clenching his fists.

XXVI

A few nights before Cranly went to the country to [recruit] refresh himself in body after his failure in the examination, Stephen said to him:

— I believe this will be an important season for me. I intend to come to some decision as to my course of action.

— But you will go for Second Arts next year?

— My godfather may not pay. They expected I would get an exhibition.

— And why didn't you? said Cranly.

— I will think things out, said Stephen, and see what I can do.

— There are a hundred things you can do.

— Are there, faith? We'll see . . . I might want to write to you. ° What is your address? °

Cranly affected not to hear this question. He was picking his teeth with a match, very deliberately ° and scrupulously, occasionally halting to insert his tongue carefully into some crevice before continuing the process of picking.° He spat out what he dislodged. His straw hat rested mainly on the nape of his neck and his feet were planted far apart. After a considerable pause he returned to his last phrase, as if he had been inwardly reviewing it:

— Ay, hundreds of things.

Stephen said:

— What is your address in the country?

— My address? . . . O . . . You see . . . it's really impossible, d'ye know, to say what my address would be. But you won't come to any decision before I come back . . . I'm almost sure I'll go in the morning but I want to see at what time there's a train.

— We looked before, said Stephen. Half past nine.

— No . . . I think I must go up to Harcourt St to see what time there's a train.

They walked slowly in the direction of Harcourt St. Stephen, refusing to nurse ill-feeling, said:

— What mysterious purpose is concealed under your impossible prosiness? Please tell me that. Have you anything in your mind's eye?

— If I had a mysterious purpose, said Cranly, I wouldn't be likely to tell you, (would I?), what it was.

— I have told you a great deal, said Stephen.

— Most people have some purpose or other in their lives. Aristotle says that the end of every being is its greatest good. We all act in view of some good.

— Couldn't you be a bit more precise? You don't wish me to write gospels about you, do you? . . . Are you really thinking of being a pork-butcher?

— Yes, really. ° Would you not think of it. You could wrap your sausages in your love-poems °.

Stephen laughed.

— You mustn't think you can impose on me, Cranly, he said. I know you are damnably romantic.

At Harcourt St Station they went up to the time-table and after a glance at it Stephen said mischievously [sic]:

— Half past nine, as I told you. You see you wouldn't take a fool's word for it.

— That's another train, said Cranly impatiently.

Stephen smiled with enjoyment while Cranly began to examine the chart, murmuring the names of the stations to himself and calculating time. In the end he seemed to arrive at some decision for he said to Stephen 'Let us eke go'. Outside the station Stephen pulled his friend's coat-sleeve and pointed to a newsbill which was exposed to public gaze on the roadway, held down at the corners by four stones.

— Have you seen this?

[Cranly] They stopped to read the [items] bill and four or five people also stopped to read it. Cranly read out the items in his flattest accent, beginning at the headline:

EVENING TELEGRAPH

[Meeting]

NATIONALIST MEETING AT BALLINROBE

IMPORTANT SPEECHES

MAIN DRAINAGE SCHEME

BREEZY DISCUSSION

DEATH OF A WELL-KNOWN SOLICITOR

MAD COW AT CABRA

LITERATURE &.

— Do you think it requires great ability to live that life successfully? asked Stephen when they were once more on the way.

— I suppose you consider literature the most important thing there?

— You take up that view of the world, I am sure, out of pure perversity. You try to prove me abnormal and diseased but it is as easy to prove that the well-known solicitor was diseased and abnormal. Insensibility is a mark of disease.

— He may have been ᶜ what you would call ᶜ an artist.

— Yes, of course ... And as for the temptation which Satan was allowed to dangle before the eyes of Jesus it is, in reality, the most ineffectual temptation to offer to any man of genius. The well-known solicitor might succumb to it but for Jesus the kingdom of this world must have been a very empty phrase indeed – at least when he had outgrown a romantic youth. ᶜ Satan, really, is the romantic youth of Jesus re-appearing for a moment. I had a romantic youth,ᶜ too, when I thought it must be a grand thing to be a material Messias: that was the will of my father who will never be in heaven. But now such a thought arises in my mind only in moments of great physical weakness. So I regard that view of life as the abnormal view – for me. A few days ago I walked out to Howth for a swim and while I was going round the side of the Head I had to take a little ribbon of a path that hung high over the rocks ...

— What side of Howth?

— Near the Bailey ... Very good. As I looked down on those rocks beneath me the thought arose in my mind to cast myself down upon them. The thought made me shiver with pleasure for a moment, but, of course, I recognized our old friend. All these temptations are of a piece. To Jesus, to me, to the excitable person who adopts brigandage or suicide after taking the suggestions of literature too seriously, Satan offers a monstrous life. It is monstrous because the seat of the spiritual principle of a man is not transferable to a material object. A man only pretends to think his hat more important than his head. That view of life, I consider, is abnormal.

— You cannot call that abnormal which everyone does.

— Does everyone jump off the Hill of Howth? Does everyone join secret societies? Does everyone sacrifice happiness and pleasure and peace to honour in the world? Father Artifoni told me of a society of mutual assistance in Italy the members of which had the right to be thrown into the Arno by their fellow-members on signing a paper proving that their case was past curing.

At Noblett's corner where they always halted, they found Temple declaiming to a little ring of young men. The young men were laughing very much at Temple who was very drunk. Stephen kept his eyes fixed on Temple's shapeless mouth which at moments was flecked with a thin foam as it strove to enunciate a difficult word. Cranly stared at the group and said:

— I'll take my dyin' bible Temple has been standing those medicals drinks . . . The bloody fool! . . .

Temple caught sight of them and at once broke off his discourse to come over to them. One or two of the medicals followed him.

— Good evening, said Temple, fumbling at his cap.

— *Druncus es.*

The two medicals laughed while Temple began to search his pockets. During the search his mouth fell asunder.

— Who has the money? said Cranly.

The two medicals laughed and nodded towards Temple who desisted from his search disconsolately saying:

— Ay, by hell . . . I was going to stand a drink . . . Ah, by hell! . . . Where's the other bob I had? . . .

One of the medicals said:

— You changed it in Connery's.

The other medical said:

— He got stuck in his first today. That's why he went on the beer tonight.

— And where did you raise the money? said Cranly to Temple, who began to search his pockets again.

— He popped his watch for ten bob.

— It mustn't be a bad watch, said Cranly, if he got ten bob on it. Where did he get ten bob?

— Ah no! said the second medical. I popped it for him. I know a chap named Larkin in Granby Row.

The big medical student who had had the political discussion in the *Adelphi* with the clerk from the Agricultural Board Office came over to them and said:

— Well, Temple, are you going to take us down to the kips?

— Ah, blazes, said Temple, all my money's gone . . . Ah, by hell, I must have a woman . . . By hell, I'll ask for a woman on tick.

The big student roared laughing and turning to Cranly, against whom he had a grudge on account of the affair in the *Adelphi*, he said:

— Will you have a woman too if I stand?

Cranly's chastity was famous but the young men were not quite impressed by it. At the same time the [little] group did not betray its opinion by laughing at the big student's invitation. Cranly did not answer; and so the second medical student said:

— Mac got through!

— What Mac? said Cranly.

— Mac – you know – the Gaelic League chap. He brought us down to the kips last night.

— And had you all women?

— No . . .

— What did you go there for?

— He suggested we'd walk through. Fine tarts there, too. They were running after us, man: it was fine skit. Ay, and one of them hit Mac because she said he insulted her.

— What did he do?

— I don't know. He said 'Gellong, you dirty [whore] hure' or something like that.

— And what did Mac say?

— Said he'd charge her if she followed him any further.

— Well, I'll stand women all round if Cranly has one, said the big student who was in the ᶜ habit of making a single inspiration serve him for a half-hour's conversation.ᶜ

— Ah, by hell, said Temple suddenly, have you heard the new parable . . . about the monkeys in Barbary? . . . Mar . . . vellous parable . . . Flanagan told me . . . O, (he said to Stephen) he wants to be introduced to you . . . wants to know . . . Fine fellow . . . doesn't care a damn for religion or priests . . . By hell, I'm a freethinker . . .

— What is the parable, said Stephen.

Temple took off his cap and, bareheaded, he began to recite after the fashion of a country priest, prolonging all the vowels [and] jerking out the phrases, and dropping his voice at every pause:

— Dearly beloved Brethren: There was once a tribe of monkeys in Barbary. And . . . these monkeys were as numerous as the sands of the sea. They lived together in the woods in polygamous . . . intercourse . . . and reproduced . . . their species . . . But, behold there came into Barbary . . . the holy missionaries, the holy men of God . . . to redeem the people of Barbary. And these holy men preached to the people . . . and then . . . they went into the woods . . . far away into the woods . . . to pray to God. And they lived as hermits . . . in the woods . . . and praying to God. And, behold, the monkeys of Barbary who were in the trees . . . saw these holy men living as hermits . . . as lonely hermits . . . praying to God. And the monkeys who, my dearly beloved brethren, are imitative creatures . . . began to imitate the actions . . . of these holy men . . . and began to do likewise. And so . . . they [left their wives] separated from one another . . . and went away far away, to pray to God . . . and they did as they had seen the holy men do . . . and prayed to God . . . And . . . they did not return . . . any more . . . nor try to reproduce the species . . . And so . . . gradually . . . these po . . . or monkeys . . . grew fewer and fewer . . . and fewer and fewer . . . And today . . . there is no monkey in all Barbary.

Temple crossed himself and replaced his hat while the audience began to clap their hands together. Just then a policeman moved on the group. Stephen said to Cranly:

— Who is this Flanagan?

Cranly did not answer but followed Temple and his companions walking emphatically and saying ''M, yes' to himself. They could hear Temple bemoaning his poverty to his companions and repeating snatches of his parable.

— Who is this Flanagan? said Stephen again to Cranly.

— Another bloody fool, said Cranly in a tone which left the comparison open.

A few days later Cranly went to Wicklow. Stephen spent his summer with Maurice. He told his brother what troubles he anticipated when the college term reopened and together they discussed plans for living. Maurice suggested that the verses should be sent to a publisher.

— I cannot send them to a publisher, said Stephen, because I have burned them.

— Burned them!

— Yes, said Stephen, curtly, they were romantic.

In the end they decided that it would be best to wait until Mr Fulham made his intentions known. Mrs Daedalus called one day to see Father Butt. She did not report her interview fully but Stephen understood that Father Butt had at first prescribed a clerkship in Guinness's as a solution of the young man's difficult case and, when Mrs Daedalus had shaken her head incredulously, he had asked to see Stephen. He had thrown out hints about some new arrangement of the college which would necessitate new appointments. These hints were fed upon by Stephen's parents. The next day Stephen [was] called to the college to see Father Butt.

— O, come in, my dear boy, said Father Butt when Stephen appeared at the door of the little uncarpeted bedroom.

Father Butt began to talk a great deal about general topics, without saying anything definite but asking Stephen over and over again for an expression of opinion which was always studiously withheld. The young man was very much bewildered. At last, after much rubbing of his chin and many blinkings of the eyes, Father Butt asked what were Stephen's intentions . . .

— Literature, said Stephen.

— Yes, yes . . . of course . . . but meanwhile, I mean . . . of course you will continue your course until you have got a degree – that is the important point.

— I may not be able, said Stephen, I suppose you know that my father is unable to . . .

– Now, said Father Butt joyfully, I'm so glad you've come to the point . . . That is just it. The question is whether we can find anything for you to enable you to finish your course here. That is the question.

Stephen said nothing. He was convinced that Father Butt had some offer or suggestion to make but he was determined not to help him in bringing it out. Father Butt continued blinking his eyes and rubbing his chin and murmuring to himself 'That is the difficulty you see'. In the end, as Stephen held his peace sacredly, Father Butt said:

— There might be . . . it has just occurred to me . . . an appointment here in the college. One or two hours a day . . . that would be nothing . . . I think, yes . . . we shall be . . . let me see now . . . It would be no trouble to you . . . no teaching or drudgery, just an hour or so in the office here in the morning . . .

Stephen said nothing. Father Butt rubbed his hands together and said:

— Otherwise there would be a danger of your perishing . . . by inanition . . . Yes, a capital idea . . . I shall speak to Father Dillon this very night.

Stephen, somewhat taken by surprise though he had anticipated some such proposal, murmured his thanks and Father Butt promised to send him a letter in the course of a day or two.

Stephen did not give a very full account of this interview to his father and mother: he said that Father Butt had been vague and had suggested that he should look for tuitions. Mr Daedalus thought this a highly practical notion:

— If you will only keep your head straight you can get on. Keep in touch with those chaps, I tell you, those Jesuits: they can get you on fast enough. I am a few years older than you.

— I am sure they will do their best to help you, said Mrs Daedalus.

— I don't want their help, said Stephen bitterly.

Mr Daedalus put up his eyeglass and stared at his son and at his wife. His wife began an apology:

— Give it up, woman, he said. I know the groove he has got into. But he's not going to fool me nor his godfather, either. With the help of God I won't be long till I let *him* know what a bloody nice atheist this fellow has turned out. Hold hard now a moment and leave it to me.

Stephen answered that he did not want his godfather's help either.

— I know the groove you're in, said his father. Didn't I see you the morning of your poor sister's funeral – don't forget that? Unnatural bloody ruffian. By Christ I was ashamed of you that morning. You couldn't behave like a ᶜ gentleman ᶜ or talk or do a bloody thing only slink over in a corner with the hearse-drivers and mutes by God. Who taught you to drink pints of plain porter, might I ask? Is that considered the proper thing for an . . . a artist to do?

Stephen clasped his hands together and looked across at Maurice who was convulsed with laughter.

— What are you laughing at? said his father. Everyone knows you're only this fellow's jackal.

— Stephen was thirsty, said Maurice.

203

— By God, he'll be hungry as well as thirsty one of these days, if you ask me.

Stephen gave details of his interview to Maurice:

— Don't you think they are trying to buy me? he asked.

— Yes, that's evident. But I'm surprised at one thing . . .

— What is that?

— That the priest lost his temper when speaking to Mother. You must have annoyed the good man a great deal.

— How do you know he lost his temper?

— O, he must have when he suggested to her to put you on the books of a brewery. That gave the show away. Anyhow we can see what right these men have to call themselves spiritual counsellors of their flocks . . .

— Yes?

— They can do nothing for a case like yours which presents certain difficulties of temperament. You might as well apply to a policeman.

— Perhaps his notion was that my mind was in such a state of disorder that even routine would do it good.

— I don't think that was his notion. Besides they must all be liars in that case for they have all expressed great admiration for your clearness in argument. A man's mind is not in intellectual disorder because it refuses assent to the doctrine of the Blessed Trinity.

— By the way, said Stephen, do you notice what understanding and sympathy exist between me and my parents?

— Isn't it charming?

— Yet, there are plenty of people who would consider them my best friends for having advised me as they have done. It seems absurd to call them enemies or to denounce them. They want me to secure what they consider happiness. They would like me to accept anything in the way of money at whatever a cost to myself.

— And will you accept?

— If Cranly were here I know how he would put that question.

— How?

— 'Of course, you will accept?'

— I have already told you of my opinion of that young gentleman, said Maurice tartly.

— Lynch, too, would say 'You'd be a damn fool if you didn't take it'.

— And what will you do?

— Refuse it, of course.

— I expected you would.

— How could I take it? asked Stephen in astonishment.

— Not well, I suppose.

The following day a letter arrived for Stephen:

Dear Mr Daedalus,

I have spoken to our President *re* what we discussed a few days ago. He is greatly interested in your case and would like to see you at the College any day this week between 2 and 3. He thinks it may be possible to find something for you such as I suggested – a few hours or so daily – to enable you to *continue your studies*. That is the main point.

Sincerely Yours

D. Butt SJ.

Stephen did not call to see the President but replied to Father Butt by letter:

Dear Father Butt,

Allow me to thank you for your kindness. I am afraid, however, that I cannot accept your offer. I am sure you will understand that in declining it I am acting as seems best to me and with every appreciation of the interest you have shown in me.

Sincerely Yours

Stephen Daedalus.

Stephen spent the great part of his summer on the rocks of the North Bull. Maurice spent the day there, stretching idly on the rocks or plunging into the water. Stephen was now on excellent terms with his brother who seemed to have forgotten their estrangement. At times Stephen would half clothe himself and cross to the shallow side of the Bull where he would wander up and down looking at the children and the nurses. He used to stand to stare at them sometimes until the ash of his cigarette fell on to his coat but, though he saw all that was intended, he met no other Lucy: and he usually returned to the Liffey side, somewhat amused at his dejection and thinking that if he had made his proposal to Lucy instead of to Emma he might have met with better luck. But as often as not he encountered dripping Christian Brothers or ° disguised policemen,° apparitions which assured him that whether Lucy or Emma was in question the answer was all one. The two brothers walked home from Dollymount together. They were both a little ragged-looking but they did not envy the trim dressed clerks [that] who passed them on their way home. When they came to Mr Wilkinson's house they both paused outside to listen for [the] sounds of wrangling and even when all seemed peaceful Maurice's first question to his mother when she opened the door was 'Is he in?' When the answer was 'No' they both went down to the kitchen together but when the answer was 'Yes' Stephen only went down, Maurice listening over the banisters to judge from his father's tones whether he was sober or not. If his father was drunk Maurice retired to his bedroom but Stephen, who was untroubled, discoursed gaily with his father. Their conversation always began:

— Well (in a tone of extreme sarcasm) might I ask where were you all day?

— At the Bull.

— O (in a mollified tone) Had a dip?

— Yes.

— Well, there's some sense in that. I like to see that. So long as you keep away from those *canaille* (in a suspicious tone). Sure you weren't with Knickerbockers or some of those noblemen?

— Quite sure.

— That's all right. That's all I want. Keep away from them . . . Was Maurice with you?

— Yes.

— Where is he?

— Upstairs, I think.

— Why doesn't he come down here?

— I don't know.

— Hm . . . (again in a tone of ruminative sarcasm) By God, you're a loving pair of sons, you and your brother!

Lynch pronounced Stephen all the asses in Christendom for having declined the Jesuits' offers:

— Look at the nights you could have had!

— You are a distressingly low-minded person, answered Stephen. After all I have dinned into that mercantile head of yours you are sure to come out on me with some atrocity.

— But why did you refuse? said Lynch.

The summer was nearly at an end and the evening had grown a little chilly. Lynch was walking up and down the Library porch with his hands in his pockets and his chest well protruded. Stephen kept at his side:

— I am a young man, isn't that so?

— That – is – so.

— Very well. My entire aptitude is for the composition of prose and verse. Isn't that so?

— Let us suppose it is.

— Very good. I was not intended to be a clerk in a brewery.

— I think it would be very dangerous to put you in a brewery . . . sometimes.

— I was not intended for that: that is enough. I went to this University day-school in order to meet men of a like age and temper . . . You know what I met.

Lynch nodded his head in despair:

— I found a day-school full of terrorized boys, banded together in a complicity of diffidence. They have eyes only for their future jobs: to secure their future jobs they will write themselves in and out of convictions, toil and labour to insinuate themselves into the good graces of the Jesuits. They adore Jesus and Mary and Joseph: they believe in the ° infallibility ° of the Pope and in all his obscene, stinking hells: they desire the millennium which is to be [a] the season for glorified believers and fried atheists . . . Sweet Lord Almighty! Look at that beautiful pale sky! Do you feel the cool wind on your face? Listen to [my] our voices here in the porch – not because [it is] they are mine or yours but because they are human voices: and doesn't all that tomfoolery fall off you like water off a duck's back?

Lynch nodded his head and Stephen continued:

— It is absurd that I should go crawling and cringing and praying and begging to mummers who are themselves no more than beggars. Can we not root this pest out of our minds and out of our society that men may be able to walk through the streets without meeting some old stale belief or hypocrisy at every street corner? I, at least,

207

will try. I will not accept anything from them. I will not take service under them. I will not submit to them, either outwardly or inwardly. A Church is not a fixture like Gibraltar: no more is an institution. Subtract its human members from it and its solidity becomes less evident. I, at least, will subtract myself: and remember that if we allow a dozen for one's progeny the subtraction of oneself may mean a loss to the Church of 12^n members.

— Aren't you rather liberal about the progeny? said Lynch.

— Did I tell you I met Father Healy this evening? asked Stephen.

— No, where?

— I was walking along the Canal with my Danish grammar (because I am going to study it properly now. I'll tell you why later on) and whom should I meet but this little man. He was walking right ° into the golden sunset °: all his creases and wrinkles were scattered with gold. He looked at my book and said it was very interesting: he thought it must be so interesting to know and compare the different languages. Then he looked far away into the golden sun and all of a sudden – imagine! – his mouth opened and he gave a slow, noiseless yawn . . . Do you know you get a kind of shock when a man does a thing like that unexpectedly?

— He'll have something to do shortly, said Lynch pointing to a little group which was laughing and chatting in the doorway, and that'll keep him from walking in his sleep.

Stephen glanced over at the group. Emma and Moynihan and McCann and two of the Miss Daniels were evidently in high spirits.

— Yes, I suppose she will do it legitimately one of these days, said [Lynch] Stephen.

— I was talking of the other pair, said Lynch.

— O, McCann . . . She is nothing to me now, you know.

— I don't believe that, let me tell you.

[*The additional pages of the Manuscript begin here*]

nations. They were held out to say: We are alone – come: and the voices said with them: We are your people: and the air grew thick with their company as they called to him, their kinsman, making ready to go, shaking the wings of their exultant and terrible youth. 13 ·

[*Departure for Paris (written across between paragraphs in blue crayon*)]

From the Broadstone to Mullingar is a journey of some fifty miles across the midlands of Ireland. Mullingar, the chief town of Westmeath, is the midland capital and there is a great traffic of peasants and cattle between it and Dublin. This fifty-mile journey is made by the train in about two hours and you are therefore to conceive Stephen Daedalus packed in the corner of a third-class carriage and contributing the thin fumes of his cigarettes to the already reeking atmosphere. The carriage was inhabited by a company of peasants nearly every one of whom had a bundle tied in a spotted handkerchief. The carriage smelt strongly of peasants (an odour the debasing humanity of which Stephen remembered to have perceived in the little chapel of Clongowes on the morning of his first communion) and indeed so pungently that the youth could not decide whether he found the odour of sweat [unpleasant] offensive because the peasant sweat is monstrous or because it did not now proceed from his own body. He was not ashamed to admit to himself that he found it [unpleasant] offensive for both of these reasons. The peasants played with blackened edgeless cards from Broadstone onward and whenever it was time for a peasant to leave the company he took up his bundle and went out heavily through the door of the carriage, never closing it behind him. The peasants spoke little and rarely looked at the scene they passed but [at] when they came to Maynooth Station a gentleman dressed in a frock-coat and tall hat who was giving loud directions to a porter concerning a case of machines attracted their wondering attention for several minutes.

At Mullingar Stephen took his neat little valise down from the rack and descended to the platform. When he had passed through the claws

[*Two pages missing*]

of Lough Owel. The lodge was a whitewashed cottage at the door of which a little child in a chemise sat eating a big crust of bread. The

209

gate was open and the trap turned up the drive. After a circular tour of a few hundred yards the trap reached the door of the old discoloured house.

As the trap drew up to the door a young woman advanced to meet it with a quiet dignified gait. She was dressed completely in black and her dark hair was brushed plainly off her temples. She held out her hand:

— Welcome, she said. My uncle is in the orchard. We heard the noise of the wheels.

Stephen touched her hand slightly and bowed.

— Dan, leave that valise in the hall for the present and you, Mr Daedalus, are to come along with me. I hope you are not fatigued by your journey: it is so tiresome travelling.

— Not in the least.

She led the way along the hall and through a little glass door into a great square orchard, the nearer half of which was still a sunny region. Here, screened by a broad straw hat, Mr Fulham was discovered sitting in a basket-chair. He greeted Stephen very warmly and made the usual polite enquiries. Miss Howard had brought out a little tray containing fruit and milk and the visitor gladly ate and drank for the dust of the roads [was] had invaded his throat. Mr Fulham asked a great many questions about Stephen's studies and tastes while Miss Howard stood beside his chair in silence. At a pause in the interrogation she took up the tray and carried it into the house. When she came back she offered to show Stephen the orchard and, Mr Fulham returning at the same moment to his newspaper, she led the way down a walk of currant-bushes. Stephen had found his godfather's questions a somewhat severe ordeal and he revenged himself on Miss Howard by a counter-fire of questions concerning the names and seasons and prospects of her plants. She answered all his questions carefully but with the same air of indifferent exactness which marked all her acts. Her presence did not awe him as it had done when he had last met her and he thought that perhaps the uncontaminated nature which he had then imagined accusing him was no more than an unusual dignity of manner. He did not find this dignity of hers very congenial and his new fervour of youth was vitally piqued by her lack of animation. He decided in favour of some definite purpose of hers and against [the] a mechanical discharge of duties and said to himself that it would be an intellectual game for him to discover it. He set this task to himself all the more readily since he suspected that this purpose guiding her conduct must be inimical to his present genial impulses and would probably elude him out of instantaneous distrust and seek natural safety in flight. This fugitive impulse would be prey for him and at once he summoned all his faculties to the chase.

Dinner was served at half past six in a long plainly-furnished room. The table spread under a tall lamp of elegant silver-work wore an air of chaste elegance. It was a slight trial on Stephen's hunger to accept these cold manners and in the warmth of his relish for food he condemned this strange attitude of human beings as ungrateful and unnatural. The conversation was also a little mincing and Stephen heard the words 'charming' and 'nice' and 'pretty' too often to find them agreeable. He discovered the weak point in Mr Fulham's armour very soon; Mr Fulham, like most of his countrymen, was a persuaded politician. Most of Mr Fulham's neighbours were primitive types and he, in spite of the narrowness of his ideas, was regarded by them as a man of ripe culture. In a discussion which took place over a game of bezique Stephen heard his godfather explain to a more rustic proprietor the nature of the work done by the missionary fathers in civilizing the Chinese people. He sustained the propositions that the Church is also the chief repository of secular culture and that the tradition of learning must derive from the monks. He saw in the pride of the Church the only refuge of men against a threatening democracy and said that Aquinas had anticipated all the discoveries of the modern world. His neighbour was puzzled to discover the whereabouts of the souls of the Chinese people in the other life but Mr Fulham left the problem at the door of God's mercy. At this stage of the discussion Miss Howard, hitherto silent, said that there were three kinds of baptism and her statement was accepted as a closure.

Stephen was a long time in doubt as to the motive of his godfather's patronage. The second day after his arrival as they were driving back from a tennis-tournament Mr Fulham said to him.

— Isn't Mr Tate your English professor, Stephen?

— Yes, sir.

— His people are Westmeath. We often see him during holiday time. He seems to take a great interest in you.

— O, you know him then?

— Yes. He is laid up at present with a bad knee or I'd write to him to come over here. Perhaps we may drive over to see him one of these days . . . He is a very well-read man, Stephen.

— Yes, said Stephen.

Tennis-tournaments, military bands, rustic cricket-matches, little flower shows were [devised] resorted to for Stephen's entertainment. At these functions he remarked that his godfather was very openly humoured and Miss Howard very respectfully courted and he began to suspect that there was money somewhere in the background. These entertainments did not amuse the youth; his manner was so quiet that often he passed unnoticed and remained unintroduced. Sometimes an officer would send a glance of impolite enquiry at the cheap-looking white shoes he wore but Stephen always looked his enemy in the face. After a short trial of eyes the youth could usually procure a truce. He was surprised to find that Miss Howard discharged her social duties with such apparent goodwill. He was displeased and disappointed to hear her make a pun one day – a pun which though it was not very clever [but caused] raised a polite laugh from two scrupulous lieutenants. Mr Fulham was old and honoured enough to allow himself the luxury of admonishing publicly whenever occasion arose. [When] One day an officer told a humorous story which was intended to poke fun at countrified ideas [Mr Fulham said:

— Our peasants may be ignorant of many things]

The story was this. The officer and a friend found themselves one evening surprised by a heavy shower far out on the Killucan road and forced to take refuge in a peasant's cabin. An old man was seated at the side of the fire smoking a dirty cutty-pipe which he held upside down in the corner of his mouth. The old peasant invited his visitors to come near the fire as the evening was chilly and said he could not stand up to welcome them decently as he had the rheumatics. The officer's friend who was a learned young lady observed a figure scrawled in chalk over the fireplace and asked what it was. The peasant said:

— Me grandson Johnny done that the time the circus was in the town. He seen the pictures on the walls and began pesterin' his mother for fourpence to see th' elephants. But sure when he got in an' all divil elephant was in it. But it was him drew that there.

The young lady laughed and the old man blinked his red eyes at the fire and went on smoking evenly and talking to himself:

— I've heerd tell them elephants is most natural things, that they has the notions of a Christian . . . I wanse seen meself a picture of niggers riding on wan of 'em – aye and beating blazes out of 'im with a stick. Begorra ye'd have more trouble with the childre[1] is in it now that[2] with one of thim big fellows.

The young lady who was much amused began to tell the peasant about the animals of prehistoric times. The old man heard her out in silence and then said slowly:

— Aw, there must be terrible quare craythurs at the latther ind of the world.[3]

Stephen thought that the officer told this story very well and he joined in the laugh that followed it. But Mr Fulham was not of his opinion and spoke out against the moral of the story rather sententiously.

— It is easy to laugh at the peasant. He is ignorant of many things which the world thinks important. But we mustn't forget at the same time, Captain Starkie, that the peasant [is] stands perhaps nearer to the true ideal of a Christian life than many of us who condemn him.

— I do not condemn him, answered Captain Starkie, but I am amused.

— Our Irish peasantry, continued Mr Fulham with conviction, is the backbone of the nation.

Backbone or not, it was in the constant observance of the peasantry that Stephen chiefly delighted. Physically,

[*One page missing*]

doorway, gazed at him and answered:

— No, sir.

— O yes it was, though.

The beggar thrust his malign face down at their faces and began moving his stick up and down.

[1] Children.
[2] 'than' is written in pencil in the margin.
[3] This phrase appears, with changes, in the diary entry for April 14th at the end of the final chapter of *A Portrait o fthe Artist as a Young man*.

— But mind what I'm tellin' you. D'ye see that stick?

— Yes, sir.

— Well, if ye call out after me the next time I'll cut [yous] yez open with that stick. I'll cut the livers out of ye.

He proceeded to explain himself to the frightened children.

— D'ye hear me now? I'll cut yez open with that stick. I'll cut the livers and the lights out of ye.

This incident was stolidly admired by a few bystanders who made way for the beggar as he limped along the footpath. Dan, who had watched the scene from the trap, now descended to the ground and asking Stephen to look to the horse went into a very dirty public-house. Stephen sat alone in the car thinking of the beggar's face. He had never before seen such evil expressed in a face. He had sometimes watched the faces of prefects as they 'pandied' boys with a broad leather bat but those faces had seemed to him less malicious than stupid, dutifully inflamed faces. The recollection of the beggar's sharp eyes struck a fine chord of terror in the youth and he set himself to whistle away the keen throb if it.

After a few minutes a fat young man with a very red head came out of the druggist's shop holding two neat parcels. Stephen recognized Nash and Nash testified that he recognized Stephen by changing complexion very painfully. Stephen could have enjoyed his old enemy's discomfiture had he chosen but disdaining to do so he held out his hand instead. Nash was junior assistant in the shop and when he learned that Stephen was on a visit to Mr Fulham his manner was tinged with discreet respectfulness. Stephen, however, soon put him at his ease and when Dan emerged from the grimy public-house the two were engaged in familiar chat. Nash said Mullingar was the last place God made, a God-forgotten hole, and asked Stephen how he could stick it.

— I only wish I was back again in Dublin, that's all I know.

— How do you amuse yourself here? asked Stephen.

— Amuse yourself! You can't. There's nothing here.

— But haven't you concerts sometimes? The first day I came here I saw some bills up about a concert.

— O, that's off. Father Lohan put the boot, on that – the P.P.[1] you know.

[1] Parish Priest.

— Why did he?

— O, you better ask him that. He says his parishioners don't want comic songs and skirt dances. If they want a decent concert, he says, they can get one up in the schoolhouse, – O, he bosses them, I tell you.

— O, is that the way?

— They're afraid of their life[1] of him. If he hears any dancing in a house at night he raps at the window and pouf! out goes the candle.

— By Jove!

— Fact. You know he has a collection of girls' hats.

— Girls' hats!

— Yes. Of an evening when the girls go out walking with the soldiers he goes out too and any girl he catches hold of he snaps off her hat and takes it back with him to the priest's house then if the girl goes to ask him for it he gives her a proper blowing-up.

— Good man! . . . Well, we must be off now. I suppose I'll see you again.

— Come in tomorrow, will you: it's a short day. And I'll tell you I'll introduce you to a friend of mine here – very decent sort – on the *Examiner*. You'll like him.

— Very good. Until then!

— So long! About two o'clock.

As they drove home together Stephen asked Dan some questions which Dan pretended not to hear and when Stephen pressed him for answers he gave the shortest possible answers. It was plain that he did not care to discuss his spiritual superior and Stephen had to desist.

That evening at dinner Mr Fulham was in genial spirits and began to address his conversation pointedly to Stephen. Mr Fulham's method of 'drawing' his interlocutor was not a very delicate method but Stephen saw what was expected of him and merely waited till he was directly addressed. A neighbour had come to dinner, a Mr Heffernan. Mr Heffernan was not at all of his host's way of thinking and therefore the evening brought out some lively disputes. Mr Heffernan's son was learning Irish because he believed that the Irish people should speak their own language and not the language of their conquerors.

— But the people of the United States who are more emancipated

---

[1] 'lives' is written in pencil in the margin.

than Ireland is ever likely to be are content to speak English, said Mr Fulham.

— The Americans are different. They have no language to revive.

— For my part I am content with my conquerors.

— Because you occupy a good position under them. You are not a labourer. You enjoy the fruits of Nationalist agitation.

— Perhaps you are going to tell me that all men are equal, said Mr Fulham satirically.

— In a sense they may be.

— Nonsense, my dear sir. Our countrymen know nothing of the Reformation, as they call it, and I hope [it] they will know nothing of the French Revolution either.

Mr Heffernan returned to the charge.

— But surely it is no harm for them to know something about their country – its traditions, its local history, its language!

— For those who have leisure it may be good! But you know I am a great enemy of disloyal movements. Our lot is thrown in with England.

— The young generation is not of your opinion. My son, Pat, is studying in Clonliffe at present and he tells me all the young students there, those who are to be our priests afterwards, have these ideas.

— The Catholic Church, my dear sir, will never incite to rebellion. But here is one of the young generation. Let him speak.

— I care nothing for these principles of nationalism, said Stephen. I have enough bodily liberty.

— But do you feel no duty to your mother-country, no love for her? asked Mr Heffernan.

— Honestly, I don't.

— You live then like an animal without reason! exclaimed Mr Heffernan.

— My own mind, aswered Stephen, is more interesting to me than the entire country.

— Perhaps you think your mind is more important than Ireland!

— I do, certainly.

— These are strange ideas of your godson's, Mr Fulham. May I ask did the Jesuits teach you them.

— The Jesuits taught me other things, reading and writing.

— And religion also?

216

— Naturally. 'What doth it profit a man to gain the whole world if he lose his soul?'

— Nothing, of course. That is quite so. But humanity has claims on us. We have a duty to our neighbour. We have received a commandment of charity.

— I hear so, said Stephen, at Christmas. Mr Fulham laughed at this and Mr Heffernan was stung.

— I may not have read as much as you, Mr Fulham, or even as much as you, young man, but I believe that the noblest love a man can

[*One page missing*]

our duty to God first and then the duties of our station in life, said Mr Fulham, leaning comfortably on the last phrase.

— You can be a patriot, Mr Heffernan, said Stephen, without accusing those who do not agree with you of irreligion.

— I never accused . . .

— Come now, said Mr Fulham genially, we all understand each other.

Stephen had enjoyed this little skirmish: it had been a pastime for him to turn the guns of orthodoxy upon the orthodox ranks and see how they would stand the fire. Mr Heffernan seemed to him a typical Irishman of the provinces; assertive and fearful, sentimental and rancorous, idealist in speech and realist in conduct. Mr Fulham was harder to understand. His championing of the Irish peasant was full of zealous patronage, his ardour for the Church was implicit with his respect for feudal distinctions, and his natural submission to what he regarded as the dispenser of these distinctions. He would enforce his aristocratic notions in a homely way:

— Come now, Mr So and So, you buy cattle on fair-day in the town?

— Yes.

— And you go[1] the racecourse and make a bet or two as you fancy?

— I must admit I do.

— And you pride yourself on knowing a thing or two about coursing?

— I think I do.

[1] 'to' omitted.

— Then how can you say there is no aristocracy of breed in men since you know it exists in animals?

Mr Fulham's pride was the pride of the burgher in the costly burdensome canopy which he has exerted[1] and loves to sustain. He had affection for the feudal machinery and desired nothing better than that it should crush him – a common wish of the human adorer whether he cast himself under Juggernaut or pray God with tears of affection to mortify him or swoon under the hand of his mistress. To the sensitive inferior his charity would have offered intolerable pain of mind and yet the giver would use neither the air nor the language of the self-righteous. His conceptions of human relations [would] might perhaps have passed for a progressive conception in the ages when the earth was thought to be scaphoid and had he lived then he might have been reputed the most [tender-hearted] enlightened of slave-owners. As Stephen watched the old man gravely handing his snuff-box to Mr Heffernan, and the latter perforce appeased, inserting a large hand therein [Stephen] he thought: [to]

— My godfather is the Papal ambassador to Westmeath.

Nash was waiting for him at the door of the shop and they walked down the main street together towards the *Examiner* office. In the window [was] a white fox-terrier's [muzzle] head could be seen over a dirty brown blind and his intelligent eyes were the only signs of life in the office. Mr Garvey was sent for and presently sent in word that his two visitors were to come into the *Greville Arms*. Mr Garvey was found sitting at the bar with his hat pushed far back from a glowing forehead. He was 'chaffing' the barmaid but when his visitors entered he stood up and shook hands with them. Then he insisted on their joining him in a drink. The barmaid was 'chaffed' again by Mr Garvey and by Nash but always within limits. She was a genteel young person of a very tempting figure. While she was polishing glasses she indulged in flirty, gossipy conversation with the young men: she seemed to have the life of the town at her fingers' ends. She reproved Mr Garvey once or twice for levity and asked Stephen wasn't it a shame for a married man. Stephen said it was and began to count the buttons of her blouse. The barmaid said Stephen was a nice sensible young man not a gadabout fellow and smiled very

[1] 'Erected' (?)

sweetly over her brisk napkin. After a while the young men left the bar, first touching the fingertips of the barmaid and raising their hats.

Mr Garvey whistled the terrier out of the office and they set off for a walk. Mr Garvey wore heavy boots and he plodded along sturdily in them, tapping the road with his stick. The road and the actual sultry day had made him sensible and he gave the younger men some sound advice.

— After all, there's nothing like marriage for making a fellow steady. Before I got this sit on the *Examiner* here I used knock about with the lads and boose [a][1] bit . . . You know, he said to Nash – [Na]sh[1] nodded.

— Now I've a good house, said Mr Garvey, and . . . I go home in the evening and if I want a drink . . . well, I can have it. My advice to every young fellow that can afford it is: marry young.

— There's something in that, said Nash, when you've had your fling, that is. ·

— O, yes, said Mr Garvey. By the bye I hope you'll come and see me some evening and bring your friend. You'll come, Mr Daedalus? The missus'll be glad to see you: she plays a bit, you know.

Stephen mumbled his thanks and decided that he would endure severe bodily pain rather than visit Mr Garvey.

Mr Garvey began then to tell some press stories. When he heard from Nash that Stephen was inclined for writing he said:

— You take my tip: shorthand.

He told many stories illustrating his own smartness at his business and said that he had once got a 'par' into a London morning paper and got paid well for it by return of post.

— These English chaps, you know, they know how to do business. Pay good money too.

The day was very hot and the town seemed dozing in the heat but when the young men came to the canal bridge they noticed a crowd collected some fifty yards off on the canal bank. A butcher's boy was telling a circle of workmen about it.

—I seen her first. I noticed something – a long-looking green thing lying among the weeds and I went for Joe Coghlan. Him and me tried to get it up but it was too heavy. So then what did we do

[1] Manuscript torn.

but I thought if we could only get the lend of a pole off someone. So Joe and me, then, went down to the back of Slater's yard . . .

A pace or two from the brink of the water a thing was lying on the bank partly covered by a brown sack. It was the body of a woman: the face was to the ground and from the thick black hair a pool of water had oozed out. The body was curved upwards with legs abroad but over [word torn away] someone had drawn down the [word torn away] nightdress. The woman had escaped from the asylum the night before and Stephen heard many criticisms of the nurses.

— It'd be better for 'em mind the patients than traipsing about with every Tom, Dick and Harry of a doctor.

— It's them has the style.

Mr Garvey's dog wanted to sniff the body but Mr Garvey kicked him heavily and the dog curled up yelping. Then there was silence for some time, everyone remaining at his post watching the corpse, until a voice said 'Here's the doctor!' A stout well-dressed man came down the path quickly without acknowledging the salutes of the people and after a few moments Stephen heard him saying the woman was dead and telling the people to get a cart and have the body taken away. The three young men then continued their walk but Stephen had to be waited for and called to. He remained behind gazing into the canal near the feet of the body, looking at a fragment of paper on which was

[*The additional pages of the Manuscript end here*]

The world's greatest novelists now available in Triad/Panther Books

Aldous Huxley

Brave New World	£1.95	☐
Island	£1.95	☐
After Many a Summer	£1.95	☐
Brief Candles	£1.95	☐
The Devils of Loudun	£1.95	☐
Eyeless in Gaza	£2.50	☐
Antic Hay	£1.95	☐
Crome Yellow	£1.50	☐
Point Counter Point	£1.95	☐
Those Barren Leaves	£1.95	☐
The Genius and the Goddess	£1.95	☐
Time Must Have a Stop	£2.50	☐
The Doors of Perception/ Heaven and Hell (non-fiction)	£1.95	☐
The Human Situation (non-fiction)	£1.95	☐
Grey Eminence (non-fiction)	£1.95	☐
Brave New World Revisited (non-fiction)	£1.95	☐
The Gioconda Smile and other stories	£2.50	☐
Ape and Essence	£1.95	☐

Hermann Hesse

Stories of Five Decades	£2.50	☐
Journey to the East	£1.95	☐
Demian	£1.95	☐
Pictor's Metamorphoses	£1.95	☐
My Belief (non-fiction)	£1.25	☐
Reflections (non-fiction)	95p	☐
Hermann Hesse: A Pictorial Biography	£1.50	☐

To order direct from the publisher just tick the titles you want and fill in the order form.

The world's greatest novelists now available in Triad/Panther Books

Ernest Hemingway

The Old Man and The Sea	£1.50 ☐
Fiesta	£1.95 ☐
For Whom the Bell Tolls	£2.50 ☐
A Farewell to Arms	£1.95 ☐
The Snows of Kilimanjaro	£1.95 ☐
The Essential Hemingway	£2.95 ☐
To Have and Have Not	£1.95 ☐
Green Hills of Africa	£2.50 ☐
Men Without Women	£2.50 ☐
A Moveable Feast	£1.95 ☐
The Torrents of Spring	£2.50 ☐
Across the River and Into the Trees	£1.95 ☐
Winner Take Nothing	£1.95 ☐
The Fifth Column	£1.95 ☐
Death in the Afternoon (non-fiction)	£2.95 ☐

Richard Hughes

A High Wind in Jamaica	£1.25 ☐
In Hazard	£1.50 ☐
Fox in the Attic	£1.50 ☐
The Wooden Shepherdess	£1.50 ☐

James Joyce

Dubliners	£1.95 ☐
A Portrait of the Artist as a Young Man	£1.95 ☐
Stephen Hero	£1.95 ☐
The Essential James Joyce	£2.95 ☐
Exiles (play)	£1.25 ☐

To order direct from the publisher just tick the titles you want and fill in the order form.

All these books are available at your local bookshop or newsagent, or can be ordered direct from the publisher.

To order direct from the publisher just tick the titles you want and fill in the form below.

Name _____

Address _____

_____

Send to:
Panther Cash Sales
PO Box 11, Falmouth, Cornwall TR10 9EN.

Please enclose remittance to the value of the cover price plus:

UK 45p for the first book, 20p for the second book plus 14p per copy for each additional book ordered to a maximum charge of £1.63.

BFPO and Eire 45p for the first book, 20p for the second book plus 14p per copy for the next 7 books, thereafter 8p per book.

Overseas 75p for the first book and 21p for each additional book.

Panther Books reserve the right to show new retail prices on covers, which may differ from those previously advertised in the text or elsewhere.